Hunting

for

Crows

IAIN CAMERON

To find out more about the author, visit the website:

www.iain-cameron.com

DEDICATION

For Vari

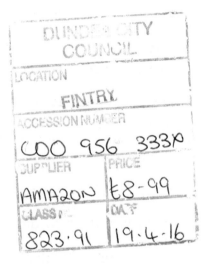

ONE

The water slapped at the banks of the river; angry, cold and with a hint of menace. It was the rain that did it, the relentless rain that came down over the last six months, only stopping for Christmas when it started to snow. He flicked the toothpick over with his tongue in one movement; five minutes one way, five minutes the other.

A man walked towards him with a giant poodle at his side, but not the man he was looking for. What the dog-walker made of this individual, sitting alone and content on a riverside bench at this hour of the morning he couldn't guess. The man strolled past without saying a word. Not many people came down here on a cold winter's morning, as the River Arun gave off a fine mist which seeped through thick clothing and chilled the bones.

A few minutes later he spotted him: Lucky out in front, the stupid Labrador as happy as a sand-boy to be out on this freeze-your-bollocks day and not lounging beside a warm hearth in his master's house. He rose from the bench, ducked behind a bush close to the river and removed a piece of liver from a bag. The dog padded along the path and, sensing his presence, turned his head towards him.

'Lucky, come here boy,' he said. 'What have I got?'

He held out his hand and on seeing the food, the daft mutt walked over to him. He gobbled the meat in seconds. If man's best friend refused to play ball, it was laced with a little something extra to increase his compliance. He reached down and picked him up, surprised at first by the weight of the greedy bugger, then turned and threw him into the deep, fast flowing current.

He waited a few seconds until the man's footsteps approached before rushing from his hiding place and shouting, 'There's a dog in the river, there's a dog in the river!'

The idiot took a few moments to react, his mushy brain still tucked up in his warm bed and not registering what this handsome stranger was saying to him.

'There!' he said again, pointing. 'Can you see it? I think it's a Golden Labrador.'

Lucky's master shook his head out of his daydream and gazed at the water. 'It looks like Lucky,' he said, edging closer to the riverbank. 'My God, it is him! Lucky! Lucky! Come over here boy!'

Amidst the turmoil of rushing, surging water the plucky pooch heard his master's shout and turned. The dog tried to paddle towards him, but against the strong current all his fine efforts were in vain, as he didn't move at all; ah what a shame.

'What can I do?' the man said to him, his face pale and anxious. 'What can I do?'

'Go in after him. The poor dog's going to drown!'

'What? Do you think so? The river's high and it's moving so fast.'

'I'll look after your jacket and call the Emergency Services. Go now, before he drowns.'

Lucky's owner stared at him for a moment before whipping off his heavy jacket and handing it to him. At first he thought he was going to dive in, but there was hesitation in his voice. 'I'm not sure, the river looks so dangerous.'

The target turned to look at the dog, leaning around a bush to get a better view. He moved behind the tilted figure and shoved him hard in the back. Lucky's owner made an ungainly splash when he hit the water and was soon whisked away by the swirling, rushing river. He was obviously a good swimmer as he didn't panic, but turned and looked around for a tree or bush to grasp, but the bank was receding from his view, the current dragging him towards the centre of the river.

For a moment, water surged over his head, submerging him and when he reappeared moments later, he was gasping for air. Bits of debris rushed past: bottles, tin cans, branches. A piece of wood whacked him on the head leaving him dazed.

He turned and walked downriver towards the bridge, whistling his favourite song, *How Long* by Ace. With a newly acquired set of house keys in his pocket, there was a little place in King Street he wanted to search.

TWO

He collected drinks from the bar and returned to the table in the corner. DI Angus Henderson of Surrey and Sussex Police knew that Brighton possessed many trendy and modern pubs in its canon, much better hostelries to drink in than this crappy dump, so he couldn't understand how places like this still survived.

'Cheers mate,' his companion said when a pint of chilled lager appeared in front of him. The words sounded pleasant enough but his furtive, nervous gaze didn't stop scanning the faces of fellow drinkers, even as grubby fingers circled the glass, raised it to his lips and he took a large gulp.

If Henderson wasn't facing away from the body of the pub, he would be looking around too, not for a snitch or a rival as Davy seemed to be doing, but in trying to spot some of the contraband being passed around. The pub was notorious to regulars and the police as a place where dope and burgled goods could be bought, and at this moment any number of iPhones, packets of coke, credit cards and watches would be changing hands.

'So, how are you, Davy?'

'Ah you know, Mr Henderson, ducking and diving, ducking and diving.'

'Still hanging out with the lanky bloke who always wears the Harvard University t-shirt, even though I don't think he could spell it?'

'Billy? Naw. He's bad news, a loser if ever I saw one. I keep well away from him.'

I bet you do, Henderson thought, until you want something from him. People like Davy here were all the same: greedy, grasping and self-serving. They lived in a dog-eat-dog world where everybody looked out for themselves and words like 'cooperation', 'help' and 'honesty' were found only in a quality newspaper and not in their lexicon.

His companion for this evening was Davy Cairns, a mid-thirties petty crook whose biggest 'score' was finding a bag containing two hundred and fifty-thousand pounds in cash, the proceeds of a drug deal that ended in a shoot-out on the South Downs. Like a good criminal, he didn't hand his fortunate discovery in to the nearest police station as he knew it belonged to Trevor Frank, one of Brighton's biggest drug dealers. If he kept the money and ran off to Spain or Argentina, it wouldn't be far enough to prevent Frank finding him and removing his liver, spleen and heart and feeding the lot to two aggressive Dobermans who patrolled the grounds of his Spanish-style villa in Hove.

As a consequence of his good fortune, Frank now treated Davy Cairns like a long-lost cousin. He gave him easy jobs to do, paid him well and allowed him to attend meetings when he and his boys discussed business and future projects. Cairns was one of the DI's long-term narks. He wasn't so naïve to believe Cairns would tell him anything important about Frank's activities, as he valued the aforesaid body parts as much as the next man, but was always happy to pass to him any information which would put the proverbial boot into one of their rivals.

'So what's new, Davy?'

'Did you bring the...?'

Henderson passed across a copy of *The Brighton Argus*, an edition of the paper not sold by street vendors and newsagents, as a tidy sum lay within its pages. It didn't count as an unusual occurrence in this pub, cash passing between two punters, in fact the trade in illicit goods most likely surpassed the takings in the till. He was being discreet, as he didn't want to draw attention to his conversation with Cairns and involve the younger man in an awkward and painful bout of questioning.

Without missing a beat or changing body position, *The Argus* disappeared into a sports bag and his nark's usually taciturn mouth began to move.

'In the last few months a load of cheap skunk has flooded into Brighton. It's potent stuff, based on a Dutch strain. It's all over the place in schools, the universities, you name it and if it's not stopped now, who knows the sort of damage it'll do to our young folk.'

Henderson tuned out. Scum drug dealers getting sanctimonious about other scum drug dealers didn't sit well with him and was almost as hard to stomach as the chemical flavour of the beer.

'I know some people—'

'Who's behind it?'

'A couple of Chink businessmen.'

'Names?'

'I dunno, couldn't pronounce them if I did, but I can tell you where they grow the stuff.'

*

Henderson drove back to his flat in the Seven Dials district of Brighton in a contemplative mood. He had hoped Davy Cairns would let something slip and lead him to his boss, but the wily bastard only told him enough to take out one of his rivals. Even so, such an operation might offer a few brownie points because of late, there hadn't been many of them around.

He climbed the stairs. He liked living on the top floor, well away from traffic noise and drunks shouting in the street about their undying love for a woman in an apartment nearby or their favourite football team. He also liked having no one above him, stomping around in work boots and playing hip-hop music at all hours. What he disliked was having to climb up there, laden with bags, or tired after a long day at the office, or heaving a stomach filled with beer and curry.

He dumped his jacket on the chair in the hall, grabbed a packet of crisps from the cupboard, and poured a large whisky into a glass retrieved from the draining board. The ten-year-old Glenmorangie single malt wouldn't mix well with the two pints of iffy beer he drank in the pub, but what the hell. He went into the living room, cued a CD on the stereo, and slumped into his favourite chair.

During the day, the big bay window offered fine views over the gardens opposite which followed the contours of Montpelier Crescent, but not much was visible at eleven o'clock on a cold mid-week night. There wasn't much activity either, except a couple of folks returning from a meal or the pub, and the occasional dog-walker giving their pooch the final chance for a late night leak.

Over the last few months, Henderson, a Detective Inspector with the Major Crime Team at Surrey and Sussex Police, as the recently merged group was now called, had worked on a series of stabbings, carvings and three murders, many of which were drug related. Perhaps the skunk factory mentioned by Cairns had a greater influence on the crime figures than he first suspected. He would talk to his boss in the morning and try to secure the manpower required for a raid.

Lady of the Night started at a slow tempo and soon the soaring guitar and thick bass lines grabbed him by the jugular, the ideal antidote to lift his sombre mood. The song came from the fourth album by an eighties rock band from Brighton, the Crazy Crows, thought by many to be their best, but at the time press interest had focused not so much on their musical abilities as their bad-boy antics.

They'd had a reputation for trashing hotel rooms, appearing drunk on television and radio, and bedding any woman who strayed too close, although much of it had been exaggerated by their PR company to differentiate them from other clean-cut groups around at the time. Henderson, and his brother Archie, were once in a rock band, if humping speaker stacks and driving an old rusty Transit van could be called being in a band. On one occasion, he'd taken his thirteen-year-old brother down to Glasgow from Fort William to see the Crazy Crows, the first such outing to the big city for both of them and a rock concert first for Archie.

The Crazy Crows were a four-piece comprising Derek Crow, his brother Barry, Peter Grant and Eric Hannah. Derek started the band, played rhythm guitar, wrote and sang most of the songs and did his best to keep things in order. After they split, he became a successful businessman with a big house in St. John's Wood and the ear of the new Labour Prime Minister. Henderson knew this without resorting to the web or talking to Archie, as

Derek Crow's rough-hewn features were a regular sight in the business sections of the Sunday papers.

Eric Hannah played lead guitar and his performance on the band's acclaimed fourth album was, in the DI's opinion, nothing short of brilliant. He could also be an unreliable character as he took too much dope, drank as if suffering from a permanent thirst, and found rock infamy by missing the start of the Trevor Lamb talk show as he was too busy having sex with a production assistant in a broom closet. He didn't known if Hannah still played or performed, but if his copious consumption of illicit substances in the past was anything to go by, it would be a miracle if he did.

On drums, Peter Grant. He knew Peter, as he ran a health supplement business in Brighton. In the early days, when he'd owned only one shop and the man himself served behind the counter, Henderson would pop in for a chat. At the back of the cupboard under the sink, there still lurked some bottles of energy tablets and muscle building powders, purchases he'd felt obliged to make to justify his visit.

Derek Crow's brother Barry played bass guitar. In any rock band, the drummer and bass player are the driving forces, laying down a bedrock of sound over which the lead guitar or keyboard adds melody, and makes the music shine

He also knew what Barry was doing now and why he was listening to their album and thinking about the Crazy Crows. This morning, Barry's body had been fished out of the River Arun.

THREE

The squad car cruised down the street, the slow pace mimicking a big cat waiting to pounce on an unsuspecting mouse. Inside the car, driver PC Harry 'Jake' Jackman and his partner, not the real one he shared a bed with, although if she asked nicely she could be, PC Sandy 'Saks' Atkinson, were arguing like an old married couple.

'Are you sure this is the right address, Saks?' he said, trying to sound calm as she could be a prickly so-and-so first thing in the morning, and if he rubbed her up the wrong way now, she could make it last until tea-time.

'Of course I'm bloody sure.' She grabbed the folder that was tucked down the side of the seat and flicked through the pages as if they were on fire. When she found the correct page she stabbed an accusing finger at the text. 'It says here, and I quote, 15 Oak Avenue. So Jake,' she said snapping the folder shut, 'can we please get a bloody shift on and find the place ASAP, as I'm gasping for a fag.'

'Oak Avenue did you say?'

'You heard me, Jake, don't try to be a clever dick, not today.'

'So, why did you direct me to Beech Avenue?'

The sudden acceleration of the car scattered a couple of dogs engaged in sniffing one another's reproductive organs and in one small gesture, Jake saved the world from feeding another six skanky mongrels. He turned right into Cedar Drive and left into Oak Avenue and even he would be forced to admit he found a certain similarity in the names and styles of the houses here in this part of Chichester.

'There it is,' he said, trying hard not to sound as triumphant as he felt.

He parked the car and without another word they got out and headed towards the front door. A girl aged seven or eight answered their knock, surprising as it was still term-time, but by the look of the Disney pyjamas, pale face and spotty complexion, she wasn't feeling well.

'Is your mother in, love?' Saks said in a kindly voice.

The girl turned her head and hollered, 'Mum! It's for you!'

Jake turned to Saks. 'I guess it's not tonsillitis.'

No response.

'Tell whoever it is to come in,' another voice shouted back. 'I'll be there in a jiffy.'

It was late morning but the living room felt like Jake's house at eight in the evening. The gas fire and the central heating were blazing, a large LCD television was showing some kids' programme, dirty tea cups and plates were lying around and an ironing board stood idle in the corner. In his world, all it needed to complete the scene were a few empty beer cans and an overflowing ashtray.

Valerie Lassiter came into the room wiping her wet hands on a towel and didn't seem surprised to find a couple of cops sitting on her sofa. She looked a big lady with a pleasant, ruddy face, dark brown eyes, wiry, unkempt hair, and wearing baggy tracksuit bottoms and an ill-fitting home-knitted jumper.

She collapsed into an armchair, the springs and floorboards squealing with displeasure. 'This isn't

11

something to do with my Josh is it? He's always getting into trouble in school, but it's never involved the police before. Well, only once when he broke the window in the library.'

'They might be here to take him away Ma,' said a voice from the floor where the little girl sat cross-legged, her eyes never leaving a cartoon on the television.

'Shurrup you little madam. She's got it in for the boy 'cause he switches her programmes off so he can watch the music channels.'

'When I'm bigger I'm going to break his nose if he does it again.'

'I'm warning you missy.'

'No, this isn't about Josh, Mrs Lassiter,' Jake said as quickly as he could, trying to regain control of the conversation.

'My divorce just came through, so it's *Miss* Lassiter from now on. It took ages because of stupid lawyers—'

'It should be Miss Crow,' the little voice said.

'I told you to shut up and watch the telly; now do it, will you? I always hated the name 'Crow', you know, ever since I was a little girl and there's no way I want to go back to it. It reminds me of those ugly black things in the garden, peck-pecking away at worms and dead birds at the side of the road. I hate them.'

'Fine, *Miss Lassiter,* but our visit is nothing to do with your son or your divorce. We are here to talk to you about your brother.'

'My brother? Did something happen to Derek? Is it something terrible? I kept telling him he needed to stop his drinking and smoking. I said it would be the death of him.'

'Miss Lassiter,' Jake said a bit louder than intended, 'this is not about Derek but your other brother, Barry.'

'Oh him? Why didn't you say so? Me getting so het up about nothing. You nearly gave me a heart attack.'

'Sorry.'

'So what's happened to him? I mean I wouldn't put it past him to—'

'Miss Lassiter, I am sorry to inform you that yesterday morning the body of your brother, Barry Crow, was recovered from the River Arun in Arundel.'

'Wha...what did you say?'

'I said, your brother Barry drowned. Rescuers found him yesterday morning and it seems he may have gone into the water trying to rescue his dog.'

'Oh my God, how awful. How is Lucky? Is he ok?'

'No, I'm sorry to say the dog drowned too.'

She clapped her hand to her mouth. 'That's terrible, so it is. I loved Lucky.'

'Me too,' the girl said.

'How did it happen?' she asked.

Jake nudged Saks.

'As my colleague said, it appears your brother, Barry, entered the water in an unsuccessful attempt to save his dog. Local people in the town saw the body in the river and alerted emergency services. It was recovered about a mile downstream by a boatman who rowed through thick reeds to reach him and the body of the dog.'

'I need a drink,' she said. 'Can I get you folks something?'

'No thanks,' he said. 'We're still on duty.'

Saks gave him one of her looks, not because he refused a drink for both of them, but expressing her dislike for

Valerie Lassiter's lack of sensitivity about her dead brother. The deceased's sister had proved to be a difficult woman to locate, as they didn't find any reference to her in Barry's house, and only when a police researcher called them this morning did they even know he had a sister.

The bottle and everything else rested on a plastic tray on the sideboard, close to hand and set out for quick access. She returned a few moments later with a glass of vodka topped up with lemonade and sat down.

'Does Derek know?' she said, after downing a large slug. If Jake drank like she did, the miserly 25ml measures they served at his local wouldn't last two minutes.

'By Derek, I take it you mean your other brother?' he asked.

'Yes.'

'Officers are attempting to make contact with him as we speak. Does Barry have any other relatives, aside from yourself and Derek?'

She shook her head. 'Barry's wife died a few years back and they didn't have any kids; couldn't. She blamed him for shooting blanks but he said it was her fault, barren as the Gobi Desert he liked to say. Don't bother trying to contact my ex, I want nothing more to do with the swine, nothing more.'

'Were you and Barry close?' Saks asked.

'Derek's an important businessman and needs to be told, but he's a very busy man and difficult to pin down. I know this from personal experience because when I went through a bad patch with my ex, he's called William if you must know, I could never get hold of him.'

'Is there anyone else we need to inform, for example, work associates or friends?'

'There's no one I can think of. Barry worked on his own after the band split up and set himself up as an internet entrepreneur. I don't know what he did, but he made a lot of money doing it. As I was saying about Derek...'

She carried on yapping about Derek; she didn't seem to be talking to them, but giving a little speech made dozens of times in the lounge of her local pub or at the bowling club, telling anyone who would listen about Derek, her important brother.

Jake supposed if anyone in his family became famous or rich he would want to tell all and sundry about them, but not when being informed about the death of his brother. It was similar to cracking a dirty joke at a funeral. The sombre circumstances might call for it but if you did let fly, your wife would always remember her embarrassment and never let you forget it.

They left the house ten minutes later, the freeze between him and Saks thawing as they discussed the woman's indifferent attitude to her dead brother and the genuine level of concern she expressed for the very-much-alive brother, Derek. The question which hung in the air and caused an altercation between Valerie and her daughter whenever it came up, was where were they going to bury the damn dog.

FOUR

DI Henderson stepped out of the car and locked it. Before leaving Sussex House, the Brighton home of the Major Crime Team of Surrey and Sussex Police, he'd told colleagues he was following up his earlier encounter with Davy Cairns. In fact, everything was already in place and he would put a team together and raid the skunk factory, after some bits of paperwork were signed-off. Instead, he was in Arundel, home of the recently deceased Barry Crow, as his untimely accident had piqued his interest.

He walked out of the car park, situated beside the River Arun, and strolled along the road running parallel to the riverbank. The spot where they'd found Barry's body proved easier to find than he first thought, as a nearby fence was resplendent with floral tributes, messages and cards from appreciative local people and breast cancer charities. Despite several days of dry weather, the river lapped close to the top of the bank and gave him some sense of how dangerous it could be and only increased his bewilderment as to why anyone would consider jumping in.

He headed back towards the High Street and climbed the steep hill past the Red Lion pub, numerous antique shops and banks, towards the cathedral, but received no reply from a knock on the door of Barry's house in King Street. It was a pretty, white-painted terraced house with the front door opening straight onto the pavement. On the negative side, it didn't provide enough space to position a chair and chat to the neighbours or set down a few geranium pots to add a bit of colour in summer, but on the positive side, he didn't have a path to sweep, garden to dig, and there wasn't a squeaking gate to keep anyone awake at night.

He knocked on the door of Barry Crow's next door neighbour. He half-expected it to be answered by an old hippy with long, grey hair in a pony-tail or a groupie, way past her sell-by date, but instead there stood an elderly lady wearing a flowery dress and sensible slippers. He should have known better as Arundel was a sedate tourist town, famous for quaint pubs, a castle, and dozens of antique shops, not for loud music and dope-smoking rock fans.

'Hello,' she said, smiling. 'Can I help you?'

'Good afternoon, I'm Detective Inspector Angus Henderson of Surrey and Sussex Police.'

'Are you investigating the death of poor Mr Crow next door?'

'Yes, I am.'

'You better come in.'

That was easy. He half-expected to be faced with a nosey neighbour who would ask him why anyone was spending valuable time probing a clear accident, or if they were really on the ball, why the case of a drowning man required the presence of a senior murder detective. Whatever the response, he was prepared with a stock reply. He was there to collate information about the dead man, building a picture for their files. In fact, if he tried digging a bit deeper, he still wouldn't know the real reason as he didn't know either.

Mrs Partridge served Darjeeling tea in china cups with saucers, accompanied by a plate of plain and chocolate biscuits, all neatly laid out on a lace tablecloth. This was in stark contrast to the way he treated his guests, as the best they could hope to receive at chez Henderson was a faded Brighton and Hove Albion mug and a pack of biscuits that had probably been lying at the back of the cupboard for months. The living room felt warm and chintzy, full of photographs and commemorative plaques and mugs, mainly of the Queen and Duke and Duchess of Cambridge, all shimmering in the flickering light from a vigorous coal fire.

The room reminded him of an elderly aunt's house in Glasgow, as she was big on the royals and loved her soft fabrics but she didn't live so close to her neighbours that she could see a figure moving around in the house opposite, in spite of the obligatory net curtains. If she was still alive, she would soon be battling through deep snowdrifts just to get her newspaper and milk. Central Scotland was scheduled to receive a large dump of the white stuff this afternoon, while Mrs Partridge's house in Arundel, was bathed in weak Sussex sunlight under clear, blue skies.

'I knew Mr Crow better than anybody around here as he didn't talk much to anyone else, but you see I always looked after his dog when he travelled anywhere.'

'What did he do?'

'My, that's a very good question. I'm not really sure.'

'The report I read said he was an internet entrepreneur.'

'I don't know what that is, but I do know he invested in lots of businesses.'

'Did he do it with any degree of success?'

'I think so.' She took a sip of tea. 'You see, this isn't his only house. Oh no, he's got one in London and another one in Spain and travelled overseas on business about two or three times a month. He only bought the house next door to be close to his wife.'

'Does she still live in the town?'

She smiled. 'No, no. She died six years ago and she's buried in the local churchyard. They used to live in Worthing and came to Arundel most weekends. She loved it here and always said it was the place where she wanted to be buried. When she died of breast cancer, the money raised by local people was used by Barry to start a breast cancer charity. Before he died, he was its chairman.'

'Ah, that explains the cards I saw down at the river. Does, or should I say, did his brother Derek ever come down to see him?'

'Oh, now and again. Barry used to say he saw more of him on television than he ever did in person, but only yesterday I received a call from a nice young lady at his office in London who said they would be sending someone down in a few day's time to clear the place.'

'They don't hang about, do they?'

'I thought so too, but I suppose his brother wants to sell the house, although I suspect he doesn't need the money.'

This dovetailed into a request to take a look inside Barry's house, but far from responding in the negative as he expected, Mrs Partridge offered him the keys and apologised for not taking him there herself, but she suffered from arthritis and found it difficult moving around.

His suspicions that Barry's house was a mirror image of Mrs Partridge's appeared well-founded, but with less furniture and fewer personal items. It looked as though he didn't stay there often, or he was a man of few needs. If the ground and first floors were much as he expected to see in a small terraced house, the basement wasn't.

'Welcome to Kennedy Space Centre' declared a photograph of Barry in front of a gigantic space rocket. The rocket was long and sleek but Barry was fat and dumpy, and gripped in his hand, his own brand of rocket fuel, a large drum of popcorn. The 'space centre' description might well be used to describe the room as it was kitted out with all manner of computer gear: giant screens along one wall, printers, keyboards, scanners, little encryption pads and a Spaghetti Junction of cables.

Henderson drove back to Brighton in a reflective mood. Barry's basement was surprising and intriguing but indicative of what? He was a switched-on investor who used technology to monitor stock markets and track investments? Or did he manage the personal affairs of his rich big brother and use the apparent modest lifestyle to shield it from nosey buggers like journalists and the Inland Revenue?

It was clearer in his mind now why he came to Arundel. He had been deluding himself into thinking something suspicious was going on, and that he could become involved in something that interested him for a change, but having seen the winking lights of Barry Crow's computer set-up, it was obvious he'd intended coming back and this wasn't some elaborate cover-up.

It was foolish of Barry to enter a river as fast-flowing and menacing as he'd seen today, but the more he thought about Barry Crow and added it to the information given to him by Mrs Partridge, the more he realised such an act of unselfish bravery was in his nature. He was always the quiet one, ready to follow the lead carved out by his brother without drama or fuss, but willing and able to step up when circumstances demanded it.

It would always be a mystery why he did what he did, but if the words of the local paper were anything to go by, the headline of which he saw as he walked past a newsagent, the people around here were calling him a hero.

FIVE

Peter Grant edged the big BMW into a parking space and sat there for a few minutes with his eyes closed. He was enjoying a song by Bruce Springsteen on Planet Rock, coming through a twelve-speaker Bose system, while held in the sumptuous grip of a body-moulded seat clad in soft Napa leather. All the time, trying to decide if the car was a good omen or bad.

It was less than three months old, but in that time, his company's first out-of-town superstore had opened here, in Redburn Retail Park in Croydon, the turnover of the whole business had passed the thirty-million mark, and one of their products had been voted muscle-builder of the year. On the negative side of the equation, he'd lost one his best friends, Barry Crow, in a drowning accident, and the divorce from his wife of over twenty-six years had just come through.

Until the opening of this superstore, Grant's Fitness Emporium had consisted of twelve city-centre shops stocking their own brand of fitness and weight-gain powders, food supplements and various items of sports clothing, backed by a growing web-based business. Now, the monster he was walking towards, where the sign proclaiming the name of the business looked taller than him, had over ten times the square-footage of his biggest shop. This allowed him for the first time to realise his dream of selling a wide range of fitness equipment, including rowing machines, multi-gyms, tennis, squash and badminton racquets, racing, road and city bikes, and with a cafe upstairs serving good food and fitness drinks.

He walked into the shop and moments later the manager, Ben Young, came striding towards him and shook his hand.

'Good morning, Mr Grant.'

'Good morning, Ben. How are you? How's Martha keeping?'

'I'm fine. She's getting better day by day, thanks for asking.'

'Glad to hear it.' Grant started walking. 'Let's take a wander around the shop before we start our meeting. How's it going?'

'It's a lot bigger than my old shop, and now that we're dealing with a much larger product range, I can offer a more complete fitness package to our customers.'

'What about you?'

He puffed out his cheeks and blew a blast of air, flicking up a lock of jet-black hair. 'It's been a big learning curve for sure, but I think I'm getting there.'

'I'm pleased to hear it.'

'Pradip', the badge said, was demonstrating an expensive rowing machine to a young couple, clearly impressed by his ability to row and talk at the same time. It was not hard to feel jealous of this tall, rugged individual who moved without breaking sweat and enthralled his audience, and even though Grant was as fit as any office-bound forty-seven-year-old could hope to be, he didn't feel the urge to take over the demo and show the young Turk how it should be done. He knew what he was good at and this wasn't it.

Peter Grant was a businessman and no matter the sophistication of the machines or the palatability of the weight-gain and muscle-building powders, it was nothing but a bag of beans unless the same magic was being pushed through the tills.

Ben did not disappoint with his assessment of the shop's progress to date or his three-month projections, and when Peter Grant left the new face of Grant's Fitness Emporium an hour later, he was a happier man than when he'd arrived. He could now see the idea, one he'd championed in the face of deep reservations by many of his colleagues, was living and breathing in the big wide world and taking its first tentative steps.

The head office and main warehouse of the company was located in a modern industrial unit on the Woodingdean Business Park, to the east of Brighton and close to the University of Sussex. By the time he got there it was almost two o'clock and, feeling hungry, he headed straight for the cafeteria. He could have purchased a pack of sandwiches from the service station he passed on the M23 and eaten them at his desk, but doing so would make him feel like some lab-raised hamster, fearful of stepping off the treadmill in case he missed an important phone call or an interesting email. He didn't see many people about as most of the staff in the building stopped for lunch at one, but after collecting his food, he spotted his Human Resources Director, Sarah Corbett, and walked over to join her.

'This is a bit late for you, Peter.'

'Are you checking up on me, making sure I'm eating well?'

She smiled. 'Sorry if it sounded like I was. No, what I

meant was you are usually down here by about twelve-thirty.'

'I know, I'm only teasing. I visited the Croydon shop this morning. It's the first time I've seen it since it's been stocked.'

'What did you think?'

'It's marvellous, and if the numbers over the next few months back it up as I expect they will, we'll be opening a few more and refocusing our other shops to compliment them.'

'How do you mean refocusing, in what way?'

It never ceased to amaze him how skilful HR people were at making conversations flow with continual use of 'open' questions, those which could not be answered with a simple 'yes' or 'no'. At times, it could be irritating, in particular when he was in a hurry, but at the moment he was happy to indulge. He explained his rationale and told her he would raise the subject in their next management monthly meeting, a week on Tuesday.

'You seem to pack away a pretty big lunch,' she said, 'but you never seem to put on an ounce of weight. What's your secret?'

He smiled. 'Don't think I'm about to reveal the details of a new, radical diet just so you can write a book and make millions. Not because I don't want to lose you, but because I don't have one. I only eat here to save me cooking at home.'

'It makes sense. How are you coping on the domestic front?'

'What, with Emily gone?'

She nodded. 'But don't tell me if you think I'm being nosey.'

'It's all right, I'm a big boy. I'm doing ok, I suppose. I mean, I'm a bit limited in what I can cook but I can read the instructions on a packet and operate a microwave, so I won't starve although I have to admit, it's not much fun cooking for one.'

She sighed. 'Tell me about it.'

'Oh. Did something happen between you and Andrew?'

'We split up...two weeks ago.'

'I'm sorry to hear it. You kept that quiet.'

'I did. I didn't want to broadcast it and have everybody talking about me.'

'You mean like I did?'

'No, I didn't mean it like that. In any case, it's different for you, you're the boss and everyone in here knew Emily, so it would have thrown the whole place into gossip-overdrive if you'd turned up at one of our regular restaurant get-togethers on your own or on the arm of someone else.'

'Ha, fat chance of that happening at the moment, but you're right. What happened between you and Andrew, if you don't mind me asking?'

She looked down at her empty plate; he was only halfway through his lasagne. 'He said we were moving in different directions and we weren't the same people we once were.' She shrugged. 'I guess it was a polite way of saying he fancied somebody else.'

'I didn't know him too well, but whenever we met I always thought he was a nice guy.'

'Maybe too nice, if you know what I mean.'

'Don't do yourself down, Sarah. You'll soon find someone else.'

'I haven't yet.'

'You'll see. You'll be inundated with offers if you haven't been already.'

He meant it. She was forty-two with a pretty face and styled shoulder-length blonde hair which was trimmed every three or four weeks. She wore stylish clothes and had what he would call a 'womanly' figure, as she wasn't stick-thin like the bulimic clothes-horses he often saw in the fashion pages of newspapers, or so fat that the material on her blouse was put under continual strain.

'I thank you kind sir,' she said reaching out and putting her hand on his arm. 'I regret to say I can't sit around here listening to any more of these fine compliments. I've got three more interviews to do this afternoon.'

'What a shame, but I'm sure you'll enjoy it.'

She stood and waved a dainty hand. 'Bye, Peter. See you later. We should do this more often.'

He spent a large part of the next few hours on a succession of phone calls and in two long meetings, and only returned to his desk at six-thirty after a tedious session with the marketing team. If he was tired, he would usually check his messages and emails and if nothing required his immediate attention, he would pack a briefcase and head home, but tonight the prospect of microwaved meatballs in front of the television somehow didn't have its usual appeal. Instead, he went down to the cafeteria for something to eat and came back to the office and continued to work for another couple of hours.

He began by reviewing a report sent to him by a firm of property consultants, the same company who were responsible for finding the Croydon shop. The report listed a number of similar sites in various towns across the UK, and he enjoyed an intriguing half-hour reading the descriptions and trying to locate the places on a map. By the time he'd finished, the scribbles on his notepad suggested three sites met his criteria, and he was about to send the consultants an email to arrange viewing appointments, when Sarah Corbett walked in.

'Do you have a few minutes, Peter?'

'Sure, take a seat.'

'I wanted to give you the heads-up on a guy I've just finished interviewing for the web marketing position. I think he may be the right person for the job.'

He pushed the property details to one side. 'Ok, let's take a look.'

She opened a folder and passed him some papers. He didn't spend much time reading the CV as he often found them cold and featureless, and if newspaper reports were to be believed, full of blatant lies and flagrant embellishment. Instead, he concentrated on Sarah's assessment, as she was good at homing-in on a subject's main accomplishments and unearthing hidden deficiencies and failings.

'He's an interesting guy,' he said when he finished reading. 'With bags of experience. I mean, he designed and maintains a web site for his current employer and is doing the same for his own music news website. I don't like dance music myself, so I'm not the best judge to determine if it's any good or not.'

'Don't worry, I've taken a look and I think it's very good.'

He didn't think she was the type to attend acid parties in a ripped t-shirt or noisy basement clubs dressed in her best leathers, but he let the thought pass.

'Good. We both think he could do the job. What do you

want to do now?'

'I'd like to bring him back in, let him see the people and the place where he might be working, and to meet you.'

'No problem. You go ahead and agree a date with him and I'll try and be here. My diary is quiet next week, as I left it free to go over the initial data from the Croydon superstore. That might be the best time.'

'Great,' she said, writing it down. 'Thanks.' She gathered her papers together and stood, but as soon as she did so, her arm caught the back of the chair and the papers she was holding fell out of the folder and scattered across the floor.

'Blooming heck,' she exclaimed. 'How could I have been so stupid and clumsy?'

Her skirt was tight and Peter doubted she could bend far without bursting a seam or hiking it up too much and leaving little to the imagination.

He rose from the chair to help her. 'Don't worry about it, Sarah, I'll get them.'

He bent down and picked up the sheets. He stood and handed them over but as their fingers touched he felt a surge of electricity and when he looked into her eyes, it was obvious she felt it too. He leaned closer and without any reproach or hesitation on her part, her face rose to meet his.

SIX

DI Henderson walked into the Detectives' Room and headed towards DC Phil Bentley's desk.

'Morning, sir. How are you today?' Bentley said as he approached.

'Not bad Phil. How are you? How are you getting on with the new baby?'

'Fine. I had a good night's sleep as it was my wife's turn to get up and do the two o'clock feed.'

'Good to hear. It wouldn't do to see you sleeping at your desk. How did you get on with the recon of our drugs warehouse?'

'Grab a pew and I'll show you.'

Henderson took a seat beside his desk while he searched through a large wad of papers. He found what he was looking for and handed the DI a thin report.

'As you suggested, sir,' Bentley said, 'I contacted EDF and they sent a helicopter armed with a thermal imaging camera over the site two days ago.'

Henderson flicked through the report, which included a series of photographs.

Bentley pointed at the first photograph, a black and white still of various buildings taken from about one hundred feet where one, a large barn, glowed white.

'They detected a significant heat signature from the barn, consistent with a strong heat source, such as multiple lights and heaters.'

Henderson looked at the other pictures, taken at lower altitude and with more zoom, so he could make out the shape of the barn, and almost all of it glowed white.

'What about their electricity usage?'

'There's one meter for the farm and EDF say the usage is what they would expect from a large, working agricultural outfit.'

'Good. So what we know is something hot is going on in the barn and they're by-passing the electricity meter to power it.'

'I would say so, and if they're not growing dope, I'll eat the report.'

Henderson stood. 'Good work, Phil. Is DS Walters about?'

'I haven't seen her this morning.'

'When you do, tell her to come into my office. Cheers, Phil.'

He walked back to his office in a cheerful mood. The little snippet his nark, Davy Cairns, had given him about a drug growing operation at a farm on the outskirts of Burgess Hill was starting to look like the real deal. All he needed now was some intel on the owner and they would be ready to pay the farm a visit.

When he arrived at his office, DS Walters was standing outside.

'Morning Carol, you've been missed.'

'Sorry, sir. I couldn't get out of bed this morning.'

'Late night?'

They walked into his office and sat down at the small meeting table.

'I didn't finish here until gone nine and afterwards went out for a drink with a few mates.'

'How did you get on with researching Potter Farm?'

'I thought you might ask,' she said opening the folder she had been carrying. 'It's owned by a man called Tristan Hunt and the farm's been in his family for four generations. They grow corn, wheat, and rapeseed.'

'Interesting. Did you check his record?'

'Yep, he's clean.'

'Anything else?'

She lifted out some papers from the small pile. 'I took a look at the accounts for the last few years. Three years ago the business made a loss, the year after, an even bigger loss, but ever since they've made healthy profits.'

'This suggests to me that the farm has been in decline and Hunt approached the dope growers, or the dope growers came to him with the idea at just the right time. Either way, I think Hunt is complicit in what's going on and not a poor farmer trying to make a buck by renting out a barn, unaware of what's going on inside it.'

'I agree.'

'Good. Talk to Sergeant Gary Brown over at John Street and see if you can rustle up half a dozen uniforms for a raid on Wednesday.'

'Would you like them armed?'

He thought for a moment. 'No. If it's Chinese or Vietnamese guys tending the plants inside, the most we'll see is knives or baseball bats.'

'Famous last words before we face a small platoon carrying AK47's.'

'You've been watching too many Vietnam War movies. The reason I don't like taking guns is not because I fear one of our guys will shoot someone, accidentally or in the heat of the moment, as they're trained to avoid these situations, but they'll be overpowered and then the bad guys will be armed.'

'I understand. I'll get it organised.'

When Walters left the room Henderson woke up his computer and ran a search on Google. When he found the company he was looking for, he dialled the number listed for the switchboard.

'Good morning, Grant's Fitness Emporium.'

'Good morning. I'd like to speak to Peter Grant, please,' he said.

'I'll see if he's free. Who should I say is calling?'

'Detective Inspector Angus Henderson, Surrey and Sussex Police.'

'Just a moment, sir.'

She came back on the line thirty seconds later. *'I'm afraid he's not around, Inspector, he's out on a shop visit. This morning he's in Hastings and this afternoon, Brighton. Can I take a message?'*

'No, it's all right. I'll call back.'

Henderson continued working on a project for his boss, CI Edwards, for the rest of the morning. At lunchtime, he ate a sandwich at his desk and at two he left the office.

He could see his car without too much trouble, a dark blue Audi Avant. It was sandwiched between two other dark cars, both of which were clean and sparkling, while his car hadn't seen the inside of a carwash since January.

He drove into town in a reflective mood, his usual temperament when wrestling with a new case or trying to put some facts into a semblance of order, such as why had Barry Crow jumped into a fast-moving torrent. He turned into the car park at Churchill Square, relieved to see it back to normal after the long queues and the fight for spaces he experienced the last time he was here, a week before Christmas.

Inside the shopping centre, he took an escalator to the top level. He easily found the Brighton branch of Grant's Fitness Emporium, wedged between an American gents' outfitter and a kitchen shop. He walked in and approached a young man stacking shelves from a trolley that included big tubs of muscle-building powder, so huge it would take someone with large muscles to even attempt to place them on the top shelf.

'Excuse me. Is Mr Grant around?'

'He's in the office at the back.'

'Can you get him for me?'

The guy grunted something, annoyed to have his work interrupted, and sauntered away towards the back of the shop.

A minute or so later Peter Grant appeared. Instead of the sweater or t-shirt he used to wear when he once manned the till in his shop, he wore a smart two-piece suit and open-neck shirt. Mr Grumpy Shelf Stacker went back to his toils.

'Angus, good to see you,' Peter said shaking his hand.

'You too, Peter. How are you?'

'Good. You've heard about Barry?'

'Yes, sorry to say.'

'I'm just trying to come to terms with it, myself.'

Henderson nodded.

'Are you here in a personal or a professional capacity?'

'A bit of both to be honest. Is there a place where we can talk?'

'Sure. Follow me.'

He turned and walked past shelves of food, drink,

powder and potions; the products of an apothecary for the fit and healthy who wanted to be become more fit and healthy.

Through a door at the back of the shop, Peter led him into a small office. In his experience these places often resembled an overflow stockroom with boxes of product and overloaded hangers with extra uniforms or staff clothing, but this one looked neat and tidy.

Peter took a seat behind a desk which faced the wall, and Henderson sat on a chair at the side.

'Can I get you anything?' Peter asked. 'Tea, coffee or a Tai Chi pick-me-up?'

'No, I'm fine. Can I ask you Peter, what did think when you first heard how Barry died?'

He leaned back in the chair. With his jacket off, short hair, lean face and muscular frame, he looked like a sportsman masquerading as a businessman, but looks could be deceptive, as the growth of his fitness company had been meteoric and much lauded by local media and business leaders.

'I felt shock at first, as I'd lost a good mate, but when it finally sank in, I couldn't understand why he jumped in the water at all.'

'An article I read said he was a good swimmer.'

'He was, and went to the pool a couple of times a week, and in the summer he swam in the sea. But the thing is, I still don't see him jumping in the river after the dog.'

'Why not?'

'He loved animals, and the papers down in Arundel were treating him like the Patron Saint of Dogs, but he wasn't like that.'

'How do you mean?'

'Would you jump in a river after your dog?'

Henderson had thought about it before. 'No, I don't think I would.'

'Me neither, and in my opinion, Barry was no different. He was a caring, loving dog owner who would feed it, walk it and look after it, but would he risk his life? I don't think so. He had too much riding on it.'

'Like what, his business?'

'Yeah, his business and the charity work he did. What's your interest?'

'Curiosity, nosey copper syndrome, call it what you like. I went down to Arundel to take a look and like yourself, I was surprised he jumped in, as the current in the river looked strong and would deter better swimmers than him.'

'You couldn't even say Barry was into taking risks, because he wasn't. In the band, that was Eric's role, and a couple times we were convinced he had a death wish.' Peter smiled at the memory. 'Barry would take one look at Eric and tell him he was an idiot.'

'Does Barry have any living relatives?'

'Derek Crow, who I assume you've heard about.'

'Henderson nodded.'

'There's him and a sister, who lives in Chichester, I think. Now you mention it, I don't know if you're aware, but Barry was rich. He started investing in web-based companies way back when people didn't know what the internet was about. Some of them took off in spectacular fashion and made him millions. I don't know if he left a will but if the money is split between the two siblings, his lazy sister who never did a day's work in her life, according to Barry, will become a millionaire overnight.'

SEVEN

Dusseldorf, Germany - 1984

Derek Crow strode across the stage, his face fixed in a stony stare. 'What the fuck are you guys doing there?' he shouted at two men, hunched over the rack that was holding Eric Hannah's guitars.

They turned, rabbits caught in the headlights.

'Vee are trying to fix–' one of them said in guttural English.

A strong hand gripped Derek's arm and steered him away from the mess of wires, a partially set-up drum kit, electricians hoisting lights, and roadies positioning speaker cabinets. It was Kurt Manneheim, Stage Manager for the band they were supporting, an Irish band called the Awakening, a tall, handsome German who spoke flawless English with an American lilt.

'Derek what are you doing here? You should be relaxing with your friends. It is only two hours until the soundcheck; you should be saving your energies for then and the concert tonight.'

'I just thought I would come over and see how things are going.'

'Things are going fine. You have nothing to worry about.'

He led him down a flight of steps at the side of the stage, down a dimly lit corridor and out through the emergency exit to the street.

'I know this gig is the biggest your band has done, but there is no need to fret. We have everything in hand. Now please go back to your hotel and relax with your friends until the soundcheck.'

He walked across the road from the Philipshalle to the Rheinbahn station, his mood nervous and black. He always felt tense before a concert, but then it was in front of two hundred people in Aberdeen or three hundred in Cardiff, not five-and-a-half-thousand bloody Germans in Dusseldorf. No wonder he felt nervous.

The train swished into the open-air station on time, sleek, streamlined and itching to go like a tethered mountain lion, the very embodiment of Teutonic efficiency. He liked Germany. He liked the order he saw around the place, from street cleaners who appeared as if by magic at 6am, hotel staff who delivered food and drinks when they said they would, and the hotel maintenance team capable of returning any room back to its original configuration after a riotous end-of-show party.

They even worked their magic on Eric Hannah's room. Each night, he would screw at least two women, burn the bed covers when he fell asleep with a fag in his mouth at some ungodly hour of the morning, and break lamps, showers and televisions when he crashed into them in a booze or drug-fuelled haze.

They were staying in the Excelsior Dusseldorf and far from finding the boys in their hotel rooms, relaxing on beds and preparing for the biggest concert of their careers, they were in the bar. As usual, Eric Hannah was at the centre of the action.

'Derek, there you are. Where the hell have you been?'

Eric said.

'I went out for a walk,' he said, as they all shifted up and made room for him on a long, padded bench seat.

'To the Philipshalle, to check on preparations, I'll wager my favourite Gibson SG upon.'

'You guys have nothing to worry about,' Steve Minihan said in a Cork drawl, barely comprehensible after a few pints. His slow speech wasn't the result of too much booze or an earlier bout of pill-popping, he always spoke each word as if it tasted good and a sentence was something to be savoured. 'Our fellas have done this hundreds of times, and take it from me, it will work like a dream. All you guys gotta do is go out there and furkin' play.'

A glass of German lager appeared in front of him. He liked Germany, its organisation and efficiency, but he hated the beer. He liked the real ales of Sussex, Dorset and Derbyshire, but none of this light, amber-coloured stuff that tasted of nothing and made him piss twice as often.

Around the large table were all the guys in the Crazy Crows: lead guitarist Eric Hannah, drummer Pete Grant, and bass player, Barry Crow, younger brother of Derek. In addition to the four Crazy Crows, were a couple of guys from the headlining band, the Awakening, Steve Minihan, their rhythm guitarist and Haden O'Rourke, the Irish band's manager.

Derek was pleased to see everyone taking it easy on the booze, sipping down a couple of pints, or litres as it was in this part of Europe, to calm the nerves. He started to relax and was laughing at a joke made by O'Rourke when the manager of the Crazy Crows, Frannie Copeland, showed up. As usual, he had a serious look on his face and chomped on a trademark cigar.

'Hi Frannie, how are you doing?' Derek asked. 'You wanna join us for a drink?'

'No, I won't Derek, thanks. Can I see you a minute?' He nodded towards the far side of the lounge.

Derek left the noisy group, and after finding an empty table in the corner, they both sat down.

'How are you feeling about tonight?' Frannie asked.

'Good. I'm a bit nervous as you might expect, but good.'

'I'm pleased to hear it. Everybody will tell you, playing a big venue like the Philipshalle, you do it as if you're playing a smaller one. Just imagine you're in a small club in Bolton or Basingstoke and you'll be fine.'

'Sometimes all I can see are the first five rows because of the lights, so it wouldn't matter how big the venue is.'

'There you go then. But just remember, the fans are here to see the Awakening so don't get pissed off if they talk amongst themselves and seem more interested in their beer or the person in the seat next to them, than you lot.'

'I know, I know.'

Frannie Copeland looked and behaved like the manager of a band, as he dressed in a suit, could talk the talk with record company executives, and chomped on a big cigar, giving everyone the impression he was very successful, and yet he was only a couple of years older than Derek. They met not long after the band formed in 1982 and by then, Frannie had ten years of the music business under his belt: scouting clubs for talent, organising and promoting tours, and managing several other acts, so he wasn't a rookie like they felt themselves to be.

'I spoke to Kingsley this morning.'

'What, the guy at the record company?'

'Yeah, the guy at the record company who's been championing our cause. He told me the word on the exec floor is they all like the new album. That's not bad praise for a first attempt.'

'It's good to hear. It might stop the bastards from dropping us.'

'It might, but if you can't halt the self-destructive behaviour of our Mr Hannah, you might leave him no option.'

'Is that a threat?'

'Take it how you like, Derek,' Frannie said, his face impassive. He doubted he had ever seen the man smile, granted it was not an easy thing to do with a cigar in permanent situ. 'Hannah is a brilliant guitar player and you guys could go places if you can keep him on the straight and narrow. You never know, next year you could be headlining venues like this all by yourselves.'

'I wish.'

'Don't wish, make it happen but you need to see this as a final warning. Record companies nowadays will tolerate only so much bad publicity. What's the point of paying for PR people and marketing guys to get you guys on the radio and in the newspapers, if it all gets undermined by one story in a tabloid about a trashed hotel room or one of you lot is photographed fighting with a cab driver?'

He sighed; he knew it was true. The first album, *Breakaway,* was out and while a few reviewers were negative about the raw sound and hints about riffs nicked from other records, many were full of praise for Eric Hannah's guitar work and suggesting the best was yet to come. He was worried now, in case the carpet was pulled

41

from under them before they even got started. He loved music, but hated the music industry and their faceless corporations.

'I'll speak to Eric again, but the problem I've got is he'll walk if I piss him off. I know plenty of other bands that will take him.'

'Are you telling me there are no better guitarists out there, because I could name you twenty off the top of my head.'

'Yeah, I know what you mean, but I think Eric's got something special and he's the one who'll take us places. If I say to him, play me a new riff, he can make something up on the spot. How many in your twenty could do that?'

'Yeah, but if his head's not right, the only place he's going to take you is back to the dole queue.'

'Trust me Frannie, I'll sort it.'

'I do trust you Derek, but the trust is wearing thin.' He looked at his watch. 'We all better get down to the soundcheck. I'll go over to reception and see if the car's here.' He eased his thickening frame out of the seat. 'Get over there,' he said nodding at the table where the band were sitting, 'and pull everyone together.'

Derek walked back to the noisy group feeling energetic and full of purpose, despite the sober warnings of their manager. All thoughts of being dropped and record company hassles were cast from his mind, as it was close to time and for him, that was the best part of doing a concert: the anticipation of what was to come.

'Right guys, it's time to go. The car will be here in a minute.' He looked around at the faces. 'Where's Eric?'

'He went outside to get some air,' Barry said. 'At least that's what he said, ten minutes ago.'

'Cheers, Barry. I'll go out and get him. I'll meet you guys at Reception.'

He walked out of the hotel but Eric was nowhere to be seen. He walked along the street and crossed an alleyway at the side of the hotel. He peered down the alley, the stonework of the buildings black from recent rainfall, and there was Eric Hannah, about half-way down, talking to someone.

He headed towards them. When the two men saw him coming, they turned in surprise and pulled their arms into their bodies as if they had something they didn't want him to see.

'Who the hell's this?' Eric's stocky companion said.

'It's ok, Fredrick. He's a mate. We're cool.'

'Ah, good. Maybe he wants some of this too.' He opened the satchel at his side and Derek could see exactly what the two of them had been doing.

'What the fuck are you up to, Eric?' Derek said, his face red. 'This is the biggest gig of our careers and you want to screw it up by taking dope and getting out of your fucking head?'

'Nah, nah, Derek it's not what you think.'

'No? Well, I don't care, I'm not having any of it.' He turned towards Hannah's companion and pushed him hard in the chest. 'Get the fuck out of here you druggy scum. We don't want your sort around here.'

Some of his produce fell to the ground, small packets of powder, wrapped in cellophane and taped together. He kicked the packets in the direction of the dealer.

'And you can take this load of shite with you.'

'We are not finished yet,' the dealer said. 'He owes me money.'

Derek turned to Eric Hannah and grabbed his arm in a strong grip.

'Open it,' he said.

He opened his hand and Derek removed the four or five packets he was holding and threw them at the dealer.

'There's your stuff. Now clear off, he owes you nothing. C'mon Eric,' he said taking hold of his arm, 'we've got a soundcheck to do.'

They turned and Derek pushed Eric up the alley. Seconds later, he heard a noise behind him. He turned and saw a blade coming towards him. He pulled back and the slash missed his face, but cut a slice through his favourite leather bomber jacket. His anger returned big style.

The dealer squared up to him with an evil look in his eye as if he wanted to kill him. The guy sprang forward with a straight jab, which he side-stepped. As he passed to the side, Derek locked his big mitts together and brought them down on the back of the guy's head, like wielding a two-handed axe. The druggy collapsed in a heap and dropped the knife. Derek kicked it away.

The guy made to get up but before he could, Derek booted him in the balls and punched him in the face. He slumped down on the damp pavement, the blood from his face seeping into a small pool of rain, discolouring it.

He turned to Eric. 'C'mon, let's go.'

'Christ almighty, Derek,' he said, his face like a five-year-old who had just dropped his sweets in the mud. 'I was starting to like the guy.'

EIGHT

It was early, not yet seven o'clock, when DI Henderson walked into Sussex House. After dumping his document case in his office, he entered the small kitchen at the side of the CID offices to make a coffee. Surprise, surprise DS Walters was standing there and not only had she cleaned out the coffee machine but it was bubbling away making a brew.

'Morning sir, how are you today?'

'Stunned is the best description. You're more often than not tucked up in bed or looking like a half-shut knife at this time of the morning.'

She busied herself trying to find clean mugs and testing the milk for freshness, not a job for the faint hearted. 'Maybe I'm turning over a new leaf.'

'You don't fool me, Ms Walters. There wouldn't happen to be a new boyfriend on the scene?'

'Could be.'

'If there is a new boyfriend, doesn't it mean the opposite, more late mornings because...'

'Don't go there,' she said. 'We're still at the 'getting to know you stage', if you must know.'

'What I was trying to say is, you might be needing more sleep as this liaison could involve you in more socialising with late nights and parties.'

She gave him a sceptical look and handed him a mug. 'No more speculation, I'll tell you all about it when I'm ready.'

A few minutes later they headed downstairs and into a small briefing room. The four heavily-kitted individuals allocated to this operation were already seated there and after introductions, Henderson walked to the front of the room.

'The target this morning is this building here,' Henderson said, pointing to the brightly lit screen behind him, currently displaying a photograph of a large warehouse. 'This warehouse is located at the back of Potter Farm, a cereal farm two miles south of Burgess Hill. The farm and the warehouse are owned by a man called Tristan Hunt and we don't know if he is involved, but we do know he rents the building to a Chinese businessman.'

Henderson stopped to take a drink as his mouth was parched. The previous night he went out with his girlfriend, Rachel, for a curry in Hove and it must have contained more garlic than he realised.

'We believe there is a cannabis nursery in this location for two reasons,' Henderson continued. 'One, a nark with his nose close to the drugs business says there is, and he's been reliable in the past. Two, EDF, the local electricity supply company, identified a high infra-red signature when they made a pass over the premises in a helicopter equipped with a thermal imaging camera.'

'No chance it could be something more exotic, sir,' one of the coppers said. 'Like Aloe Vera or some new tea?'

'Need something smooth for your rough skin, do you Alex?' said another.

They all laughed.

'I can't think it might be something else, because if it is a legitimate business, why would they need to by-pass the electricity meter?'

'True.'

Henderson spent the next few minutes discussing door entry, covering the exits, and chasing down and arresting everyone there, including the owner, Tristan Hunt. He and Walters would interview him at the site and make an assessment of his culpability, but if tenants were growing dope on his property he would need either to be a saint or a cabinet minister to escape arrest.

'I think I've covered everything. Are there any questions?'

The raid team travelled to the farm in an unmarked blue van, and to ensure everyone arrived at the same time Henderson told them to follow his car. It was a grey morning, thick clouds blanketing much of Sussex with no sign of the sun lurking behind. Last night, heavy rain pounded the seafront and they'd got soaked coming out of the curry restaurant, now it left the leafless trees all around looking damp and feeling sorry for themselves, dreich, as his father in Fort William would say.

Twenty minutes later, Henderson turned into the farm, the unmarked van following close behind. His fear in approaching a place like this was not in discovering it was empty, or that the people inside were growing something else, as he believed the intel to be sound, but in not finding anyone at home. He didn't know a lot about cultivating cannabis but he assumed most plants could look after themselves, so he was steeling himself just in case this time they were unlucky.

He needn't have worried as three vans were parked close to the large, brick-built building. After the raid he would take a closer look in each of them, as it was likely they were used for carrying seeds and fertiliser, and to find something else would only strengthen the case against them. The police vehicles came to a halt and everyone got out and ran towards the entrance. One of the team disappeared around the back to look for and cover any other exits.

The door appeared to be locked from the inside and without waiting to knock and give the occupants time to scarper, the door banger rushed up to the front. Two bangs later and the door swung loose. Henderson piled in behind the running officers and once through the heavy PVC curtain, his senses were assailed by the intense brightness and the heat and the humidity of the heavy, moisture-soaked air.

He had seen several cannabis nurseries before but this one took top prize for the scale of operation. The walls of the massive warehouse were insulated with acres of plastic sheeting draped all the way round and in front of him, a sea of luxuriant green plants.

They were all sprouting from their own big plastic pots, like you could see in any garden centre, and resting on more plastic sheeting. He could see ten rows of pots but had no idea how many were in each row as they disappeared into the mist created by the irrigation system, and bathed in the ghostly yellow light from radiating heat lamps.

If the plant growing system looked elaborate, the electrics above their heads seemed equally so. It was a dull morning outside, but inside was like standing under the floodlights at the Amex Stadium. It was also hot, and mixed with the amount of water around the place, Henderson's shirt clung to his body and his face perspired as if at the end of a long run along Brighton seafront.

He heard much scuffling and after a few minutes, PC Davis lined three Chinese people against the wall, cuffed and ready to be escorted out to the van. He couldn't see Walters and hoped she wasn't sampling the merchandise as she was hard enough to handle when a new boyfriend appeared in her life without the complication of exotic stimulants.

Henderson walked towards the suspects when a ruddy faced-man walked into the warehouse and approached him. 'What the hell's going on here?' he asked. 'What are you people doing in my warehouse?'

If this new arrival experienced surprise at the array of electrical expertise and the large-scale replica of the Malaysian rainforest, he didn't show it. Tut, tut, his first mistake.

'Who are you?' Henderson asked.

'I'm Tristan Hunt, I own this place. Who are you?'

'Good morning, Mr Hunt. I am DI Henderson, Surrey and Sussex Police and I have a warrant to search these premises.' He flashed his ID card and the search warrant, but Hunt knew well enough what was going on and didn't need to look too closely.

'What the hell are you looking for?'

'I don't know if you are aware, Mr Hunt, but your warehouse is being used to grow illegal substances. Due to the high levels of electricity needed to power all this,' he said spreading an arm in a semi-circle, 'your tenants are also by-passing the electricity meter. A foolhardy and dangerous thing to do and another serious offence they are guilty of committing.'

'What do you mean, illegal substances! They told me

they were growing a herbal remedy widely seen in China and sold by health shops all over the world to treat rheumatism. My mother has severe symptoms from the condition and I tried some of it on her and it works. So how can it be illegal?'

'Don't give me your lame excuses. You're a cereal farmer. Most farmers I know can tell the variety of corn or wheat just by looking at it. You're not trying to tell me you didn't know what these plants were, or if you didn't, looked them up on the web or in one of your seed catalogues.'

'No, I did not.'

Just then, Henderson heard a shout coming from the small office at the back. The door flew open and a Chinese guy appeared. He ran, and moments later a raid officer emerged from the same door and chased him, blood running down his face.

'Stop that man!' the officer shouted.

Henderson set off after the fleeing man and on passing DS Walters coming towards him, said, 'Carol, read Hunt his rights, he's coming with us.'

Outside, Henderson caught up with PC Davis. 'I didn't see which way he went,' Henderson said.

'Me neither.'

'You go that way,' he said, indicating the back of the building, 'and I'll go this way.'

'Ok.'

Henderson ran in the direction of the three small, dirty vans, figuring the guy might be heading there to try to make a getaway in one of the vehicles rather than attempt to run across fields at the back of the warehouse. He stood back from the vehicles and bent down to look underneath.

There and unmoving, he spotted a pair of legs.

He waited a few moments until PC Davis arrived at the far side of the warehouse and held his hand up to stop him running. Henderson pointed to the vans and mouthed, 'he's in there.'

Davis nodded in response and as quietly as possible made his way towards them.

The guy was crouched down between the first and second vans and when Henderson appeared in his vision, he turned to run the other way but ran into the bulky form of PC Davis.

The guy ran at Henderson, Kamikaze style, wielding a rock. Henderson flinched when he swung it towards him, his head missing direct contact with the stone but it still caught the side of his face. It stung like crazy but he didn't move from his position and the guy, half the height of the DI, barrelled into him in an attempt to get past.

Henderson grabbed him but it was like trying to bag a wildcat as he threshed about, all arms and legs while still attempting to have another swing of the rock. Just then, a long-handled baton swished through the air and hit the guy in the shoulder and he crumpled in an untidy heap on the ground.

'I feel much better now,' Davis said as he pressed a knee into the guy's back and applied the cuffs. The guy was small, and in the confined space between the vans having a sixteen-stone weight on top of him must have felt claustrophobic.

'In my book, nobody smacks a copper and gets away with it.'

NINE

Over a week had passed since Peter Grant had kissed Sarah Corbett in his office, but this was the first time they were both free of diary commitments to go out on a proper date. Without much discussion, as they seemed to like the same things, they settled on Graze, a 'modern British cuisine' restaurant on Western Road in Brighton.

The restaurant was busy, which was to be expected on a Friday night, but at least they weren't seated near the window. It was still early days for both of them and there was no point in giving the gossip-hive a good poke if their relationship was going to fizzle out in a couple of weeks' time. Now, did this sort of thinking make him a pessimist or a realist? He couldn't decide.

Despite the time constraints of leaving work and getting ready to go out, it was obvious Sarah had made good use of her time. Her green eyes sparkled, her hair had lost the formal, business look and was now bouncy and full of life, while a set of pearls given to her by her late grandmother gave him a good excuse to have the occasional peek at her ample cleavage easing over the top of her dark blue dress.

'It's a nice place,' she said as pre-dinner drinks were served, and after he took a surreptitious look around the room to make sure no business colleagues were dining close by. 'Have you been here before?'

'Once,' he said, cringing at the memory. 'About

eighteen months ago, I came in with Kevin and Mike but I got so plastered, I don't have any idea what I ate or how good it tasted; it could have been a Big Mac or a plate of whelks from a seafront seller for all I knew.'

'Tut, tut,' she said trying hard not to smile. 'I didn't know I was spending the evening with a drunken bum.'

'Nor is it a good advert for a fitness company to see the MD lying in the gutter in his best suit, gazing at the stars with a stupid grin on his face. In my defence, it wasn't long after Emily and the kids left home and I was going through my angry phase. For a few weeks I didn't know what I was doing.'

'You seem much better now. At least I think you do.'

'You sound just like my therapist.'

She may have been a skilled HR professional, but she couldn't hide the look of consternation creeping across her face.

'Hah, got you there,' he said. 'Do I look like the type to go to a therapist? I mean, if I acted any calmer I'd be asleep.' He picked up the glass in front of him and drained the last of a gin and tonic. 'If I have any issues I need to work through, I head down to the gym.'

'Thank the Lord for that. For a moment I thought I was going out with a drunk and a basket case.'

'I have my moments.'

'Does it still bother you, Emily leaving?'

'I'm over the hurt and the anger I felt at the time when she walked out. The practicalities of lawyers, money and houses, I must admit, didn't trouble me as much as they should have, and now I'm trying to forget about the whole thing and move on.'

'What caused the break-up in the first place, if you

don't mind me asking?'

He was about to speak when a wine waiter arrived with their selection. It was one of the most expensive bottles on the list and so it was only right he should treat it with respect. He took a sniff and a slurp, but in truth he was only going through the motions as he couldn't tell Tannat from Tempranillo; he knew what he liked and how to drink it. Deference duly observed, the waiter poured the wine into glasses so large he could have emptied the bottle into both, but the amount he did pour only succeeded in creating a small puddle at the bottom of the glass.

'Stop me if you've heard it before,' he said when they were alone again. 'We hadn't been getting along for some time, mainly because she couldn't get used to me being away on business as often as I was.'

'I remember when I first started in the company,' she said, 'you were scooting off on business just about every week. If it wasn't the US and Germany, it was the Far East and China. I don't know how I would have coped with such a punishing schedule, although it's calmed down a lot since then.'

'Yeah, I did all that, plus I visited equipment manufacturers in Holland and Scandinavia as I was trying to flesh-out the idea for a mega-store, even at that time. As you say, it's eased off since then, because the company is bigger and now it's not only me who's out there meeting suppliers and landlords; but by then the damage had taken its toll and she'd found someone else.'

'I'm sorry it ended the way it did, it's a real shame. I liked Emily.'

'It is and it isn't. If you believe in fate as I do, you'll know it was meant to happen. Plus, it's better for it to have occurred now and not later when we're both too old and set in our ways to do anything about it.'

'You have a very philosophical way of looking at it.'

'Yeah, maybe, but the bit I can't take is living alone. The house seems so empty without the kids running up and down the stairs and leaving dirty clothes everywhere else but in the washing basket.'

'I felt the same after Andrew left, but if it's any comfort, it does get better.'

'I bloody hope so.'

'It took me a while, but I soon got into a new routine and the hours I used to spend with him talking, arguing, shopping and all the rest are now filled with doing loads of other stuff. If you're lucky, they can be just as fulfilling as the things they've replaced.'

'You should be in HR, you're good at making people feel better.'

The influence of the food and the wine gradually shifted the conversation onto lighter topics and he found out that she liked photography and gardening and swam twice a week, while she learned that his spare time was centred around his kids, taking them to coffee bars and the cinema or up to London to see a concert or an exhibition at the Barbican or Tate Modern.

'What sort of access do you have to the children?'

'God, it sounds so formal, so legal.'

'It often is.'

'Emily and me are pretty relaxed about it as they're not young kids anymore. I mean, Graham's sixteen and Danielle's eighteen. Danielle comes to see me whenever she wants as she's got her own car, although her visits will stop when she goes away to Durham University in

September. Graham, well Graham has always been a bit of a mummy's boy and so he'll only come if Danielle or Emily are coming over, which is a shame.'

They left the restaurant at eleven-thirty, leaving behind two clean plates, an empty bottle of St Emilion and a handsome tip for the waiter, and this time Peter could say he enjoyed his meal and it would be remembered. If he was counting, her consumption of the 'chateau's premier wine, redolent of blackberries and fine wood shavings' was more than his. It was not a thinly-veiled ploy to take advantage of a drunken woman and hope for a quick fondle as they stumbled into a doorway, but he'd taken the car; Brighton cops had a sound reputation in the pursuit of drunk drivers and he didn't want to be the next name in their little black book.

The car was parked at the bottom of Brunswick Square and as they walked down the slope towards the seafront, a strong wind whipped up from the sea into their faces, bringing with it a tang of salt and seaweed. She snuggled in close and while it was good to have a warm body beside him, he was under no illusion it was the result of the inclement weather and not his expensive after-shave or any rough-boy-made-good charm.

Peter Grant lived in a four-bedroom, mock-Tudor detached house in Woodland Drive, Hove and if the floral parlance of estate agents was to believed, he lived in a 'much sought-after road with a favoured south-westerly aspect.' Despite the closeness of other neighbours, the house did have a double garage, a long back garden and ample parking space out front to accommodate three or four cars, which was just as well as a few years ago he'd converted the garage into a gym.

His ex-wife used to call the gym his 'folly', as the company offices in Woodingdean were equipped with a well-appointed gym and there were any number of clubs and sports centres in the Brighton and Hove area. He wanted one at home as he liked to exercise whenever the notion took him and couldn't do so in a public gym, not after drinking a bottle of wine or at some time past eleven o'clock at night when most of the clubs were closed.

While he made coffee, Sarah rummaged through his record collection. Before starting the fitness business, he was the drummer in the Crazy Crows rock band and through this and his love of music, he had accumulated a vast amount of cassettes, CDs and vinyl albums.

Unlike most other people he knew, his LPs did not end up on the council waste tip or boxed-up and hidden away in the attic like an embarrassing relative; they were displayed in a floor-to-ceiling wall unit which also included a high-output amp, floor-standing speakers with a twelve-inch bass and played on a two-grand Linn Sondek turntable.

If pressed, he would have to admit he was 'old school' when it came to recorded music, and critical of the march of CDs and MP3 downloads, although he knew he couldn't ignore them completely. To his ears, vinyl produced a much warmer and fuller sound than the treble-heavy CD or the top-and-tailed MP3, and he loved listening to an album while poring over a beautifully drawn cover like Cream's *Disraeli Gears* or one stylishly photographed such as *Abbey Road* or *Sergeant Pepper*. Anyone who had ever peered frustratingly at a CD flyer in a vain attempt to read the minuscule song lyrics, or tried to identify the faces in a tiny photograph, would not dispute the LP's superiority on this score.

He removed two coffee mugs from the cupboard, when he felt warm hands circling his waist. Slowly, as he enjoyed the little tingles the gentle massaging action of her fingers were causing and didn't want to put her off, he placed the mugs back in the cupboard, closed the door and turned to face her. Her kisses were passionate and demanding, her lips caressing his with sensuous delicacy, while her tongue dipped in and out his mouth leaving him gasping for more. He ran his hands down her body with a burning desire to touch everything.

They staggered towards the stairs, he without his shirt and she without her dress, both of which were now lying on the kitchen floor. She wasn't wearing a bra, a brave thing to do in the middle of winter, revealing large, rounded breasts which he found hard to keep his hands from touching. The belt of his trousers had been loosened and when he tried to climb the stairs, he almost tripped as his trousers fell to his knees. It was touch and go if they would make it to the bedroom or stop where they were and make love on the landing, but if working for a fitness company guaranteed one thing, there would be no shortage of stamina. It was going to be a long night.

TEN

With a sigh he turned and walked back to the van. He flicked the toothpick over with his tongue in one movement; five minutes one way, five minutes the other.

It was quiet here, full of big houses and flash cars but he knew from the web they could be a stroppy lot. Commuters often used this road as a rat-run to the by-pass at the top of the hill, and a few years back annoyed residents had tried to block access with rubbish bins. Not to be outdone by this petulant display of anger and frustration, the motorists dumped the contents of the bins on their smart driveways. Oh yes, he would have liked to have been there.

He had been watching the house for several days now, and was starting to believe this guy was a boring bastard, as his routine never varied. He left for work at the same time every morning and came back at the same time almost every night. He knew what he ate, how much he drank, what time he headed into the home gym and what time he went to bed, but it all changed this evening when he brought a woman home.

He liked the guy's gym. It was better than the one he'd used in the nick which was full of big bastards with elaborate tats on their muscular arms that stretched and moved when biceps were tensed. He didn't bother them and they left him alone, until he proved he could lift the same as they could and only then did he gain acceptance into their circle. It suited him fine inside as it was Category A and they protected him from a lot of serious nutters.

In this guy's place there was a multi-gym, a running machine, exercise bike, loose weights; the dog's bollocks. In all the time he'd been watching him, he never once did any of the aerobic stuff like running or cycling, and often he heard him grunting under the weight of the barbell. It would be a different sort of grunting he would be doing tonight, he thought, giggling.

He could see his van, a customised Mercedes Vito Euro parked in front of a row of shops, close to a wine shop and a posh hairdresser. Subtle it wasn't with matt black bodywork, a flame effect along one side, chrome wheels, tinted windows and a sound system capable of blowing a pedestrian's clothes off.

For doing surveillance, it was crap and stuck out like a tart at a vicars' convention, more so in a snobby place like this where he often saw curtains twitching. He climbed in, closed the door and pulled out his phone.

'Hi man, it's me.'

'Hi mate. Did you do it?'

'Nope, he came back with a woman.'

'What him, that ugly bastard? She must be a pro.'

'Na, na. You forget summat.'

'What?'

'He's rich. Birds go for that.'

The voice on the phone grunted disapproval, but he knew he was right. 'When you gonna do it?'

'I told ya, I'll do it when the time's right. To do this stuff proper with no comeback takes planning. You know the score.'

'Ach, sooner the better, is all I'm saying.'

'You getting heat from Blakey?'

'No more than usual. He wants the job done.'

'Let me know if he hassles you. I'll take him on, see if I don't.'

'It's not him you need to be worrying about as he's getting on, same as me. It's his sons; they're bastards.'

'Yeah, they're a bad bunch.'

'You look after yourself, man. Be seeing.'

The phone went dead; a man of few words.

He started the van and a deep rumble shook through the bodywork. If he revved it harder, it would shake through the windows of nearby houses and wake up their children, but it didn't make sense to attract unwanted attention. Oh no, he liked being anonymous.

He drove away slowly, the big engine straining at the leash, urging him to go faster, but he wouldn't put his foot down until he reached the A23.

ELEVEN

DI Henderson walked out of the cinema at Brighton Marina deep in thought. It wasn't because the film was so interesting and left him with a new way of looking at life, quite the opposite, in fact. He was racking his brains trying to think of something positive to say, as Rachel had been looking forward to seeing it for ages and would be annoyed if he dismissed it without justification.

'Did you like it?' he said, getting his question in before she could ask him. 'Did it live up to your expectations?'

'No, it didn't. I found it overlong and I hated the way they switched the location of the story from London to L.A. as it is in the book. How about you?'

'I haven't read the book, as I told you before, but yes, it did go on a bit too long and I found my mind drifting at times.' A lot of times, in fact.

She reached over and kissed him. 'Sorry for dragging you there H, I'll do better next time.'

'No, you won't. The next time it'll be my choice.'

It was dark and the wind whipped across the wide open spaces in the centre of the Marina, swirling items of litter and bringing an instant chill to anyone not attired in warm clothing. Rather than drive back into Brighton and face the problem of finding a parking place, they walked up the stairs to The West Quay pub and entered.

Standing at the bar Henderson could see out to the army of masts and pontoons of the Marina, an impressive sight in the day but not much to see at night. It reminded him, if a reminder was required, that his boat was moored out there somewhere and he hadn't been down to see it in a while.

It was close to the end of February and not a lot of sailing was being done by him or anyone else until the weather improved and the sea warmed, sometime in April or May. Until then, he was reassured to know it was securely tied and covered with tarpaulins to protect it from whatever Mother Nature could offer over the next few months.

The last time he'd taken *Mingary* out for a long sail was August when he took Rachel west along the South coast to Salcombe in Devon. They'd hit a purple patch of weather as it didn't rain once and most of the evenings were warm, calm and balmy. The trip involved two firsts. It was the first time Rachel had spent more than one night on *Mingary*. In fact, she managed four nights aboard and felt disappointed when the voyage ended. It might have been something to do with her companion, but he was nothing if not modest.

The second 'first' was to have a first-class seat to view the Perseid meteor shower. He liked astronomy, ever since studying the rudiments of sailing as a teenager, as every sailor worth their salt needed to know how to navigate using the stars, just in case the electrics went haywire.

Perseid's are loose rocks and other material from the tail of the comet Swift-Tuttle which the earth passes through once a year. When the rocks and dust enter the earth's thick atmosphere, they burn creating a brief but bright streak of light across the sky, a modest fireworks display without all the crashing and banging. A boat on a calm night is the ideal place to watch something like this, almost impossible in Brighton with interfering light pollution from shops, street lights and houses.

He carried the drinks back to the table and sat down. Rachel, in common with many of the pub's other customers, was looking at something on her mobile phone.

'No phones at the table,' he said, 'remember.'

'I didn't know it included this table in this particular pub. Only joking, as I hate people looking at their phones when they should be talking to the person next to them. It's just that I received a text from my mum.'

'At ten-thirty at night? I thought they were early to-bed, early to-rise people.'

'They are, but because Dad's away in Japan at the moment she's got no one to talk to.'

'He's always away. No wonder they pay him so much.'

She gave him a reproachful look before dropping the phone into her handbag with a practised air. 'I suspect she's lonely but I'll give her a call tomorrow.' She took a sip of wine. 'So what did you get up to this week, H? I've hardly spoken to you as I've been so busy and you're always in meetings.'

'Did I tell you how I received this mark on my face?'

'No, I was going to ask but I'm not sure I want to hear all the gory details. What was her name?'

'Very funny, but the story's not so gory.' He outlined the Burgess Hill drug warehouse raid and told her about the amount of drugs seized. It had earned him a ten-second spot on *South Today*, the regional television news programme, his bashed face made more presentable for a television audience tucking into their lunch, with a dab of the presenter's makeup. If this incident constituted the highlight of his week, he omitted to mention the meetings, the paperwork or the staff issues, as even he couldn't make that lot sound interesting.

'Did your fine newspaper make anything of the Barry Crow story?' he asked.

'Remind me. Who's Barry Crow when he's at home?'

'The guy found drowned in the River Arun at Arundel trying to save his dog.'

'Yeah, I remember the story. We first reported it as a regular news story, you know what I mean; a man drowns, body recovered, the police calling it a tragic loss of life, all that sort of thing. By the time the funeral took place, Becky had done a piece about a local hero who died trying to rescue his dog, with quotes from the RSPCA and other dog charities praising his actions. Why are you so interested? Was he on the police radar and doing something he shouldn't?'

'Nothing like that. He was the bass player in a band called the Crazy Crows.'

'I remember reading the name somewhere. When were they around, as I'd never heard of them before?'

'You've never heard of them because you were too busy listening to pop music when you were growing up and missed out on an essential element of your musical education. They were around in the mid-eighties, to the early-nineties.'

'I take it when you say something like, 'my musical education', we must be talking about a rock band.'

'Correct, but not any old rock band. One who looked destined for greater things but packed it all in before they got there.'

'Interesting, as the Sunday papers are always full of gigs by bands from decades ago. According to you, they're still playing the same clubs and halls they did in their twenties and most of them are now in their sixties. Why did this lot pack it in?'

'Is this you feigning interest, the seasoned reporter thinking she might use it to fill a space in the newspaper sometime in the future?'

'No, you cynic, I'm interested as it sounds like a good story.'

'If you think you can add it to your 'human interest' collection of interviews and profiles, you're a few years too late. It's already been done.'

'I guessed that. So come on tell me, what happened?'

Henderson had called his brother, Archie, last night and asked him what he remembered about the Crazy Crows. No longer in the Army, he was working now as an estate agent in Glasgow and, strange as it may seem for a guy who liked dressing in fatigues, carrying a gun and heading out on patrol, flogging flats and houses to people with harder accents than his seemed to suit him just fine.

Archie then trotted out a potted biography of each member of the Crows and his assessment of them as musicians. He knew a lot about the band's leader, Derek Crow and admired him for his single-minded approach in the way he dealt with record companies and journalists, and how he marshalled the disparate factions of his band.

Henderson took a sip from his pint. 'There's not much to tell. As I was saying, the guy who died in Arundel used to be in the Crazy Crows, a band I liked in the eighties, still do. In fact, it was the first rock concert I took Archie to see.'

'Do bands play places like Fort William?'

'You are joking. Unless they play fiddles and acoustic guitars, they've got no chance. It was in Glasgow.'

'How old were you then?'

'About seventeen.'

'So, Archie was what, thirteen? Surely you didn't travel to Glasgow together?'

'No, my dad took us down and while he visited his brother in hospital, we went to the concert.'

'Were they good?'

'They were brilliant. Now, continuing my story. Their first album wasn't bad, a bit reminiscent of many other bands around at the time, but by the second, there were signs of a marked improvement and good things to come.'

'Have you got them?'

'What?'

'The albums.'

He nodded. 'Of course.'

'I might give them a listen, if I can stand the racket.'

'I'll ignore that. By the third album they'd introduced a keyboard player, I forget his name, but he expanded the sound and improved the song writing and all the rest, and it was much better than the previous two. When they released the fourth album, they were flying. The music press were calling them the next best thing since Led Zeppelin.'

'I take it that's a good thing.'

'Of course it is, Philistine.'

'So what went wrong?'

'The keyboard player, Danny Winter, I remember his name now, was killed in an accident and afterwards the band just fell apart.'

'Just like that?'

'Yep, just like that. The main singer and songwriter in the band, Derek Crow–'

'Not the guy who owns all those fuel tankers and who came to the country's rescue in its hour of need?'

'Him.'

'He was in the papers only the other day, shaking hands with Rob McNaughton, our new Labour Prime Minister, for his role in averting a petrol shortage.'

'Yes, the very man.'

'Hasn't he done well? I thought you said there wasn't a story?'

'I remember what happened now. Derek Crow was devastated by the accident and told the rest of the band he didn't want to continue.'

'That sounds like Derek Crow: this is what I'm doing and you lot can go and sling your hook if you don't like it. What sort of accident killed the keyboard player? Did he take an overdose like all the rest or blow his liver on too much booze?'

'No, but this is where the story takes on a little twist and is one of the reasons why it caught my eye in the first place. You see, the keyboard player drowned.'

TWELVE

Ludwigshafen, Germany - 1985

The gear from the last concert was safely stowed away, packed in vans that were now sitting immobile over in the car park. Derek and the rest of the boys were in the lounge of Friedrich Ebert Halle, drinking while waiting for the Guns of Detroit to finish their set. If it was up to Eric Hannah, he would piss-off right now, but Derek insisted they had to be nice to the folks they met on the way up, as they didn't know when they might need their help in the future. Amen to all that.

It was brass monkeys outside as he was still wearing his stage clothes, thin cotton shirt and jeans. They felt damp and his body sweaty but it was more from the dope in his system than any form of exertion as he didn't run around the stage much when performing.

Standing at the back of one of the vans was Fast Eddie, chief of the roadies. He was a slow-mover, but strong as an ox.

'Hey Eddie,' he said as he walked towards him.

'Hey there, Eric.'

'Is all the gear packed away?'

'It's all shipshape and ready to go back to good old Blighty.'

Eric leaned on the van beside the fat roadie, a man who liked curries and beer a couple of times a week.

'I'm looking forward to going home,' Eddie said.

'Oh, yeah, what's so special about it?'

'I miss two things. A decent pint of ale and a bloody good fry-up. The fucking stuff they serve up for breakfast here, bits of meat and rolls you can't get your teeth into, doesn't hold a candle to a full English breakfast.'

'You've got a point there, mate. How's our little hideaway?'

'All waiting to be filled.' He nodded towards the open rear doors of the Transit. 'Take a butcher's.'

Eric pulled open the doors. The amps and guitars they had been playing at the concert about an hour ago were packed at the front with the big speaker cabinets standing behind. Three vans were being used for this tour, two full of gear and one for the band, but the difference here was the backs of a couple of speaker cabinets were off, exposing the rear of the speaker and electrical wiring.

'When does your guy get here?' Fast Eddie asked.

'He's late.'

He offered Eddie a cigarette and they both sparked up.

'You played a blinding set tonight, Eric, you were on fire.'

'I was, right enough. The tracks from the new album really suit a live venue, you know.'

'The crowd could sense it. They came to see the Guns of Detroit, but I think they went away liking the Crazy Crows.'

'If we could only bottle all the energy generated from a live performance and pour it into an album, we would sell shed-loads and get ourselves on the cover of *Rolling Stone*.'

'I think you're right.'

A silence descended between them, he thinking about

the set tonight and if this, their second album, would be the making of the band. Eddie, on the other hand, was maybe trying to decide whether he should go back to his painting and decorating job after this tour or join another band's road crew.

'Is this him?' Eddie said, nodding towards a Mercedes saloon driving fast around the car park, not easy as it was full of cars, vans and trucks as the Guns of Detroit were still on stage.

The car pulled up beside them. The rear door opened and a tall man approached them.

'Eric,' the man said grasping him in a bear hug. 'It's so good to meet you. Any friend of Heinrich is a friend of mine. Call me Max. Did the concert go well?'

'It sure did. Your people seem to like us.'

'This is good. Did you bring the money?'

Eric handed him an envelope and Max flicked through the pile of notes with a practised eye.

'Good, good,' he said. He walked to the rear of the car and opened the boot. Removing a holdall, he dropped it at Eric's feet.

Eric bent down, unzipped the bag and rummaged through the merchandise. It was the largest consignment he had ever seen and indeed the largest he had ever bought, so he had to make sure he wasn't being sold garden weeds and talcum powder. He pulled out a small knife, one used for trimming cables and splicing piles of coke, and pierced the bag.

Five minutes later the Mercedes screeched away, almost at the same time as fans were starting to stream out of the concert hall. Working fast, they transferred all the packages into the back of the speaker cabinets and using Eddie's speedy battery-powered screwdriver, sealed them again.

He left Eddie to round up the rest of the road crew for the long drive back to the UK tonight, and headed back into the Friedich Ebert Halle and up the stairs to the artists' lounge. The Guns of Detroit had finished their set after completing two encores, and there they stood, bathed in sweat and guzzling bottles of Becks Bier as if lives depended on it. There was a lot of mutual back-slapping, the Crows telling the Guns what a great band they were and the Guns doing the same to them.

It was the last date on the Crows' mini-tour of Germany and for them it was back to the UK to start thinking about a third album, while the Guns were soldiering on through Europe bringing their own brand of blues-infused Southern rock to a new legion of fans.

For Eric, the tour was an enlightening experience, as he'd spent a lot of time talking to the Americans. They had been in the same place as the Crows were now, and within five years, they had conquered America and this month were doing the same all over Europe. Far from making him feel overawed or jealous, he desperately wanted to hear their stories and craved a piece of the action for himself.

He and the Guns' guitarist, Henry White, spent many a happy hour trading licks and yakking about equipment and playing techniques. Looking back, it brought a smile to his face to think that even though White was a couple of years older than him and had worked as a professional musician since leaving school at sixteen, most of the tutoring came from him to the American.

He started talking to Emily Grant, the flirty, sexy wife

of Peter Grant, the band's drummer. So far, and despite his best overtures and chat-up lines, she'd still resisted all his attempts to get into her pants. To her credit, she was the only wife or girlfriend to make it out to Germany to watch them, moving her up a couple of notches in his estimation and making him want her all the more.

They left Ludwigshafen, a town near Stuttgart, around midnight, although none of them had much of a chance to see either place, and headed west. They drove in convoy, Fast Eddie driving the first van, Nathan Connelly driving the second, and Derek behind the wheel of the third. The third van was reserved for people but still it included some items of kit they couldn't fit elsewhere, so they were fighting for space with coils of cables, effects pedals, and several unyielding guitar cases.

He was in the back with Peter, and at the front sat Barry, Derek and Peter's wife, Emily, who was saving her train fare by hitching a ride home. It was a good job Barry was sitting there and not him, as the desire to slip a hand under her pretty, floral dress would be a temptation too far and most likely earn him a slap from Emily and a punch in the face from Pete.

It wasn't so bad where they were, as they had a couple of mattresses to sleep on, but he hoped the gear was well tied-up, as he didn't fancy being woken from a dreamless kip with a guitar or an amp bouncing off his head. He bedded down and in combination with the number of Becks he had consumed earlier plus a small toke from the new consignment, he fell asleep almost immediately.

He woke with a start, not because gravity had set loose a piece of kit, but on hearing a loud noise. He waited a second or two for his groggy head to clear before sitting up. The van was no longer in motion and yes, he could hear shouting outside, suggesting something was going on; he hadn't imagined it.

'What's the beef out there, Pete?'

Peter Grant stretched. He didn't seem to sleep much and even though he did the most physically demanding job in the band, he was still the fittest and healthiest of the bunch. Now, how did that work?

'I dunno, some ruck about waiting too long or something.'

'Where are we?'

'In Dover, in a long bloody queue waiting to go through Customs.'

'Christ, did I snooze through Germany and a Channel crossing? That has to be some kind of record.'

'You did, and boy do you make some strange noises in your sleep.'

'Yeah,' he said as he got up, careful to avoid hitting his head on the low ceiling, and tensed tired muscles. 'I must have been dreaming I was humping your wife.'

Pete flexed those big drummer arm muscles and a few other ones on his face.

'Only in my sleep mind, nothing else.'

'Better not be,' he said through gritted teeth.

'Bloody hell, when you put on a face like that, you could play a villain in one of the Bond movies instead of playing drums in a rock band. I'm going out to see what's going on before you explode.'

He pushed open the doors. Before he could adjust, he was assailed by a combination of fresh sea air, the bright sunshine of a Dover morning and the rumble and grind of a traffic queue, making him flinch.

A long line of vehicles, including their three vans, were waiting to be cleared by Customs but at least they were near the front of the queue. The shouting he'd heard was an argument going on between a Customs officer and a lorry driver, the latter complaining about the time he'd spent waiting and the Customs guy giving him back as good as he got.

He wandered up the line to Fast Eddie's van as the Customs guy seemed to lose the plot with the mouthy lorry driver and decided to give his load the complete tooth-comb treatment.

'Christ, we're gonna be here for ages,' he said as he scrounged a light from Eddie.

'That's what you get for giving a bloody jobsworth too much lip. Be nice to the buggers is my approach.'

'Yeah, you can be nice as ninepence because all our stuff is sprayed with Eddie's custom-made pooch fooling perfume.'

'Too true brother, it never fails.'

Eric yawned. He wasn't a morning person, never had been. It was an old rock cliché to think all musicians slept during the day and worked at night, not getting to bed until regular folks were heading off to work. For him, there was nothing rock 'n' roll about it. He preferred working this way and often came up with his best guitar licks at three or four in the morning, stoned out of his skull and a long way from a warm bed.

He wandered back down the line of cars, buses and trucks to talk to Derek, who was stretched out in the passenger seat with a snoozing Emily beside him, her head on his shoulder, the jammy bastard. Barry sat behind the wheel and the taciturn bass player with the voracious sexual appetite acknowledged his pleasant salutation with a barely perceptible nod.

'We sail through border controls in France and Belgium,' Derek said by way of greeting, 'and get stuck here. No bloody wonder Britain's in such a mess. I've got a meeting with a promoter at one and don't think I'm gonna make it.'

'What's that about?' Eric asked, only mildly interested, as he would willingly play anywhere the band were doing a gig and didn't care if it was called Aberdare, Aberdeen or Aachen.

'He came to one of the gigs in Germany and wants to put a tour together with us headlining.'

'You're kidding?'

'No, straight-up.'

'Fuck me, it'll be brilliant. Hang on, we're not heading back to the Bramley Scouts Hall or that dive of a pub we played in Brum when a drunken bastard came on stage and thumped me?'

'Nah, don't be daft. He says he'll get us into decent-sized venues like The Dome in Brighton and Sheffield City Hall.'

'Yeah, and there will be us strutting our stuff to big empty spaces.'

'No chance. Watch out mate, we're on the move.'

He stepped back to see the mouthy truck driver drive his big truck away, clearly not pleased with the treatment he'd received from the gentleman from HM Customs and Excise if a middle finger out of the window was anything to go by. The cars, vans, and trucks in the queue all edged forward and Fast Eddie was next.

Three of them were in on the deal: him, Fast Eddie and

another roadie, Smelly Dave. He and Fast Eddie could represent England, an Olympic pair in the pill-popping and weed-smoking events, but Dave was too fond of buying the latest hi-fi gear and records, a way more expensive habit than dope, and as a result he was only interested in the money.

If Customs found the dope, they would claim it must have been there all this time as the cabinets didn't belong to them, they were rented from a dodgy outfit in East London. At the very least, it would encourage the cops to raid their place which would serve the bastards right as they were always rude to him.

Eddie opened the van's doors and the Customs guy looked in. 'Fucking stinks in here,' the jobsworth said. 'What have you guys been doing?'

'Had an oil leak,' Eddie replied, his sad, hangdog face devoid of mirth. 'I thought we'd fixed it but maybe it's started up again.'

An oil leak? Where the hell did he get that little belter from? Their kit was either electric or acoustic and didn't require more than a dab of WD40 now and again to loosen a hinge or free a stiff tuning peg. Nothing he could think of needed oil, except maybe Fast Eddie's muscles and joints after sleeping outside in the van when he'd had a few too many.

'Take the stuff out and we'll let Bobby sniff around.'

'For fuck's sake mate, it'll take hours,' Eddie said.

'Less of the mate. Just do it and shut up.'

Eric went over to help. Ten minutes later and with most of the large gear removed and piled up against the side of the van, the dog was let loose.

He cringed as the dog did its stuff, sniffing and moving

around like a mad, wind-up toy. It was ten, half-ten in the morning and it looked like a nice sunny June day was in prospect but he was sweating as if standing in the middle of the Arizona Desert, his shirt sticking to his back, his eyes clouded in moisture like he was crying.

He was lost in a cloud of fear and anxiety, not for the shame he would bring on his parents or his vilification in the press, as they were constantly out to get him, but his inability to play guitar and hear the crowd roaring his name.

He was so engrossed in the melancholy of his own thoughts that he failed to hear the Customs guy say, 'On your way.' It was only when Eddie slapped him on the back and said, 'Told you so mate, now come on and give me a bloody hand,' did he realise they were free to go.

THIRTEEN

He was walking down the road as if looking for an address, and after spotting a house with no one at home, turned into the driveway. He continued to walk as if he knew where he was going, but as soon as he was enveloped in darkness by the shadow of the house, he stopped and listened.

He was listening for the sound of Neighbourhood Watch opening their doors and switching on torches, or passing around the matches and lighting them, knowing this area. Instead, the only noise breaking the night's silence was an owl hooting in the trees. He flicked the toothpick over with his tongue in one movement; five minutes one way, five minutes the other.

It wasn't this house he was interested in, but another a few doors along, and so he made his way to the back of the garden and began climbing over neighbouring fences. The gardens of these houses were extraordinarily long, no doubt the reason why properties around here were so expensive. Personally he hated gardens and gardening, many years in prison saw to that, but they provided good cover for him just in case someone decided to take a look out of their back window.

When he reached the house he wanted, he headed straight for the back door. The target would be in his garage pumping iron, as it wasn't yet time for bed. He quietly lifted the small sturdy table at the side of the barbeque and positioned it under the kitchen window. He placed a long screwdriver under the hole he'd cut a few days ago and popped the lever holding the window closed. A minute or so later, he was standing in the kitchen.

He made his way to the hall and then towards the integral garage; he knew the way. Peter Grant lived alone now; even if he hadn't known, it would have been easy to tell as there were gaps on the walls where pictures were once hung, indentations on the carpet where heavy furniture had once stood and several rooms were devoid of the soft, frilly touches a woman usually brought to a house. Mind you, what did he know about women? He couldn't go out with a girl without giving her a black eye or something worse, and his mother before she died, was a drug addict. The closest she ever got to decorating was barfing on the walls and pissing on the carpet.

Standing at the door of the garage he could hear loud music. He didn't know much about anything, but music was his thing and without hearing the track too distinctly, he knew it was *Street Fighting Man* by the Rolling Stones. In prison, he liked quiz nights. They were designed to be a bit of light entertainment for the boys, but often led to serious punch-ups with simmering recriminations.

He pushed open the door just a sliver and peered in. The target was at the start of his routine, lying on his back on the bench and lifting a heavy bar which was usually fifty kilos to start and progressively increased to eighty or ninety, or if he was feeling especially manly, one hundred. He waited until he dipped the bar and it began moving on its journey up towards the rest, his grunts almost drowning out the next track, Bad Company and *Can't Get Enough*, before stepping up behind him. Gripping the bar with both hands, he pushed it back down.

The sap was so surprised to find someone standing there, he lost concentration and his arms buckled. The bar, 60 kilos of solid metal, fell against his chest with a deep thump. Not allowing him the time to appreciate what was happening and give him a chance to offer resistance, he pulled it up towards his throat.

'Stop it, you bastard! I can't...breathe. Who...the fuck are you?' he said, gasping for air.

Frantically his fingers were clutching at the bar, trying to move it away from his throat, but the angle wasn't good for the man on the bench and his assailant's grip was strong. If Grant wasn't panicking so much he might have noticed that his attacker was standing in a position where his balls were within easy reach of a good punch; good job as anyone who could potentially lift one hundred kilos could pack quite a thump.

'What's the combination of the safe?'

'How...how do you know...I've got a safe?'

'Call it a lucky guess.' He pressed the bar down harder on his throat.

'Ahhh. Stop it!'

Momentarily he eased back; the man needed to speak. 'I won't say it again, the combination of the safe?'

'653...ah, ah 425.'

'653425?'

'Yes.'

He applied more pressure, and soon Peter Grant struggled no more.

FOURTEEN

What a morning. It took until ten-thirty before householders stopped reporting false alarms at houses in the Elm Grove area, temporarily incapacitated by a power cut, and then they had to return to Churchill Square to pick up yet another shoplifter. To cap off a lousy start to this week's shift, the intruder they caught climbing through a kitchen window in Patcham was only the son of the stone-deaf woman inside who couldn't hear him knock and didn't see the bell alert on her visual display. All PC Cindy Longhurst wanted to do now was get back to John Street nick and enjoy a well-earned mug of Rosie Lea.

The patrol car turned into Kingswood Street and they were close enough to John Street nick for Cindy to almost taste the heavy aroma of a hot Tetley brew. Just then, Telepathic Tina, otherwise known as TT, the masochistic controller who possessed an uncanny sense of knowing when they weren't busy or were making their way back to the station for a break, came on the squawk box and sent them to Hove. Cindy's driver, Dave Gosling executed an angry U-turn, causing a mini-hold-up behind and giving pleasure to the twisted bastard, as his face creased into the first smile of the day as they roared off in the opposite direction.

Cindy was new to Traffic, a welcome relief from pounding the beat which she'd done for four years, but she'd always liked cars and helping people and so far the job had lived up to her expectations. This was in spite of the behaviour and attitude of her ill-mannered and all-round misogynist companion, a twenty-two-year veteran who was passed-over, pissed-on and more often than not, passed-out. In fact, he didn't believe women should be in the force at all, but stuck at home doing his washing and ironing, and in such a comment lay the reason why no one had volunteered to marry the cranky sod.

'When TT said this bloke didn't turn up for work yesterday, did she say if anybody had made any attempt to contact him because if they haven't–'

'Yep, she did,' Cindy said glancing at her notes and heading off another moan at Gosling Pass. 'Friends tried his mobile and the home phone but they didn't receive a reply. He might be inside and incapacitated in some way.'

'How do we get in? I know the Woodland Drive area, my uncle used to live there, it's full of big houses with smart-arsed alarm systems and big dogs. I don't want to be the one standing there for the third time this morning with my dick in my mouth while this screeching thing wakes the whole neighbourhood, and then having to face an angry Alsatian, spitting venom because its master's gone and tripped down the bloody stairs.'

'Don't wind me up Dave, you know how I hate dogs. TT said a neighbour, a Mr Charles Whiting, has the key and he'll be there to meet us.'

'He better be because...'

She tuned out. Life as a new-minted Traffic cop began in the enclosed space of a police squad car five weeks ago, and in this short time she now knew his views on politics, football and women. It varied little, from 'string 'em up', 'they're rubbish' to 'they should all be at home' and talk of his impending retirement only made matters worse. She couldn't wait until the spring really kicked in, as he was a keen gardener and he could then bore her rigid about flies on his fruit trees and slugs on the lettuce.

They turned into Woodland Drive and about a hundred yards down, into a driveway, and parked behind a pristine BMW Six Series. She knew it was the owner's car, but it didn't half make their grubby Mondeo patrol car look old and shabby.

'Nice set of wheels,' Dave said after easing his beer-bloated frame out of the door and stretching, as if at the end of a long journey and not a couple of miles between two adjoining towns. 'I might buy one of them when I retire.'

'I don't know what sort of package you've been promised, from what I hear you'll be lucky to afford a well-used pool car.'

'I wouldn't touch a heap of crap like this if you–'

'Good morning officers.'

Cindy turned and came face to face with a small, elderly man with thinning grey hair, clad in an ill-fitting cardigan, either his wife's first attempt at knitting or the poor man needed to use his glasses whenever he went shopping. They didn't hear his approach as the daft old goat was still wearing his slippers, despite the presence of many puddles from an overnight deluge, leaving drains in the road gurgling with running water.

'I have the keys,' he said, before turning and heading towards the house.

The door opened without drama and the piece of paper clutched in Mr Whiting's bony fingers containing the alarm code jotted down in neat blue writing was not needed, as there was no ominous countdown and no wailing siren to spin the wheels of PC Dave Gosling's moan-meter. Mr Whiting was standing in the hall waiting to follow them, but Dave placed a firm hand on his elbow and steered him back the way he came. 'Sorry sir, but you'll have to wait outside,' he said. 'Thank you for opening the door but this is police business.'

He closed the door on the crestfallen old-timer. No doubt he was a fan of cop shows like *CSI* and Scandinavian murder mysteries like *The Bridge*, and was gung-ho to discover his first pool of blood, a bashed-in skull or God-forbid, a dead body. With four years under her slowly expanding belt, Cindy still found the sight of a corpse disturbing, and with Mr Whiting on the wrong side of seventy, she doubted if his heart could stand the shock of finding his neighbour lying at the bottom of the stairs or impaled on the tines of a garden fork.

'You take down, I'll do up,' Dave said, his foot on the first step effectively ending any discussion.

She had no choice and nodded in agreement, but she made a face behind his back. For once, she would like to take a look at the places where other people slept, and find out what clothes they owned and what toiletries they used. Dave did it, he said, as it required more detective work than looking at a cooker and the contents of the fridge, but she suspected he wanted to take a look through the wife's underwear drawers. She didn't have the heart to tell the big, sad lump that if he listened to TT a bit more carefully instead of sounding off about being sent to Hove and missing his morning cuppa, he would realise the man of the house was divorced and lived alone.

The kitchen was big, much too big for a single man

who, in her experience, ate mostly take-aways and drank beer straight from the tin and whose idea of home cooking was an M&S meal for one. The oven was clean and looked unused, and despite the presence of a dishwasher, numerous dirty dishes were lying on work surfaces.

The downstairs loo and study were small, making it obvious the master of the house was not lying inside and so with little enthusiasm, she walked into the lounge. It was a large, L-shaped room, light and airy and it was clear the current owner, or the previous one, had knocked down a few walls to create the space, as a couple of big RSJs crossed the ceiling. The furniture was a bit minimalist for her taste with two settees, a few chairs and a flat screen TV, but she assumed the lack of it was more likely a consequence of a family break-up than any strict adherence to the principles of feng shui.

If the furniture was a little on the sparse side, the hi-fi kit looked full-on, the shelving occupying a sizeable section of wall. There were CDs, hundreds of LPs and cassettes and all the equipment to play them on, including an amplifier, tuner and CD player, most of which looked top-notch stuff, although she couldn't believe anyone still owned a turntable. The only people she had seen using one of those were DJs in nightclubs down on the seafront.

The other thing to catch her eye were two paintings on the wall. At first she thought they were copies of one another, but on closer examination she spotted a few differences. She liked art, a fact she didn't mention to any of her colleagues. Coppers were a funny bunch when it came to stuff like art, poetry and reading and before she could say, 'heterosexual' or 'I like men,' she would be branded a dyke and the moniker would stick for evermore.

Both were signed 'Joaquin' and although not a name familiar to her, she would look him up as she liked what he was trying to do. Most visitors to art galleries spent no more than a couple of seconds gazing at each painting, but with these two the artist was encouraging them to spend a bit more time looking at his pictures by inviting them to participate in an adult version of 'spot the difference.' You had to admire the man for his cheek.

She left the lounge and opened the door to the room next door. It was another sitting room with a settee and coffee table, but no television or music, a 'parlour' as her granny would have called it. Like the room in her granny's house in Bodmin, it smelled musty and looked unused. She closed the door and opened the door to the garage.

She didn't receive a blast of cold air, often the result of opening an integral garage door, and it didn't take the skills of a seasoned detective to understand why. The garage had been converted into a gym, and a sophisticated air conditioning/heating system hung from the ceiling.

She shut the door behind her and walked in. It was perhaps the way the light was shining from the large windows, dotted all around the room, but at first she didn't realise someone else was in there too. It was the owner, Mr Peter Grant. She knew what he looked like, as his picture had been in *The Argus* and there'd been a short piece about him on Southern Television the other day when he'd talked about the new superstore his fitness business had opened in Croydon.

The reason she didn't spot him at first was he was lying on the exercise bench, his face as pale as snow, the weight of a 60 kilo barbell pressing down on his neck.

FIFTEEN

DI Henderson headed back to Sussex House after attending the site of a stabbing in Southwick. He was driving slowly along the Old Shoreham Road due to heavy traffic when he heard the news about Peter Grant's death on Southern FM. He changed direction and headed for Woodland Drive. In a way, he was more shocked now than when he had heard about the death of Barry Crow, not because Peter was the second of the Crazy Crows to die, but because he knew him. He wouldn't class him as a close friend, but whenever they saw one another on the street they would always stop for a chat. In fact, he last spoke to him the previous week when he visited him in his Brighton shop.

He drove slowly along Woodland Road, in part due to road calming measures designed to slow commuters, keen to make their way to the A23 link road at the top of the rise, but also as a result of the melee outside Peter Grant's house. The house was surrounded by incident tape and on the roadside he could see a number of cars and vans, reporters, neighbours, and a crew from the local television station. He walked towards the constable guarding the front door and flashed his ID.

'Who's the SIO?' Henderson asked.

'DS Hawkins. He's inside.'

'First name?'

He looked confused. 'What?'

'Of DS Hawkins.'

'Oh, I see, sorry sir. Denis.'

He stepped inside. Most of the noise seemed to be coming from behind a door at the end of the hall which he assumed to be the garage. Henderson headed there. A small crowd were gathered inside, a few cops, detectives, the pathologist and a photographer. He approached the crumpled figure in the dark sports jacket, pens sticking out of his top pocket, looking more like a local government official here to talk about planning permission than a detective.

'DS Hawkins?'

'Who wants to know? If you're a reporter I want to know how you got in here.'

'I'm DI Henderson.'

'Ah, right, sorry sir. You're in the Major Crime Team over at Sussex House?'

'Yes, I am.'

'What brings you here, then? From what the doc tells me our man here took too much drugs and booze, did a workout and got out of his depth and Bang!' he said thumping his fist into his open palm, 'the bar fell on his throat and he couldn't get it off.'

Hawkins was around forty with thinning grey hair, a podgy face and a podgy frame, suggesting this was probably the closest he'd ever come to standing in a gym. He was a detective from John Street nick, more used to dealing with burglaries and shop thefts than dead bodies, so he could be forgiven for being too irreverent in the presence of the dead. If he worked for Henderson on one of his murder investigations, he would now be outside helping the young officer outside to maintain order.

'I'm not here in any investigative capacity. I knew the victim.'

'Well, perhaps you can tell me if he was in the habit of drinking before starting a workout.'

Henderson walked towards the pathologist. 'I don't know but I do know you won't find the answer standing around here.'

He bent down beside the body. He could see it was Peter Grant. He was dressed in a t-shirt and shorts, displaying the muscles that had once made him such a fine drummer.

'Still got the Healey, Grafton? I didn't see it sitting outside.'

'I left it further up the road,' the pathologist said, 'as these TV crews and reporters can be a bit careless. When they come out of their vans carrying all manner of cameras and recording equipment, they only have eyes for the story.'

Grafton Rawlings was in his late-twenties but drove an old car, wore old-fashioned tweed jackets and sensible shoes, and if he possessed a mobile phone it would either be a brick or a tiny un-smart unit, only able to make calls.

'There's no need for me to ask you the cause of death,' Henderson said, 'as I can see the heavy bar, but DS Hawkins mentioned something about booze and drugs.'

'Yes, there's an empty wine bottle in the kitchen and a half-empty glass in here, and what I believe from a cursory sniff is the remains of a joint in the ashtray. It's purely speculation at this stage, as I won't know if my supposition is correct until the post-mortem and we've analysed his blood and stomach contents.'

'I'll try and come along to the post-mortem.'

'Please do so, you're welcome. Why the big ballyhoo outside? Is he a celebrity or some sort of television actor? I don't watch much television, so I wouldn't know.'

'I suppose him being a local businessman is the angle they're interested in. He owns Grant's Fitness Emporium, based out in Woodingdean.'

'Oh yes, I know it. They've got a shop in the mall.'

'They do and also, he used to be the drummer in a rock band called the Crazy Crows but I expect you've never heard of them, as they were a bit before your time.'

'You're right, I haven't heard of them, but then I do only listen to opera and on occasion, Radio 4. Ah here's the ambulance crew.'

Henderson stood back as two male paramedics brought a stretcher into the room. They were both a bit porky and out of condition and it made him smile as they tried to lift the heavy barbell and return it to its rest. It took the intervention of slightly-built Rawlings to prevent it crashing to the ground.

Ten minutes later, the gym now devoid of people, Henderson wandered through the house. It was a big place with four bedrooms, two sitting rooms and a large garden out back; too big for one man. If Henderson lived here, he would have moved when he finally realised the marriage was over.

He returned to the gym. His vision of a garage-cum-gym was of whitewashed breeze-block walls, shelves of paint and tools, with a myriad of bikes, mattresses and children's toys stacked in a heap at the back of the room, leaving barely enough space for a few weights and a dusty bench. Now that he had a chance to take a proper look, he could see this place was the polar opposite.

The walls were painted a cool blue, and if constructed from breeze-block, he couldn't see the joins. The windows were fitted with vertical blinds in a shade to match the walls, the room was lit by dozens of recessed LCD down-lighters and the polished wooden floor had a gentle spring he could feel as he walked.

He had seen less equipment in many hotel gyms. There was an exercise bike, running machine, a huge multi-gym with a range of attachments and handles, and smack-bang in the middle of the room, a padded bench with a built-in aluminium stand, upon which rested the barbell which had killed Peter Grant. There was little sign to indicate something tragic had happened here; no incident tape, no body outline in chalk, no photographic markers and no blood. With everybody gone, it now looked all set-up and ready for another keen amateur to use.

On a shelving unit with a cupboard underneath, he found a selection of nutrition bars bearing the GFE logo, weightlifting gloves and those strange hand tensioning grips which he assumed weightlifters squeezed while watching TV or reading a muscle-man magazine. Nearby, a small fridge looked to be well-stocked with a variety of GFE energy drinks, some of which were of unusual colours, making him think they would have greater appeal to children than body-builders.

A well-thumbed notebook with a sticker on the front which warned, 'Not To Be Removed From Gym' caught his eye. He flicked through the record of the dead man's progress on various machines. In columns, he'd recorded the date, the machine used and the level achieved. The entries for the bike and the running machine were old, as if he no longer worked out on them, while the dates for the bench press were current and marked until the end of last week, presumably the last time he completed an exercise routine.

It took a few seconds to realise what the little book was telling him: Peter was killed lifting sixty kilos but he often lifted in excess of this. In fact, most days, he lifted seventy and seventy-six kilos and on a couple of occasions, eighty. Had he felt tired, or as DS Hawkins would be saying to the press in a few days' time, had he been so drunk or stoned that his judgement was impaired? It certainly looked that way.

Henderson drove to Sussex House with the radio playing loud, trying to drown out the two voices vying for attention in his head. The first one saying how terrible it was for two members of the same band to die within weeks of one another, and the second one warning him something didn't look right.

*

The door to Chief Inspector Lisa Edwards' office was open. There was no one sitting inside occupying the visitor's chair and no one standing out in the corridor waiting to see her, so he knocked and walked in.

'Hello, Angus. Give me a tick, I just need to finish this.'

CI Edwards returned to reading a report she had annotated copiously with her big, black pen. This report was one of dozens landing on her desk throughout the day, everything from information about a new forensic test to the overtime analysis of all the officers under her command. The climb up the police promotion ladder inevitably meant more pay, but with it came additional paperwork and way more hassle. The administrative workload increased all the way up to the ACC level, a man who rarely shifted from his desk except to make a speech at the Women's Institute or attend a lunch hosted by the Lord Mayor.

'Right, it's done,' she said. 'How did you get on at Southwick?'

'The stab victim is now in a coma, but his injuries are not thought to be life threatening. A witness who didn't want to be named fingered the perpetrator, and myself and two officers went to his house. His mother let us in, we headed upstairs to his room and kicked in the door. We found a blood-stained fleece and a knife in a plastic carrier bag, all ready to be taken to the dump. I arrested him, charged him with attempted murder and possession of a weapon, and later today it will be sent for testing.'

'A serious case wrapped up in a morning? Good work.'

'Thank you.'

'Keep me posted on any developments. I want to see scum like him, who would take a life for the cost of a bicycle, locked up. I don't want him walking free on a technicality.'

'Don't worry, it won't happen.'

She lifted her pen, ready to attack another report.

'There's something else.'

Henderson explained about the drowning of Barry Crow in Arundel and now Peter Grant's death at his gym in Hove, and his suspicions, as yet unfounded, that both deaths might be related. Even as he said the words, he could hear how unconvincing the story sounded and he wouldn't blame Edwards for telling him that conspiracy theories were for journalists and to come back and see her when he had some solid facts.

'Two members of the same band?'

He nodded. 'Two out of four.'

'Were they popular? The reason I ask is, if this is one of those cases where their deaths will upset a lot of fans, the press and social media will be on my case every day, demanding a result.'

'No, you don't have to worry on that score. They were popular at the time, but it was over thirty years ago. Their fans are all middle-aged and would worry more about their expanding waistlines and moss on the lawn than the death of a couple of former rock musicians.'

'Thank goodness it's not One Direction or someone as popular, I don't think I could cope.'

'I didn't know you were one of their fans.'

'I'm not, but my daughter is and she would be devastated if one them died. If it was two, I can't imagine the grief it would cause.'

She paused, thinking, and he knew not to say anything if he didn't want his ear chewed off.

'I can see why something like this would bother an inquisitive copper like yourself,' she said. 'The odds against losing fifty per cent of the surviving band members in the space of two weeks are high, but–'

'Before you say 'no', and tell me about all the other stuff we've got on, which is more important than this, I'm not talking about a staffed-up murder investigation...'

'I sincerely hope not.'

'No, I was thinking more about a low-key enquiry. I'll talk to the surviving members and people associated with the band and find out if someone has got it in for them, or if we're looking at something more innocent.'

'You're not selling it to me, Angus.'

'The lead singer of the Crazy Crows was Derek Crow, the tanker fleet owner and a man hailed by the new Labour Prime Minister as the saviour of British industry when he averted the recent nationwide fuel strike. What if there is something going on with the band and he becomes the next victim?'

'The same Derek Crow? Well, blow me, I would never put that pugnacious growler down as a former rock musician. I don't want him or anyone else to die, if that's what you're suggesting, but I don't see how this is a vendetta against the Crazy Crows. From what I've read about the cases, both men were killed in two separate and unfortunate accidents.'

Henderson didn't say any more. He'd made the case and if she wasn't buying, he didn't have anything else to add.

'Knowing you,' she said after a few moments, 'you'll investigate this case even if I forbid it, so here's the deal. You can investigate both accidents and interview surviving members of the band but no more. I want to see a report on my desk in two weeks' time which I'll assume will close the case once and for all, and while you're about it, I don't want any of your current work to fall behind.'

'You drive a hard bargain, Chief Inspector, but I accept.' He stood and made to go.

'One other thing, Angus, under no circumstances is this to be called a murder investigation.'

'Credit me with a bit of sense.'

'I do, but I want to make the point perfectly plain as I don't want this story coming back and biting me on the rear with headlines about wasting police resources. Do what you need to do, but keep it low key. That's an order.'

SIXTEEN

Derek Crow returned to his office, his face sullen and his mood sour. He called a special meeting of his IT people to discuss his concerns about computer hacking. Instead of filling him with confidence at his company's ability to withstand malicious data intruders, they left him with a feeling of helplessness at their lack of assurance at being able to stop anything but an out-and-out amateur.

A few days back, he had attended a conference where the main speaker, a professor in cyber crime and hacking at Bristol University, made it clear the number of attacks zipping into government agency computers had reached an unprecedented rate, something the previous administration failed to mention. The principal targets were the Ministry of Defence and GCHQ, the Government's secret listening post in Cheltenham, with less intensive but nevertheless damaging attacks aimed at many large commercial organisations.

It wasn't an area where he could profess any special knowledge, as his inability to keep up with conversations in the last meeting demonstrated, but he also knew responding with a knee-jerk reaction and throwing a shed load of money at the problem was not the answer either. He needed time to think and listen to the opinions of experts, but he had to do something, as he didn't want to be the one standing up in front of the press when his IT systems went up the spout.

The phone rang. It was his secretary.

'Mr Crow, I have a Mrs Emily Grant on the line.'

All thoughts of insidious hacker emails and the security of the tanker and parcel business IT systems evaporated like a petrol spill on a hot summer's day at the mention of Emily's name.

'Derek?'

'Hello, Emily. It's been a while since I last heard your voice. Much too long in fact.'

'You're right, it is. So how are you keeping? How's your wife and family?'

'We're all well. Edward, the nine-year-old from Hayley's first marriage, took a long time to accept me but the little one, Nathan, is a diamond and always full of smiles. How are Danielle and Graham?'

Derek Crow had known Emily Grant for almost thirty years, since Peter Grant introduced her to him and the guys in the Crazy Crows all those years ago. They talked families for a few minutes, but he knew most of it, as he talked to Pete at least once a week. When Pete and Emily first split up, he worried in case his name was brought up during divorce proceedings, as things like this could be embarrassing to him and the PM, now that he was considered a public figure and a free target for the tabloid press. It hadn't been, and he knew then as he did now, Emily could be discreet even when at her most vulnerable.

'The reason I called you, Derek, is to pass on some sad news.'

'What?'

'Pete's dead.'

'What!' He held the handset at arm's length, staring at it, as if it was the telephone's fault. If it wasn't Emily on the line, he would probably have smashed it against the desk until it shattered into a thousand plastic fragments.

'Derek, are you there? Are you all right?'

'I can't believe it,' he said. The trade unions often said he was a tough bastard for the way he called their bluff when they threatened to go out on strike last month, but now on hearing of the death of his friend, tears tumbled down his cheeks.

'How did he die?' he said after a few moments.

He listened as she recounted the heavy barbell, the gym, the drugs in his system, the booze.

'So, what they're saying is he died because his judgement was impaired by booze and drugs?'

'Yes.'

'That's bullshit. I've seen Pete go into the gym in every state you can imagine, from stone-cold sober to blind drunk and I've never seen him make a mistake like this.'

'Me too.'

Ten minutes later, he put the phone down; it took another five for the news to fully sink in. In fact, he had such trouble believing the words Emily had said, he researched the story on the web and when it was displayed there in front of him on the screen, he could no longer ignore it. He had loved the man like a brother; the phone conversations, the dinners in London and the hearty reunions they held in some posh hotel in Shropshire or Dorset when they got so pissed they had to help one another up the stairs.

Pete was dead, killed by the bloody thing that was supposed to keep him fit and healthy well into old age. He buried his head in his hands and wept tears of sorrow for a good friend. Almost without bidding, his brain began running through a slideshow of concerts, radio interviews, rehearsals and wild, drunken parties, all the things they'd experienced together.

He wiped his face, picked up the phone, instructed his secretary to cancel all meetings for the rest of the day and closed the office door. He needed time to get over the terrible news, but he could also see, clear as day, what the implications might be. First Barry, now Pete. It had to be him next.

In the space of a month, he had lost a brother and a good friend, but try as he may, he could see nothing to connect their deaths other than they were both members of the Crazy Crows and friends with him.

He reached for the phone and dialled a number from memory.

'Hello,' a gruff voice said. 'Bill Paterson.'

'Bill, it's Derek Crow.'

'Hello there Derek, how are you? Don't answer, I saw your mug in *The Mirror* the other day, in the company of your young lady and if you don't mind me saying, you looked like the cat that had supped all the cream.'

'Jealousy will get you nowhere.'

'True, but what would I do with it at my age? So Derek, what can I do for you?'

Chief Inspector Bill Paterson used to work for the Metropolitan Police, where he specialised in vice and sleaze, and spent the years before his retirement lining up clients for his new business venture as a private investigator for harassed senior executives. Derek explained about the deaths of Barry and Pete and his concern that his former band members were dropping as fast as a groupie's knickers.

'You have my deepest sympathies Derek, and if I can offer a crumb of comfort, I'll say that any copper who believes in coincidence has never solved a bloody crime in his life.'

'So you think the deaths might be connected?'

'I obviously couldn't comment further without seeing some evidence, but off the top of my head, I can think of a couple of other ways of looking at this.'

'Such as?'

'Granted I don't know much about your band, but I know many bands at the time led what might be called boisterous lifestyles with drugs, women, booze and all the rest. I'm thinking the guys might have died from the drugs they once took, you know, it might have weakened their hearts or given them diseased livers or something. Then, there's the sexually transmitted diseases picked up from some tart, or a tropical disease copped on a foreign tour and you know, some of them can lie dormant for years. In Peter Grant's case, his accident might have resulted from weakened shoulder muscles, his years of drumming catching up with him.'

'Bloody hell, I didn't think of any of this. It makes perfect sense.'

'I'm only chewing the fat, Derek, trying to give you something else to think about. I'm not saying any of this stuff is the answer to what you're looking for, and I won't know any different unless I take a closer look.'

'I know Bill, I know, but you hear of businessmen dying when they get bitten by spiders when travelling to the Far East or South America and people getting infected with diseases that lay undetected for years until one day they suddenly drop dead. I didn't think along those lines.'

'That's the reason you became a successful businessman and I became a copper.'

'If we take this a stage further, my turn to chew the fat if you like, what if someone has cast a spell and is hitting us with some bad karma?'

Paterson laughed. 'I've known a lot of tarts from Jamaica who practiced this voodoo stuff, or went to see a witch doctor when they felt ill, you know?'

'Yeah.'

'But I never saw anything to convince me it worked. In my mind, these so-called witch doctors were just a bunch of charlatans who only did it for the money and to have sex with the girls, and my view on this score hasn't changed.'

Derek smiled. Bill Paterson might have left the streets of London, but the streets of London had never left him.

'The reason I mention it,' he said, 'is I went through a phase in the late eighties when I only wore black clothes and hung a big metal cross around my neck. In combination with one or two of our songs with devil and occult references, it attracted a few crazies to our concerts. One time, we went back to our rooms and found four Hare Krishna characters camped outside in the corridor praying for our blackened souls.'

'Ha, I can believe it with them.'

'Bill, can you do me a favour?'

'Name it Derek, but it'll cost you. As you know, I'm no longer funded by the great British taxpayer.'

'I know this might sound a bit daft, but could you take a look at the deaths of Pete and my brother Barry and tell me, in your considered opinion, if it looks like both guys genuinely died in accidents?'

'I could Derek, but I'll tell you now, I think you'd be wasting your money.'

'What, you're telling me your former colleagues don't make mistakes?'

'Sure they do, but as much as I criticise modern policing, I do think cases like these are meat and drink to the average Bobby, and any investigation of this nature would be done by the book. They don't often get stuff like this wrong.'

'I understand what you're saying, but it would make me feel a lot better. At least I'd know whatever the problem might be, it doesn't lie there.'

'Let me see what I can do.' He paused for a couple of seconds and Derek could hear heavy breathing down the phone, perhaps a legacy of Paterson's time in Vice or his high cigarette intake.

'I might still know a few friendly faces down in Sussex, and maybe I can get a swatch at the Accident Reports. I'll visit the loci and talk to some of the witnesses. How does that sound?'

SEVENTEEN

Eric Hannah attempted to make his way to the back of the shop without being seen. Despite his best efforts, clothes hangers started rocking in his wake and he grabbed a large cardboard cut-out of a topless bloke wearing tight jeans before it could fall and damage his well-developed pecs or scratch his bronze-toned skin.

Even with some major impediments blocking their view, such as tall clothes stands, in-your-face 'sale' cards and a couple of concrete pillars, his two staff members spotted him, as the shop was quiet and they were both standing around chatting.

'Good morning, Eric. How are you this morning?'

'Morning Fran, I'm fine. How are you? Morning Cassie.'

He made it to the sanctity of his untidy office without being buttonholed by either of his two assistants with their never ending list of issues and problems; he didn't want to talk to them as he was unshaven and stank of booze and garlic. It didn't pass muster as a good look for the owner of a gents' clothes shop and he didn't need to give his well-togged underlings anything else to gossip about. He slammed the office door shut, took off his jacket and slumped into the seat.

He sat back with his eyes closed, and moments later, an arm snaked out and felt for the large latte, bought from a coffee shop two doors along. Fingers tapped their way up to the lid and removed it. The hand then moved down the desk, opened a drawer and fumbled inside for paracetamol. Two were gulped down in rapid succession followed by a large glug of coffee made from the finest Columbian beans, harvested at the optimal moment by local farmers and brewed to perfection by a highly trained Italian barista. He bought one every day to give his non-morning body a boost, but in the dank, swampland of his mouth, the fine coffee tasted bitter and metallic and couldn't penetrate the deep cave where his hangover lurked.

Last night was bad. In fact most nights these last few months were bad. These were not the guilty feelings of the remorseful hangover victim, as he was well used to its corrosive effects and the negative impact it had on his moods, but his life was in a rut and he didn't know how to get out of it.

Most evenings he would head down to his local in Farnham, The Horse & Groom, and team up with a few regulars. From there, they would go to a curry house or a Chinese restaurant and afterwards, end up back at someone's house and raid the booze cabinet. Night after night it seemed a good idea at the time, but it left him with a physical pain which nagged in his side and an emotional pain at the emptiness which refused to go away.

Last night might have improved if the barmaid at The Horse & Groom had joined them for a curry, but she was a smart kid and refused because she knew what he was like. Instead, he'd shared onion bhajis, chicken dalfrezi and enough rice to feed two families with a bunch of hard core losers: a redundant banker, an alcoholic window cleaner and a crooked car dealer.

On such occasions, his return to the marital bed in the wee small hours might often be rounded off with a third-degree grilling and a nasty slanging match, but these last few weeks she'd been giving him the silent, cold-back treatment. A clear indication his good lady didn't give a toss anymore.

Suzy, Mrs Hannah number three, was fast becoming a royal pain in the arse. They were married after a whirlwind romance and it was followed by a fantastic honeymoon on the Caribbean island of Antigua, fuelled by copious amounts of sex, the best ganja he could find, and a valiant attempt to drink every rum-based cocktail ever made. It created a spark to re-ignite the Soufriere volcano on nearby Montserrat, but they'd left it behind in the sand of Hermitage Bay and nothing said or done since had even come close.

Her list of complaints loomed almost as large as the shopping list she tacked on the kitchen wall. She didn't like him drinking, didn't like sex, didn't like the way he dealt with his children, didn't like being left short of money, blah, blah, blah. She was twenty years his junior and could easily start again if they divorced, but what about him? A few weeks back he'd turned fifty-three. The suggestive charm and boyish good looks, once responsible for removing the pants from seven different women in one riotous weekend, faded with each shower, shave and broken night's sleep, the result of a nagging bladder filled with too much beer and a stomach irritated by high doses of turmeric and monosodium glutamate.

By eleven, more caffeine and additional painkillers were beginning to make inroads into his debilitated condition, so much so, he made a momentous decision.

Today would be the day he would start to make positive changes to his life. The source of his malaise was this damn clothes business; he felt manacled to the office and weighed down by the paperwork, the moaning staff and a business that no longer inspired him.

If having once played in a rock band had taught him anything, it was that he was better suited to owning a small bar in Jamaica than forever tied to a Farnham shop selling jeans and t-shirts. When Suzy was out of the way, he decided he would sell the house and business and use the money and the stash he had hidden away, safe from the grasping hands of his free-spending wife, and move to the Caribbean.

Without much enthusiasm, he reached for a pile of invoices, all requiring his approval, but as he tried to focus red-veined eyes on the first, the phone rang.

'Hello Eric.'

'I would recognise your animalistic growl anywhere. Derek Crow my man. How's life treating you?'

'I'm fine mate, how about you?'

'Nothing a new liver and a new woman couldn't fix but fuck, what do I have to complain about? Listen man, I haven't heard from you for ages but you're in the paper just about every bloody day, you and Mr Soundbite.'

'Who, Rob McNaughton?'

'Yeah.'

'Who calls him that?'

'Me, I just made it up.'

'Christ, it seems like some of your brain cells are still working. Take it easy mate, you could hurt yourself.'

'Ha, chance would be a fine thing.'

'I mean, nobody took a blind bit of notice of me before

Rob became Prime Minister and back then I spent just as much time with him as I do now. Such is life. So, how's business?'

'Ach, its all hunky dory, you know.'

'You can't catch me out, that's another one of your bloody album titles, is it not? Don't tell me.... Yeah, David Bowie.'

'Very sharp Derek, my man, I can't sneak one past you. There's no need to ask you how your business is doing, as all I need to do is look in the paper and there you are, jabbering on about what another fine year you're having, blah, blah blah.'

'There's no secrets nowadays. Listen mate, the reason I called was to find out how you are—'

'Stop worrying, I'm fine. What's the sudden concern for my health? D'you know something I don't?'

'Eric, read the fucking papers. We lost Barry and now we've lost Pete. Schoolboy logic says it's either you or me next.'

'Whaaat? Don't be daft man. Pete's death was an accident with all those bloody weights he liked playing with, and you know Barry, he would help any animal in distress. Where's the connection? At a push, someone might call it, I don't know, a suicide pact or something, but knowing the guys as we both do, no fucking chance.'

'I agree on that score, but don't you see?'

'See what?'

'Somebody's fingering the band, Eric. Somebody out there has put a curse on us.'

Fucking hell. The great Derek Crow's gone gaga, he never thought he'd see the day.

'What do you mean, like witches, spells and mixing

potions around a fire in the woods? What a load of phoney baloney. If you ask me, Derek, you've been spending too much time reading *Harry Potter* to those kids of yours.'

'Don't you remember the time in Denmark when we supported a band from Leicester, Hazard Warning.'

'How could I forget? Copenhagen's got to be one of my favourite places in the world, free drugs even freer sex and the only thing expensive was the booze and it tasted like piss. Hazard Warning were shite, as they were coked out of their heads most of the time. The guitarist often couldn't remember the running order and more than once he started playing the wrong intro. Remember?'

'I do, but their singer told me about a tour they did in Jamaica when he watched a witch doctor as he treated boils and fever. He waved some smoke around, repeated some incantations and in a matter of minutes, the symptoms were gone. He said it was amazing to see.'

'What was the guy's name again?'

'Hal Lester.'

'Yeah, Hal Lester. His real name was Hayden or something but he didn't think it sounded too rock 'n' roll so he changed it to Hal.'

'Bloody hell, you do surprise me with some of the rubbish you still remember.'

'I mean he was such a pisshead I'm not sure if he knew what day it was or what city he was in, never mind give you an accurate account of something he'd witnessed. Listen, if there's a curse on the band, don't you think someone would have come forward by now and told us about it? I mean we haven't played together since 1989.'

'I know, I know, but what if it's the work of some twisted bastard who's been harbouring something we did to him way back when? Maybe he's come back here after twenty-five years in the States, or just left a commune or kibbutz where he's been living all this time, I don't know, and sees me in the paper? It might bring the grudge he's been keeping back to the surface all over again.'

'Do me a favour, man. How warped would you need to be to hold a grudge for twenty-odd years? Listen to me, Derek. You need to catch a grip. You're as fit as a greyhound and I'm as healthy as a pissed fruit fly, so nothing's gonna happen to you and nothing's gonna happen to me. Now tell me, how are Hayley and the little ones getting on?'

EIGHTEEN

With only two weeks to investigate the deaths of two members of the Crazy Crows, DI Henderson didn't waste any time in setting up interviews with Peter Grant's friends and associates. He expected the process to take a while, as no one liked talking to the police, but to his surprise, Sarah Corbett wanted to.

He'd called Peter Grant's office to find the names of friends and business acquaintances of the dead man, and he was put through to the HR Department. It was a surprise when he spoke to the head of the department, as not only did she know all the people he needed to speak to, she'd also been Peter Grant's girlfriend. Now, she was sitting across from him at a table in a coffee shop in the centre of Brighton.

She'd come straight from the office and was wearing a lilac skirt and matching jacket over a white blouse, looking every inch the HR professional.

With the introductions and preliminaries out of the way, Sarah fingered her latte, as if trying to decide where to start. He decided to help her out.

'Had you and Peter been going out for long?'

'Three weeks, but we'd worked together for over four years.'

'Can I ask why both of you left it so long?'

'He was married when I started working at the

company and I was in a long-term relationship. He recently got divorced and my relationship also ended around the same time so...we just got together. It wasn't pre-planned in any way.'

'What do you know about Peter's accident?'

'Only what I read in the paper, and I've looked for the story in every newspaper I could lay my hands on. After a time you realise they must all have access to the same press release or witness statements as it all started to sound the same.'

'I know what you mean. I attended the post-mortem and if there's anything from there you would like me to tell you about, please ask.'

'Thank you,' she said, her previous downcast expression now a little brighter. 'Did they come to the same conclusion as was reported in the press?'

'The pathologist said it was a tragic accident brought about by muscle tiredness, as he had been lifting weights beyond his capabilities at the time.'

'Did they conduct, I don't know what you call them, drug tests, toxicology tests?'

'Yes, there was alcohol in his system and a small amount of cannabis, consistent with the joint we found in an ashtray in the kitchen.'

'How much alcohol?'

'Equivalent to about three-quarters of a bottle of wine.' He looked at her face. 'You don't look too surprised.'

'What, that he took drugs or he drank wine?'

'Both, but the amount of wine consumed prior to a gym workout seems excessive to me.'

'He took the separation from his wife and kids badly; when the divorce came through, it brought it all back and he started drinking more than usual. He knew he was doing it, but said he would cut down as I... I made him feel better.' She stopped to wipe away a tear.

'Did he often take a drink before working out?' Henderson asked. 'I would have thought most people do it the opposite way round and go for a drink as a reward after going to the gym.'

She smiled. 'I used to think that too. Peter was a bit of a night owl and didn't seem to need as much sleep as everyone else. He liked to exercise at odd times. He liked wine and told me he often drank about a bottle when he wasn't going out. It helped him sleep he said. I've never seen him drunk and because he was quite a chunky person I guess he could handle it. I say he usually did these things, but of course I was only just getting to know him.'

'I understand,' Henderson said as he lifted his cup and took a drink of his Americano.

'Did the pathologist consider if alcohol or the small amount of drugs he took were a major contributing factor in his death?'

'Yes, he did. He thought Peter's judgement might have been impaired by the alcohol and as a result, he loaded more weights on the bar than he was capable of lifting.'

'I find that hard to believe,' she said. 'Peter had been doing weights since he was a teenager and knew all about the dangers. He could have written a book about it, if we didn't employ all those experts at the company to do it for us.'

Henderson had to agree as the record book he'd seen in Grant's gym suggested the same thing, but he hadn't mentioned it at the post-mortem for fear of muddying the waters. He didn't want to talk about it now either, as he wanted to hear what Sarah had to say and didn't want to confuse her.

'Sarah, this incident was investigated by the police and with all the evidence and the post-mortem results available, they decided Peter's death was an accident.'

She nodded in agreement. 'Yes, I know.'

'Why then do you give me the impression you don't agree?'

'When you say it so... starkly it does sounds pretty conclusive, doesn't it?'

'Yes, it does. I don't think there's any other way of looking at it, is there?'

'I'm finding it hard to accept. He did such a great job managing the company we both work for. I don't know if you've heard of Grant's Fitness Emporium?'

He nodded in agreement. 'I've met Peter before and I knew he worked there.'

'Then you'll know about the expertise we have. I can't emphasise this enough, but Peter lived with exercise regimes, nutrition, muscle building, protein supplements, you name it, in a professional capacity for over fifteen years. It's inconceivable he would make a mistake as basic as this.'

'How is the business doing?'

'Peter started his first shop in Western Road, now it's in the Churchill Square shopping centre, close to Hollister. From there, he opened another eleven shops and two months ago, we opened our first superstore in Croydon.'

'I knew about the shops but I didn't know about the superstore.'

'Yes, the first of many if Peter had his way, and in financial terms, we were in a good position with no bank lending, as Peter hated borrowing from banks. He made sure we had the money in the kitty before embarking on the superstore expansion plans.'

'Impressive.'

'The superstores were Peter's idea, his baby. Many in the management team were set against it. If it worked out, and Peter was confident it would, more would have been opened. Why would he want to leave all that behind?'

'Sarah, you're talking about his death as if it was a deliberate act, as if he committed suicide. I thought we decided after discussing the police report and the post-mortem that he died as a result of an accident.'

She looked down at her untouched coffee. Henderson's cup was empty and he fancied another, but didn't move.

'I know. Maybe I just can't accept he would be so stupid to die in a silly accident when there was so much in his life to look forward to. You would expect someone in his position to be, I don't know...a bit more careful and not so blasé about taking unnecessary risks.'

Henderson nodded. He'd heard of lottery winners, afraid to go out in case they were kidnapped or killed in a car accident. Perhaps Sarah expected Peter to do the same.

'If he meant to commit suicide and wanted it to look like an accident,' Sarah said, 'then I can't believe he could be so selfish. I mean, maybe he was feeling depressed about the divorce and his wife and kids leaving him, but I don't see how it could exceed his desire to manage and grow the business and,' she said in a voice barely audible, 'the affection he felt for me.'

Henderson wasn't a bereavement counsellor and didn't know what to say in these circumstances, but clearly this woman felt utterly scorned that the man she'd staked some part of her future upon had been taken away so dramatically from her grasp. He was sure there was a name for such a condition, but whatever it was, it was making him feel decidedly uncomfortable.

He explored the suicide theory with her a little further and enquired after Peter's health, his personal finances, and his emotional state, but the former drummer of the Crazy Crows ticked all the boxes and he was forced to agree with her; it didn't look as if the man had done it deliberately.

The accident theory didn't sit well with Sarah Corbett and neither did the suicide theory. It had taken forty minutes and one Americano, but it served to reinforce his belief that something in the deaths of the two men wasn't quite as it seemed.

NINETEEN

BBC Egton House, London 1987

'Guys, guys, a warm welcome to Radio 1,' the bloke holding a clip-board and wearing a pink sweater said. 'We'll get you sorted out in a few minutes. Help yourself to BBC coffee, if you can stand the assault on your taste buds, that is.'

The door closed and the five members of the Crazy Crows looked at one another before they all burst out laughing.

'Christ, I used to listen to Radio 1 under the covers late at night when I was a kid,' Eric said. 'I just can't believe we're here in the same bloody studios.'

'Make the most of it,' Barry said. 'Once they've seen us, they won't invite us back.'

'Once they've seen you, you mean,' Eric said grabbing Barry in a headlock. 'You're such an ugly bastard. Good job we're not here for the telly.'

'Knock it off fellas,' Derek said. 'I want this interview calm, ok? Remember we're here to promote our new album, not to wreck the studio or piss off listeners.'

'Right-oh, boss,' Eric said, releasing Barry and then giving him a slap on the head and mussing his long locks.

A few minutes later, Stu, the guy in the pink sweater, came back and led them into the studio. Derek had been nervous when their manager, Frannie Copeland, first suggested the idea of an interview with Radio 1, as the combination of Eric, Barry and Danny in the same room was asking for trouble. They larked and argued like a bunch of hormonal school boys, even when Eric wasn't taking dope or pissed out of his head. He breathed a sigh of relief when he heard it wasn't to be a live interview but recorded and edited later, as even though radio studios used a delayed loop to catch the occasional profanity, it wouldn't be enough to stop this lot embarrassing themselves.

Stu fussed over them for a few minutes, fitting them with headphones and easing their seats closer to the mikes. Thank goodness this wasn't a television show as he wouldn't want this guy powdering his nose and fiddling with his costume.

He'd been inside radio studios before and assumed they would all be similar, but through a plate glass window he could see the afternoon DJ at work. There wasn't one DJ inside but four, the 'afternoon crew' as they liked to be called. Headphones clamped on heads, they gathered around a large desk, upon which sat various bits of equipment and pieces of paper; tape decks, CD players, sound mixers, screens and keyboards, their voices recorded by big fat over-hanging microphones. To him it looked like chaos, but knowing the high standards employed by the BBC, it was organised chaos.

'Hi fellas.'

Derek looked round. It wasn't the whining voice of Stu this time, but Ronnie Rogan, champion of rock music on Radio 1 with a show going out on weekdays at 11 o'clock in the evening.

'Hi, Ronnie, how are you doing?' Eric said as they all

shook hands.

'Good to see you all here,' he said in a Mid-Atlantic drawl, a voice sounding as if it had been fashioned by fags, booze and copious amounts of salt water, much loved by his late-night listeners. He looked more handsome than the voice suggested, a young, lean face under a tangled mess of blonde and brown hair, and wearing a tight fitting t-shirt with the name of some sports company on the front and tatty jeans.

He gave them a preamble about what he intended to do, how it would be edited down to a fifteen or twenty minute piece for his show next week, how it would be difficult for the listener to tell who was speaking if they all talked at once, all the usual radio station guff. Ronnie nodded to the guy in the control room, who looked to be in charge of recording their words of wisdom, and gathered his notes together.

'Right, if I can make a start,' Ronnie said. 'Did the success of the new single, *Straight Up*, surprise you?'

'I'll say,' Derek said, 'because we didn't know the record company were going to release it.'

'Is that so? Then it really was a surprise.'

'Yeah, but *Straight Up* is shorter and snappier than the stuff we're used to doing, so I suppose it's more obvious single material.'

'How was *Top of the Pops*?'

'A new experience,' Eric said.

'Never to be repeated,' Barry said. 'I hate faking it.'

'Do you think of yourselves as an album band?'

'I think we do,' Barry said. 'See, you can do more with a long track on an album than a three-minute single and while I don't think any of us would say 'no' to all the additional fans and the amount of airplay we're getting for *Straight Up*, I don't think we'll make a habit of it.'

'Barry's right,' Derek said, 'but Danny just got this little tune in his head and we took it from there. Maybe he'll get another in a few weeks' time.'

'You never know,' Danny said, smiling.

'The single is a taster from the new album, *Tropical Storm*, your third, available from all good record shops on 1st September. Now I've heard you describe it, Derek, as the most complete album you've ever made. What did you mean by that?'

'Everything just sort of came together on the album, the song writing, the playing and our understanding of the techniques we could use in the recording studio. See, we were rookies on the first couple of albums and the producer took all the decisions. With this one, we knew exactly what we wanted and what the studio was capable of producing and as a result, we were more involved in its production.'

'I think it's not an exaggeration to say,' Ronnie said, 'the addition of Danny on keyboards has made a big difference to your sound.'

'Humph,' Eric said.

'For the better, I would say,' Derek said, to mutterings of agreement from the others, all except Eric Hannah. 'Plus, he's started writing a few songs himself and co-writing with me so I think the quality of the songs has improved as well.'

'It's more of a collaboration,' Danny said. 'Derek often comes up with a good idea and I add lyrics to it.'

'I've listened to the album a lot and I agree the songs are better. Eric, your role seems to have changed. Gone are the long guitar solos we heard on the first two albums, now it's a more economic, snappier sound. Do you like playing this way?'

'I can play anything,' he said, pushing back his long, untidy hair from his face, 'although I do prefer playing longer licks but,' he said looking straight at Derek, 'I do whatever the boss tells me to do.'

'The fuck you do,' Derek spat back, 'you do what you damn well please.'

'Don't give me that crap,' Eric said. 'You say to me, don't play that bit Eric, let Danny do it.'

'The hell I do. I might shorten it if I think it's too long, but nothing else.'

Voices were raised for a couple of minutes forcing Ronnie to step in and try to restore order.

'Calm down now, gents. Thank you. We'll take that bit off the tape, but hey,' he said, a devious smile on his lips, 'maybe I won't. Now we're back on script, can I ask, you've lined up a tour to promote the new album, are you planning to play any festivals?'

The interview lasted a further half hour and Ronnie assured them when the tape stopped they had captured enough to make an interesting fifteen-minute slot for his programme. He thanked them in an over-the-top radio manner and next thing they knew, they were out through the doors at Egton House, and standing in London's summer sunshine.

'Who fancies a drink?' Eric said.

No one had any plans for the rest of the day so they decamped to a pub nearby, The George in Great Portland Street. Trust Eric to know there would be a pub there.

It was a lovely old-fashioned boozer in an age when

they were all being converted into gastro pubs, wine bars and bistros, with dark oak panelling, a big ornate wall mirror and long bar with a good range of ales; none of that modern lager crap. With the lads settled around a table in the corner, Derek hauled Eric up to the bar to help him carry the drinks.

It was nearing the end of lunchtime and the pub was busy with suits from nearby offices filling bodies with the drug of their choice to help them navigate their way through a dull afternoon. Loads of drinkers were smoking, but at least the pub wasn't filled with it, as the doors and windows were open on account of it being a warm day, and a refreshing breeze wafted inside. Everyone in the band smoked, but Derek couldn't stand a room full of stale smoke.

Standing behind a bloke being served, he pulled Eric towards him by the lapels. 'Why the fuck did you pull a stunt like that in the studio?'

'What d'ya mean? Get your hands off me.'

Derek released him from his grip. 'You know bloody fine what I mean: you mouthing off to the world and his uncle that you've got a problem with Danny playing in the band.'

'I don't have a problem.'

'Yes, you fucking do. You're always on his case—'

'What can I get you, gents?' the barman asked. He was tall, blond and Australian.

Derek gave him the order and turned back to face Eric. 'You've been bending my ear for months saying you've got too much to do, as each of the songs has a long guitar solo and by the end of a gig your hand is aching. Then, if you bust a string or your effects pedal goes on the blink, the sound's screwed and there's always a tuning delay when you change guitars. Now, when I finally bring someone in, someone who can help fill out the sound and give you a break from long solos, someone who even Ronnie Rogan thinks is a major addition to the band, you go fucking apeshit. Explain it to me mate, because I don't understand what's going on.'

'I dunno. Maybe I don't feel important in the band anymore. I mean, when it was just you singing and me playing guitar, it was like we were joint front men, both of us in the limelight.'

'So, now you're having to share some of the limelight with Danny. I don't have a problem with it, why should you?'

'Yeah, but it's not only that, he's got a bigger slice of the new album. On some tracks I'm like the Yeti, a rare sight.'

'Bollocks Eric, you appear on every track, but it's true you don't play many of the long guitar solos you used to. What did Ronnie call it, 'a snappier sound' and I think it makes it more memorable. The public seem to think so as well, look at the single, it's selling well and Ronnie thinks the new album is good.'

'I dunno...'

'I'm not fucking lying to you. If you remember what that new producer Sam Schweinsteiger said–'

'What, the hippy Yank?'

'Yeah, the hippy Yank. He said the secret of good guitar playing is to make every solo memorable, not a long solo that people are waiting to finish so they can get back to the tune–'

'That's Grant's drum solos you're talking about. My playing is never boring.'

'You know what I mean. When you think of *Whisky in the Jar* or Zeppelin's *Kashmir,* you remember the guitar part as much as the song. That's where we wanna be.'

'I dunno, I'm still not happy having Danny around. It's disrupting the balance.'

'Bollocks, I don't think it is and neither do the other guys. Listen mate, you better get used to it, because Danny's going nowhere. He's joining the band full-time.'

The barman returned. 'That's three pints of lager and two pints of best. Anything else?'

'Yeah,' Derek said, 'throw in four packets of roasted peanuts and half a dozen bags of crisps: three salt and vinegar and three smoky bacon.'

'You're all heart, Derek. A big day out at the BBC and you treat us to a pint and a packet of smoky bacon crisps.'

'Whatd'ya mean?' he said picking three pints up from the bar in his big mitts and heading for the table in the corner. 'It's your treat, mate, you're paying.'

TWENTY

Leafy Surrey made a welcome change from freeze-your-bollocks-off Brighton. It was his first time in Farnham and it looked a quiet, sleepy place, full of important bankers and solicitors who worked in the city by day, leaving their pill-popping and gin-guzzling wives at home to screw the window cleaner and the postman for a bit of excitement. They were disgusting creatures, women. What was the point? He flicked the toothpick over with his tongue in one movement; five minutes one way, five minutes the other.

He stood outside a big, rambling detached house in Shortheath Road; even in the dark he could tell it had been neglected, and any lustre it had once enjoyed among its fellow neighbours had long since faded. It was a dark, leafy road with plenty of high hedges and overgrown bushes, making it easy for him to slip into the driveway and disappear around the back of the house.

Eric Hannah owned a couple of clothing shops selling jeans and leisure shirts, but like the house, the business had been neglected and it could make far more money with a smarter guy than him at the helm. It hadn't been hard to find him. If Hannah wasn't having a kip in the back office of his shop in Farnham, as he didn't often venture out to see any of his other shops, he would be occupying a bar stool in The Slug and Lettuce, a few doors down from the shop, or chatting up the barmaid in his local, The Horse & Groom, at night.

As he anticipated, the lock on the side gate was busted. He pushed the gate open but it started to squeak. He waited until a car drove past and shoved it hard; easy peasy. Standing close to the kitchen window he could hear a ding-dong argument going on inside. His wife was furious with him for something.

He might have guessed, Hannah was going out tonight to spend another night down at the pub, and by the tone of her voice, it sounded as though she was getting fed up with it. He could see her through the window, her face lined and angry, but not the anger built through decades of grief, as they had been married less than ten years.

It had taken her a while but now she was starting to realise that the handsome Lothario who once wooed her with his witty one-liners, a cheeky smile, and raucous tales of derring-do, was nothing more than a drunken, empty loser. Anyone else not preoccupied with their failing talent and fading good looks could turn this howling banshee into a compliant and dutiful wife, willing to attend to her man's every need, and eager to bring up his children in a manner to make them both proud. Instead, he chose to ignore her and the children.

He made his way back out to the road and walked over to the van. He was thoughtful, not about this guy, but the next one. He was last on the list and for a very good reason. He was the top dog and they wanted him to suffer, watching on as each of his buddies died. Ah, what a shame.

Number four required a great deal of thought as there always seemed to be people around him, but the problems weren't insurmountable for a man of his calibre, it just needed a little more planning. Soon, number three would be out of the way and he could concentrate on the big finish. He liked that, the big finish. What then? He would have to find another client to work for; but perhaps there was no need, maybe his reputation would be made on this one and now they would come to him.

He started the van and, humming his favourite song, drove away.

TWENTY-ONE

The head office of Crow Enterprises, the tanker and parcel distribution business owned by Derek Crow, was located in an unassuming, low-rise building in Dartford. DI Henderson and DS Walters drove past the petrol tanker depot a few blocks down, which might seem far enough away for the office workers to feel safe if it ever blew up, but Henderson wasn't so sure.

'It's not a nice part of London this,' Walters said, looking around as she stepped out of the car. 'It's all concrete and roads with no trees or grass.'

'I know what you mean, but distribution companies love it here as they're close to the M25, and somewhere over there,' he said pointing out towards the east, 'is the M20 down to the Channel Tunnel. In any case, I'm not sure we're still in London. This might be Kent.'

She nodded towards the head office building in front of them. 'I thought you said this guy was rich?'

'He is, lives in a big house in St. John's Wood and owns a villa in Corfu or somewhere in Greece. Look at the cars outside. One's a Bentley and the other's a Porsche, they don't come cheap. C'mon, let's go in and see him.'

She shrugged and followed on.

A few minutes later, they were seated opposite Derek Crow, his desk between them. It wasn't the most palatial office Henderson had ever seen, but a notch or two above their initial impressions outside.

'I must admit,' Crow said, 'I was surprised when you called me and told me the police were interested in the deaths of my brother Barry, and Peter Grant. I thought both men died in accidents.'

He had a reputation as a tough negotiator and for all Henderson knew, he was also a good poker player, but he was a ham actor; Henderson could see he was lying. In his position, he would be worried too.

'After a full police inquiry and two post-mortems, it's a view any rational man would be forced to take, but even you would have to admit, Mr Crow, losing two members of the same band is a high loss rate by anybody's standards. We think the situation is worthy of further investigation, not least to ensure that you and Eric Hannah are not in any sort of danger.'

'Thank you for your concern. I guess even the police need to cover all the bases.'

'If I can make a start,' Henderson said. 'I'd like to ask you about the early origins of the band, how you started, how you got your first break.' Henderson had explained to Walters in the car that he intended doing this, not as a trip down memory lane for a nostalgic ex-roadie, but to try and uncover the names of anyone the band might have upset in the past.

Derek Crow ran fingers through a thick, swept-back mop of greying black hair, a bit different from the days when it was greasy, curly and ran past his shoulders.

'I joined a couple of bands while still at school, and when I left, I played a few gigs at night and worked in a meat processing factory during the day. My brother, Barry, was with me playing bass and when the drummer and guitarist walked out in a strop, Barry suggested we take a look at Eric Hannah. Eric was good and agreed to join us and it turned out he knew Peter Grant, so he brought Pete in to play drums.'

'The four of you just clicked?'

'Yeah, we did. Eric was the kind of guitarist you only see once in a while, intuitive, eager to learn and he could play anything you asked him. After three months of solid rehearsals above a pub in Brighton, we played our first gigs and soon after, we scored a recording contract.'

Henderson heard the door open behind him and in walked Crow's secretary, Helen, carrying a tray of coffees and a number of chocolate biscuits. No wonder Crow was a tad on the porky side.

'Where did I get to? At the start, we had a good following around Sussex and Kent which was the reason we got our album deal, and after that we branched out and toured the UK and parts of Europe. The Germans and the Danes seemed to like us. We made four albums and even though the first three are pretty good, it wasn't until the fourth, *Black Saturday,* that we really cracked it. That album is a diamond. I was so proud of it at the time; I still am.'

'It's a good record and deserves more recognition.'

'Too true. I imagine your next question is going to be why did we pack it all in?'

Henderson nodded.

'I've asked myself the same thing many times, I assure you. I mean, where would we be if we'd toughed it out? In fact, even if we didn't make another album as good as *Black Saturday*, all you have to do is pick up *The Sunday Times* to realise that a lot of the bands around then are back touring and making a good living.'

'So why did you pack it in?'

'What did the record company say, due to musical differences or some crap like that, we all went our separate ways?'

'Yes, but everyone at the time knew different.'

Crow stared into space for a moment. 'When *Black Saturday* came out there was a lot of bickering going on within the band. It was mainly Eric, as his mood would change like the weather, more often than not about Danny Winter and usually with a head full of dope or booze. And then... and then Danny died. It was on the night when, if you can believe it, we were celebrating *Black Saturday's* entry into the album charts.'

Henderson waited for more.

'I couldn't go on after that. One minute I could see exactly where we were heading, I had it all planned out, and the next everything seemed to fall away like sand through my fingers. It screwed me up big time, I can tell you, and it screwed with Eric too. He went on a bender and we didn't see him for three weeks.'

'Some of the old newspapers I looked at,' Walters said, 'blamed Eric for Danny Winter's death.'

'Yeah, they did and for a time I did too. Looking back, I can see now it was an accident, pure and simple.'

'Why didn't you replace Danny with another keyboard player?' Walters said. 'I'm sure there must have been plenty of others around.'

'There were, but Danny was special and it would have been hard if not impossible to replace what he gave us. If Eric was a once in a blue moon guitarist, Danny Winter was a once in a green moon keyboard player. In the end, losing Danny and with Eric out of his head most of the time, I couldn't see a future for the band, so I decided to pack it in. Barry felt the same.'

'Maybe with hindsight it wasn't such a bad decision,' Henderson said, casting his eyes around the office. 'You haven't done badly.'

'Yeah, I guess. I look at some of these old rockers, and I've even been to a few concerts, and I ask myself, why do they still do it? I mean, some of them must have bills to pay like the rest of us, but I know for a fact some of them don't as they're worth millions.'

'Does a part of you still fancy it?'

'You bet. There's a buzz you get on stage when all the band are playing in synch and you're really rocking. Nothing comes close, not in business, drinking, sex, you name it.'

'With the recent death of your brother, Barry, and now, Peter Grant, do you think there's a connection?'

He sat back in his chair to consider, no doubt thinking how he could respond without sounding too much like a fruitcake. 'I didn't see Barry that often, once a month or so, but Pete and I were in regular contact and often went out for dinner. I'll miss them both. I know Barry loved animals, but would he jump in the river after his dog? I'm not sure, I suppose it's possible. As for Pete, it was a freakish accident that killed him and no mistake, but I don't pretend to understand it.'

'Anything else?'

He sat forward, a worried look etched on his face. 'In our early albums, we used a certain amount of imagery and sorcery in our songs, copying the likes of Marillion and Genesis. As a result, we attracted a few witches, wizards and all manner of weirdos to our concerts and it's possible one of them might have taken exception to a lyric or something we said in an interview. But if you're thinking someone has put a curse on the band, I don't believe that sort of stuff exists.'

'I agree, because if someone was taking exception to your lyrics, why stop at the Crazy Crows? Why not target all the other bands doing much the same thing?'

'That's a bloody good point, Inspector,' he said as if warming to the theme. 'Why us? Black Sabbath and Yes were into way more airy-fairy stuff than anything we ever did.'

'Can you think of anybody you might have severely offended or got on the wrong side of, either when you were in the band or starting your tanker business?'

He shook his head. 'Not with the Crazy Crows. Sure, we had the usual wrangles with record companies, managers and promoters, but nothing major and nothing that would last for over twenty-six-years. In business, I guess I've made a few enemies with trade unions and competing companies. I started this business from scratch and I guess I've trod on a few toes and put a few noses out of joint along the way.'

It was Henderson's turn to warm to the theme. 'You went from a couple of tankers to operating a fleet of over fifty with two fuel depots in the space of five years. That sort of growth is pretty meteoritic in anybody's book.'

Derek seemed to grow in stature at the last comment, or was it Henderson's imagination? 'I started out with some money I saved when I was in the band, and working with an uncle who was a tanker driver for guidance I bought a couple of tankers. I got lucky when I won the distribution contract with one of the oil majors early on and the choice was either to stay on the horse or fall off. I rode my luck a few times but when the contract went well, others followed.'

Henderson could see a crack opening up here. Did he borrow money from people who now wanted payback, or had he been involved in something nefarious back then to generate the cash, which was now coming back to haunt him? 'It still must have taken a major capital investment.'

'The *Black Saturday* album sold well around Europe and if you can believe it, in Japan and Korea. I wrote most of the songs so I got a big chunk of the royalties. I used that money in combination with a couple of bank loans and re-mortgaging my house. I'm making it sound easy but I assure you it wasn't.'

It sounded too corporate brochure for Henderson's liking. Perhaps he had told it so many times that he was starting to believe it himself, but in Henderson's mind it didn't ring true.

'Can you think of anyone who might want to do you or any of the other band members harm?' Walters asked. 'Have you or they received threatening letters or abusive phone calls, for example.'

'I know I haven't, and even though I can't speak for the other guys, I'm sure they would have told me if they did.'

Henderson and Walters left Derek Crow's office ten minutes later.

'You didn't say much, Carol,' Henderson said when they reached the car. 'It's not like you to be so quiet. Does the rock music thing turn you off so much?'

'I'm not a fan, as you well know, but it's not only that. It's the first time I've been on an investigation where we are in effect looking for a victim. It's taking a bit of getting used to.'

'I can sympathise as I often have the same feeling myself. Although if I'm being picky, I think we've got the victims, it's the motive to connect them that's proving elusive.'

'Fair enough.'

'What did you think of Mr Crow?' he said as he successfully merged the pool car into a line of slow-moving cars in the road outside.

'Much as I expected. A tough, uncompromising businessman, a man who doesn't take many prisoners.'

'And?'

'I think he has something to hide. I didn't feel he was being entirely open with us.'

'I got the same impression. I wonder why?'

TWENTY-TWO

Former Metropolitan Police Chief Inspector Bill Paterson emerged from St James's Park Underground Station looking dishevelled, as if at the end of the day and not the start. He didn't mind wearing a crumpled raincoat and shoes looking as if they hadn't been polished since the day they were bought, but he did agree with the bathroom mirror that he now needed a haircut and the use of a sharper razor blade.

He believed when interviewing anyone on police business he would have an advantage if he wasn't as smartly dressed as they were, because if the subject felt superior, their complacency might lead them into making a mistake. In any case, detective work taught him that many substances could be spilt on clothes during the working week: blood and puke of a witness or a drunk, oil and grime from wrestling a suspect to the pavement, and food and beer, as even he would have to admit he was a messy eater.

Through old contacts at Sussex Police, he had visited the accident scenes of Barry Crow and Peter Grant and found the official conclusions sound, court-sound as he used to call it. Mindful this news would not put Derek Crow's mind at rest and not deposit much in his threadbare bank account, he encouraged Derek to come up with a 'hate' list. This was a list of people from the past that members of the Crows had messed up big-time, sufficient for them to hold a long-term grudge. He was sure many people could complete the same exercise, but Derek's list was longer than most.

In Caxton Street, in an area of London called Petty France, he stopped outside a red stone town house. He reached into his pocket for a piece of paper and among the detritus: an empty wrapper of wine gums, a half-smoked cigarette, a tube ticket, house keys and an old paper hanky, he found it and pulled it out. Address confirmed, he rang the bell.

The door opened and a small dumpy woman of Mediterranean origin, wearing a simple black dress covered by a white apron, stood there wiping her hands on the apron.

'Bill Paterson here to see Mr Strider.'

'Ah, Meester Paterson,' the lady said, 'come inside, Mr Strider is expecting you.'

She guided him into a spacious living room, surprising as the house didn't look so big on the outside. It was decorated in something the west-end nobs would call minimalist modern, with pale colours on the wall, a few squiggles on canvases masquerading as art, and a few bits of furniture, all colourful and trendy. The room was trying hard to look like the inside of some up-market furniture shop in the King's Road, but it reminded him of IKEA, a place he would only return to if the barrel of a gun was being held against his temple.

He stood at the window looking down on the street when he heard Strider walk in. Derek Crow had told him he was a top session guitarist, whatever that was, and he'd imagined a long-haired spotty bloke with an ugly, pock-marked face and a beer gut to equal his own. Strider was tall and thin, with overlong fair hair, not bad for a man in his early fifties, and exuding the confidence of a seasoned businessman.

'Good morning, Detective Paterson. It's good to meet you,' he said sticking out a hand.

They shook. His hand felt cool and feminine.

'Take a seat. Can I get you tea?'

'Aye, grand.'

'We've got Darjeeling, Green, Camomile or Oolong.'

'Bloody hell, there's more choice here than Starbucks. Any builder's tea, Typhoo?'

Striker shook his mane.

'How about a coffee? Columbian, Nicaraguan, or Ecuadorian, I'm not fussy.'

'Sure,' Strider said as he walked. 'I hope instant is ok, I never touch the stuff myself.'

He must have given instructions to the cook or the housekeeper or whoever the woman who let him in was, as he came back into the room in less than a minute, empty handed.

Paterson knew little about him, only that he had been a session guitarist for over thirty years and he'd worked with the Crazy Crows for a while, and after a big dust-up, they never saw him again. From reading his autobiography, Derek said he didn't smoke or drink and claimed to have bedded two thousand women. Paterson had never met a thousand women and he used to work in Vice.

'Mr Strider...'

'Call me Boz, everyone else does.'

Boz, what kind of fucking name is Boz? He wouldn't name a parrot anything as daft and he hated parrots.

'Boz, as I said on the phone I'm investigating the deaths of two members of the Crazy Crows–'

'Yeah, I'd heard about it; tragic I'm sure.'

'Yes, indeed. Now Derek Crow has asked me–'

'Derek Crow? Fuck me, there's a name I haven't heard in a while. He must be shit-scared now, ha, ha. I bet many gravediggers are out there sharpening their shovels.'

Strider was sitting across the chair now, his long legs, shod in tight jeans, dangling over the side. This was perhaps a rock 'n' roll way to sit, or the furniture was as uncomfortable as it looked. Either way, Paterson found his behaviour disconcerting and it didn't do for a copper, even an ex, to feel this way. If he still possessed a warrant card, he would order him to sit like a normal person.

'Why do think Derek should feel scared?'

'Wouldn't you if two of your mates suddenly croaked?'

He nodded as if in agreement, but being a copper didn't endear him to many people and the odd working hours often made relationships unworkable. He doubted he could rustle up two friends if his brother and son were taken out of the equation.

In came the drinks, carried by the Mediterranean woman, a cup of the instant stuff for him and what smelled like a herbal face wash for Boz. Miss Portugal 1968 gave him a warm smile and departed.

'While it appears Barry Crow and Peter Grant both died in bona fide accidents, Derek is of the opinion some incident in the band's past may be triggering it.'

'What, like some bloke Derek fucked around all those years ago has stepped up to the plate and is doing his pals in? Do me a favour, there would be a big queue if you asked for volunteers.'

'How do you mean?'

'Derek is, and was, a cold-hearted bastard who would stamp on anyone who got in his way.'

'Perhaps we can come back to that point later. Can you tell me what you did for them? I'm not sure I know what a guitarist like yourself does.'

'I'm a session man,' he said, changing his position and sitting like a normal person. 'I'm the guy you hear on the record but the other guy gets the credit.'

'Why?' Paterson said, a bit more intrigued than he would care to admit.

'Y'see, some bands make it to the front page because they look good or sound interesting, but maybe they're not very good musicians. They call me in and I play the guitar parts and make them seem a lot better than they really are.'

'What about the Crows? Everybody tells me Eric Hannah was a good guitarist.'

'He was, might still be for all I know, but he was raw; all talent and no finesse, y'know? Big balls and a small cock as we used to call it.'

He nodded as if he did.

'The guys in the Crows would have an idea of what they wanted in a guitar solo or a riff or something,' Strider continued, 'and they would ask Hannah to play it. He would do it all right, but play it different each time and add bits here and there as he saw fit. In my mind, he was fucking about. Noodling we guitarists call it, but we save all that stuff for the rehearsal room. A studio costs big money, so you go in, do your thing and get the hell out. There's no room for pissing around.'

'So you did the guitar parts instead of him?'

'Yep, but not all the time, you understand. I did a lot in the second and a bit on the third album.'

'I'm told you had a big bust up with them. What happened?'

'Yep, we did.' His eyes clouded over, recalling a bad time.

Paterson waited and sipped his coffee. If they served this bitter and tasteless stuff to visiting tradesmen they'd leave marbles in the waste pipes and hide an alarm clock in the loft.

'Hannah didn't know I was doing it, can you believe it? The bastards didn't tell him.'

'Derek didn't mention this.'

'He wouldn't, the bastard. It was late one night while we were working in the studio at Maida Vale, adding guitar over-dubs to a couple of songs from their second album. Hannah was supposed to be shacking up with some bird in Islington, but he wandered into the studio and went ape-shite when he saw me. He called me all the names he could think of, it's all in my book if you wanna read it, but when he grabbed my guitar, I saw red and I socked him. Next thing I know, Derek is pummelling into me, and seconds later, Hannah joins in, kicking me. I end up in hospital with broken ribs and a smashed face, and you wanna know the kicker?'

'What?'

'One of those bastards stamped on my hand. I couldn't work for months.'

*

Paterson left the home of Boz Strider ten minutes later, the cup of instant grumbling away in his dickey stomach like the miserable old geezer with the stained shirt and moth-eaten cardigan living in the flat above his in Woolwich.

He headed back to the Tube and after a couple of changes, took the Jubilee Line to Kilburn. The phrase 'chalk and cheese' didn't cut it. Not only did Simon Rother's house in Charteris Road look much smaller on the outside than Boz Strider's, a two or three bedroom terrace with a bin-sized garden, inside it was a mess. Nothing minimalist or modern about this place.

While walking towards the living room, he passed the open door of a spare room, the walls festooned with posters of Jesus, religious gatherings in America and dozens of postcard-sized photographs. He didn't see any posters in the lounge except for a big picture of Jesus above the fireplace, but loads of religious books, magazines and pamphlets lay over every flat surface including the floor, and at the far end of the room, the kitchen was piled up with dirty dishes.

This time he didn't get offered a cup of tea, served by a busty maid giving him the eye, just as well as he didn't want to hang around here any longer than was necessary. He gave Rother his preamble about the accidents suffered by two members of the Crazy Crows and cut to the chase.

'Simon, you are in a cult called the Children of Jesus and you and your mates used to harass the Crazy Crows at gigs, and later, in the hotel where they were staying. I also understand you sent Derek Crow a large pile of nasty letters.'

'They deserved it,' he said, with way more venom than could be expected from a middle-aged, overwrought and overweight B&Q worker with a threadbare dead ferret for a mullet and bad teeth.

'Why?'

'Their lyrics glorified Satan and convinced many young people to turn their backs on Jesus and the word of God.'

Paterson didn't do religion and couldn't understand the zealot's fervour for ancient ideas and outmoded thinking. Why did they feel they needed to embrace restrictions on their lives when making a success of it was hard enough, as this room bore testament?

'What did you want to happen to them?'

'My followers and I wanted them to stop playing such heathen music and we would use every means at our disposal to achieve it.'

'Did this stretch to killing them?'

He looked at him, aghast. 'We are a religious order who believe in the teachings of Jesus Christ. Jesus would never condone violence, no matter how much he was provoked.'

'I beg to differ.' Paterson didn't own a computer, not because he didn't like modern technology but he couldn't be bothered learning how it worked. In any case, his local library in Woolwich had a couple of pcs and one afternoon he'd researched Rother's 'Children of Jesus' outfit.

'In a vicious campaign against the Crazy Crows, you threw paint, disrupted concerts by chanting and harassing the audience, banged on hotel room doors during the night and set off fire alarms. Does any of this ring any bells with you?'

'That wasn't me, it was some hot-heads who took our name in vain.'

'Bollocks. You've received convictions for harassment, public order offences, criminal damage and assault. But it doesn't stop there, does it? Only last month your lot were outside Tesco in this neck of the woods, annoying shoppers, maybe about using too many plastic carrier bags or the price of fish, I don't know.'

His face crumpled as if he was about to cry but then it hardened. 'You don't know the half of it. You are nothing but the soiled instrument of the capitalist machine.'

In his time in Vice, he had been called 'pimp', 'tosser', 'pensioner shagger' and a whole lot worse but never a 'soiled instrument.' He couldn't stop to ask if it was an insult or a compliment as Rother launched into a long diatribe about the corrupt morals of the young, the distorted capitalist system that favoured the rich, and was moving on to the legacy of tyrants like Mao Tse Tung and George W. Bush when he called a halt.

'Hold it, hold it, Rother. I didn't come here to listen to all this tosh about dictators or to be brainwashed into joining your little tribe of savages.'

'It's not tosh, it's the truth.'

'It's the truth to you and your blockhead friends, but quite frankly, I like to drink my beer in a different pub, if you catch my drift. Now, listen to me, mate. Two members of the Crazy Crows band are dead and it's my job to find out why.'

'You think me or one of my followers did this?'

'Did you?'

'We would never stoop so low to fulfil an animalistic desire and kill another human being.'

'I take it you mean 'no' or–'

'Of course I mean no. We didn't do it, we didn't kill those men.'

'Tell me where you were on two dates and I'll leave you in peace.' He didn't need to consult his dog-eared notebook as he knew them fine.

Rother rummaged through the junkyard that was the bookcase and produced a diary.

'On the first date which is a Tuesday, I met my...my probation officer mid-morning and in the afternoon worked at B&Q.'

'Who's your probation officer?'

He gave him her name and Paterson would call her first thing. Barry Crow was killed in the morning so if it checked out, he was in the clear for one of them.

'The second date, the last Sunday in February, I spend every second Sunday at the care home where my mother now lives. It's in Bournemouth so I drive there in the morning and come back here at tea-time.'

Time enough to get down to Brighton and kill Grant?

'That Sunday, I stayed over at a friend's house in Portsmouth.'

He blushed, suggesting the friend was a man, oh tut, tut. Paterson's son often called him an old fart, a dinosaur who couldn't tell an iPad from an eye patch, but he'd seen more than his share of trannies, homos, lesbos, cross-dressers and all the rest and nothing on that front could shock him any more.

Paterson eased himself out of the lumpy chair. 'Thanks for your time Mr Rother. I'll see myself out.'

A picture on the table caught his eye. He picked it up. A younger Rother was dressed in white robes and standing in front of a large building, redolent of a university campus.

'Where was this taken?'

Rother pulled the photograph out of his hand. He obviously didn't like other people touching his stuff. Paterson didn't like touching his stuff either and would wash his hands at the earliest opportunity.

'In St Louis, Missouri. In the early eighties I joined a monastery.'

'Is that right? I worked a case a few years back involving a monk who liked banging under-age prostitutes. How long did you stay there?'

'I lived with the brothers for twenty-two years. I only returned to the UK eighteen months ago because my father was dying.'

TWENTY-THREE

DI Henderson was seated at the desk in his office, reading the post-mortem reports of Barry Crow and Peter Grant, when DS Walters walked in.

'Find anything new in there?' she said, nodding at the reports.

'Nope, they're much as we expected. Barry died from drowning and there were no unexplained marks on his body or noxious substances inside him. Peter died from asphyxiation, and in his body there was plenty of booze and a little cannabis.'

She sat down in the visitor's chair. 'It's not much to go on, is it?'

'What?'

'This whole case. All we've got are two accidental deaths; in the context of a small group like a rock band, it looks improbable, but nothing else. I wonder how long it will be before bookies start offering odds on the two survivors.'

'Your levity is amusing but not helpful. You're forgetting two things. One is Sarah Corbett's assessment of Peter and the other is Peter's weightlifting record book.'

'I didn't meet Sarah, which is a shame as a woman might have seen her in a different light. She was in mourning for the loss of her boyfriend and as you know, grief can affect people in loads of strange ways, including not being able to accept if the person is dead, or in this case, not accepting how he died.'

'All good points, Ms Walters and I can even shoot down my own argument about Peter Grant's weights record book. He could have been tired and over-judged his capabilities due to alcohol and cannabis consumption as the doc,' he said stabbing the P-M report with his finger, 'in here says.'

'But?'

'There is still a nagging suspicion that won't go away, and you heard Derek Crow expressing surprise about Barry even going into the water. Peter Grant was killed by something he had been doing for years without mishap.'

'I went to the gym.'

'You did?'

'I joined last year but I let it lapse. Two weeks ago I went back and signed up for two classes a week.'

'Well done, I hope—'

'What I'm was about to say was, I talked to a couple of weightlifters there, for research purposes only you understand and nothing to do with their jaw-dropping physiques. They tell me they always weightlift in pairs as you never know when muscle tiredness will kick in. In fact—'

'Hang on a sec, Carol. I've just thought of something. Is there still a police presence at Peter Grant's house?'

'Nope. They're long gone.'

'Not a problem as I don't think it will make a difference to what I want to do, but I need to see it for myself. Grab your coat.'

'Where are we going?'

'Hove.'

*

Henderson eased the car onto the drive outside Peter Grant's house in Woodland Drive, Hove, carefully avoiding the other car parked there. He supposed it belonged to one of the forensic techs, returning to retrieve something left behind. He knocked on the door and to his surprise, an attractive woman opened the door. The Forensic Service didn't have techs as good looking as this, did they?

'Good afternoon, I am Detective Inspector Henderson of Surrey and Sussex Police, and this is Detective Sergeant Walters.'

'Hello,' she said sounding a touch flustered, as if they were interrupting something. 'I'm Emily Grant, Peter's ex wife. Why don't you come in?'

It was Henderson who should feel flustered as he wasn't expecting to find anyone here and didn't have a clue what to say to her. What he came to see could be examined with the house closed.

They followed Mrs Grant into the kitchen, where a copy of *The Daily Telegraph* was spread out over the kitchen table in the middle of the room.

'I was having a cup of coffee and a read of the paper. Would you like one? Tea perhaps?'

'Coffee for me,' Henderson said.

'Same for me,' Walters said.

The coffee pot must have been hot as it didn't take long until Mrs Grant placed a couple of mugs in front of them.

Henderson sat down on a seat beside the table. 'It was tragic what happened to Peter, Mrs Grant. I would like to offer you my deepest sympathies.'

'Thank you. You're right, it was tragic, but call me Emily. I've been trying to drop the 'Mrs Grant' tag for some time now.'

She was dressed in a tight-fitting blue dress, and despite her age, which he would put at about fifty, not difficult to estimate as it was Peter's age, exhibiting a figure many younger women would pay good money to have. Her hair was light brown, shoulder-length with big, luxurious curls, a fine compliment to a tanned, rounded face.

'I suppose you're wondering why I'm here,' she said, 'because as you probably know, I don't live here anymore. I moved with the children to a house in Henfield to be with my new partner.'

It hadn't crossed Henderson's mind, as even though he knew Peter Grant lived alone, he didn't know if his ex-wife was a frequent and welcome visitor or wasn't allowed to darken the door.

'I came over for one last look before I hand the keys over to the estate agents, and to see if there was anything else I could take, as Pete doesn't need it now, does he? What about you people? Everyone says he died in an accident so why does it require the presence of two detectives?'

'You're right to ask. Peter's death was an accident, same as Barry Crow earlier...' He examined her face to determine if he was telling her something she didn't know, but instead she nodded.

'All we're doing is making sure there is no connection between them, as the deaths of two members of a small tight-knit group like a four-piece rock band within weeks of one another, raises a whole range of questions and leaves many people concerned.'

'You're trying to cover yourselves in case you're proved

wrong.'

'It's not only us, Peter's HR Director at Grant's Fitness Emporium, Sarah Corbett, has also asked us to review it.'

'I've met Sarah, she's a lovely lady.'

'Why did you say, in case we might be proved wrong? Do you think we're wrong?'

'I don't know why I said it. I don't know any more than you do.'

'All we're trying to do is determine *if* there is a connection. We don't believe there is one but we would not be doing our duty if we did nothing and something happened to Derek or Eric.'

'I understand. Do you want to take a look in the gym?'

'If you wouldn't mind.'

'Help yourself, there are a couple of things I need to get on with. It's down to the right–'

'Don't worry,' he said standing, 'I know the way.' He led Walters into the gym and for the next few minutes explained to her the pathologist's findings.

'This is amazing,' she said. 'He's got a great range of kit and his own tuck shop full of health foods and drinks. I'd love to have a place like this.'

Henderson was listening to his sergeant but also keeping an ear on the movements of Emily Grant. He heard her walk upstairs and lock what he assumed to be the bathroom door. He motioned Walters to follow him.

He walked into the kitchen, towards the back door, and began examining the frame.

'What are you looking for?'

'Signs of forced entry.'

'Why?'

'If Peter didn't die as a result of an accident, the only

other conclusion we can come to, is someone broke in and dropped the barbell on his neck.'

'I get you. I'll take a look outside.'

Henderson opened the door and let Walters past. He inspected the door's outer edge, running his hand up and down the wood, feeling for imperfections or hasty repairs.

'Sir, come and see this.'

He stepped outside, and following Walters' arm, examined the frame of the kitchen window. He could see a small gap in the wood where a piece had been removed.

'This is fresh,' he said, 'maybe in the last few days as the wood is still white and hasn't gone brown.'

'It looks deliberate to me and not the result of, I don't know, weather or insects.'

'I think so too.'

He moved back into the kitchen and reaching up to the window he could see the cut was opposite the window latch.

'So,' Henderson said, 'he cuts away this bit of window frame with a Stanley knife, sticks a flat blade like a screwdriver into the gap, gives it a push and out will pop the window locking arm.' He donned a set of protective gloves and opened the window.

'Is it possible for you to climb in here, because there's nothing to impede an intruder's progress once he's inside?'

'I can't, as I'm too small to reach the window ledge.' She scanned the area around her. 'I could do it if I stood on that,' she said.

Henderson stepped outside. Standing close to the wall at the back of the house was a small, solid wooden table, probably used when cooking food on the barbecue, which he assumed was the large item under cover alongside it.

'We need to–'

'What are you doing out there?'

Emily Grant was in the kitchen watching them. He had no idea for how long or how much she'd seen or heard, but he decided to bluff it.

'I needed to make a phone call and couldn't get any reception inside.'

'You must be on EE, our friends can never get reception here.' It must have been a convincing excuse as she picked something up from the table and walked into the hall.

A few minutes later, Henderson and Walters drove back to Sussex House, not the result of being thrown out of the house by Emily Grant for his poor attempt at trying to fool her, but he'd seen what he came to see.

'Should we add this one to our list of inconsistencies?' Henderson asked as he turned off Woodland Drive and on to Dyke Road.

'Most definitely, although it could be the work of a burglar.'

'Could be, as Peter lived alone and the house is unoccupied most days, but it's too much of a coincidence and the cut made in the wood, to my eyes at least, looks new. Forensics should be able to tell us one way or another.'

'If he's been so clever in the way he's killed those guys to make it look like accidents, he'll be smart enough not to leave anything behind when he does it.'

'Yeah, that crossed my mind too, but we'll take a look anyway, you never know, we might get lucky.'

His phone rang. He pressed the button on the steering

wheel to answer.

'Henderson.'

'Angus, it's Lisa Edwards. I'm glad I caught you. Where are you?'

'DS Walters and I are coming back from Peter Grant's house in Hove.'

'The former rock band musician who died working out in his home gym?'

'Yes, him. There's been a new development and I need to talk to you about it.'

'I want you to drop the case.'

'What?'

'There's been a jewel robbery in the Lanes, a shotgun fired and one person injured. Get down there now and take it over. The press are going to have a field day as the shop belongs to the Crime Commissioner's brother.'

'This new development I mentioned suggests this case has changed from two accidents to two murders and if so, it constitutes a significant risk to the remaining members of the Crazy Crows, and with all due respect ma'am, I think this is more important than the theft of some rings and watches.'

'Angus, I haven't been working with the Sussex force for long, but I do know your antenna for spotting crime is as good as anyone I've ever met. While I think there is merit in what you're doing, it is out of my hands. When the ACC heard about the story he practically blew a gasket. Investigate the crimes we've got, not Henderson's pet projects or ones we invent for ourselves, was one of his milder comments.'

'I'm amazed he's taken this attitude.'

'You know what he's like. Vague suppositions don't

work with the ACC, he likes his evidence in concrete. I knew he wouldn't support it.'

Henderson couldn't see a way out. 'What do I do about the Crows while I'm investigating the jewel robbery?'

'Let's see if there are any more developments in the case, then we might be able to use it to persuade the ACC to authorise further investigation.'

'What, like another death?'

'Don't be a cynic, Angus. You know what I mean.'

TWENTY-FOUR

Emily Grant stood at the window watching as DI Henderson and DS Walters drove away. She knew they were up to something when they were standing outside, the DI's lame phone excuse didn't fool her. She had been an expert deceiver and liar herself for many years and could easily spot the trait in others.

Confident they wouldn't be coming back, she resumed the task she had set for herself before they arrived and interrupted. No, it wasn't reading *The Daily Telegraph* and enjoying a cup of coffee at a seat beside the kitchen table, as a better detective would have noticed the paper was dated last Friday.

She climbed the stairs to Pete's bedroom and resumed her search of the cupboard. The house looked bereft of all things loose, frilly and pretty but it wasn't as if she had taken everything; God-knows she would have liked to, but her new house in Henfield was too small. It was because Pete didn't want to be reminded of their marriage and he was a tad OCD. This meant everything he didn't want, use or like the look of had been neatly stacked in this cupboard, the one in the spare bedroom and in the cupboard under the stairs.

She'd had a good look through the cupboard under the stairs but she still had this one to do and the one in the spare bedroom. She got stuck into the task, pulling out boxes, emptying the contents, re-boxing the items, and putting the box back where it came from. A little voice was telling her to stop being so neat, as she could tip most of the stuff in a black bin bag or throw it in a skip. Pete wouldn't care what she did, and in any case, whenever the house was sold, she would have to conduct the same exercise all over again.

She suppressed the little voice as she was looking for something specific and if she didn't do this in a tidy and systematic manner, she would miss it. She plodded on for another twenty minutes before removing another box which was full of photographs.

Tears trickled down her cheeks as she looked at pictures of her and Pete during the first years of their marriage. They had gone to Spain for a cheap holiday with Pete's brother and his wife, and she picked up picture after picture of them hugging, kissing and looking at one another with love in their eyes.

This poignant reminder of how happy she'd once felt only served to bring forth a feeling lurking at the back of her mind. She didn't love her new man, Greg, as much as she used to love Pete and she knew she never would. Perhaps selling the family house would be the catalyst she now needed to force her to turn her life around.

Twenty minutes later and no further forward in her search, she picked up her phone and called her daughter, Danielle.

'Hi, Mum, where are you?'

'Are you at home?

'Yeah.'

'What happened to college?'

'Nothing. I've only got one lesson on a Tuesday afternoon, so I came straight home.'

157

'Are you sure you're not telling your dear old mum porkies and dossing off?'

'Ha, ha, would I? Have you been drinking?'

'Of course, but only black coffee.'

'Very funny. Did you call just to give me hassle or was there something else?'

'Something else. I'm over at Woodland Drive.'

'Oh.'

'Don't worry, I'm not doing a house clear of all your childhood memories.'

'You better not be, you can't do it without me.'

'I know. I'm looking for your dad's blue notebook.'

'The one with all his passwords?'

'Yes.'

'Are you trying to get into his computer?'

'Nope.'

'Shame, as I know the password for it. What do you want the book for?'

'Enough questions. Can you come over here and help me?'

'Oh I dunno. I've got work to do.'

'I didn't see you doing any last night.'

'Fair enough, but what's in it for me?'

She sighed. 'Your businessman father has taught you well.'

'Of course.'

'Let's say, I make your favourite pudding for tea and if you don't come and help, I'll make you eat rice pudding.'

'Argh, not rice pudding. You drive a hard bargain, missus. I'll be there in about twenty minutes.'

By the time Danielle arrived half an hour later, she was looking through the last box in Pete's bedroom cupboard.

'I'm upstairs,' she shouted, when she heard the door slam shut.

Danielle clumped up the stairs with the same noise and lack of finesse as her father, but he'd been a fifteen-stone bulk while she weighed a little over half that and had a sylph-like figure. Until the age of thirteen, they couldn't get her out of a dress, and now they couldn't get her in one and out of the jeans she wore all the time, except for funerals, weddings and christenings.

'Why are you looking up here?'

'I'm being a sentimental old fool looking through some of my old stuff; why do you think? It wasn't where I thought it would be, in his study.'

'Where did you look in his study?'

'In the desk where he usually kept it, then the bookcase, and then filing cabinet.'

'Did you check underneath his computer?'

'Why would I look there?'

'Because that's where he put it to hide it from me.'

She followed Danielle downstairs. 'Why didn't you tell me this on the phone, it would have saved you the bother of driving over here?'

'Because I wanted to find out what you were up to.'

'I'm not up to anything. I'm trying to open your dad's safe.'

'Dad has a safe? Cool. What's in it?'

'I don't know.'

'Don't play coy with me.' She lifted the computer and there was Pete's little blue book. 'You're not having this until you tell me what's in the safe.'

'I don't know what's in it, do I? It'll be full of important papers and such. And anyway, if it was chock-full of valuables, what do you care? He left the business to you. You're loaded.'

'True, I am. Let's open it and see what's there. Where is it?'

'In the lounge.'

'Are you sure?'

'Of course I'm sure. Come with me and learn. Your old mother still has a few tricks up her sleeve.'

She walked into the lounge and stopped in front of two pictures painted by the artist, Joaquin, the only pictures hanging in the room.

'Where is it?' Danielle said.

'Behind one of the pictures.'

'Well, I...hang on. The pictures are the wrong way round.'

'How do you know?'

'In the bottom corner of the one on the right, it has the red and black stripes, while the one on the left, black and red stripes. Dad always had the red and black stripes on the left. You know how pernickety he could be about those things.'

She did. All through their marriage she experienced Pete's funny habits, from the way he folded his clothes, ate his food or filed albums in his record collection; order and precision had to prevail. She often told him, at the risk of making him angry, that in another life he would have been a ready recruit for the SS.

'What does it mean?'

'I don't know what it means,' Danielle said, her face displaying a puzzled expression. 'Even if Dad was drunk and moved them to take a look at something, he would still put them back in the correct order before he went to bed.'

'I think you're right.'

'Now,' her daughter said, hands on her hips. 'If you did manage to find the blue book all by yourself, how were you going to get one of these pictures down? I don't know which one is hiding the safe, but they're both big beasts.'

'Now you mention it, they do look rather big.' She slapped her daughter on the arm. 'Good job you're here. I'll get a chair.'

She held the chair while Danielle climbed up and tried to unhook the painting. It was a simple enough job to do with a small painting, but even with arms outstretched and gripping both sides, she was finding it awkward to manoeuvre.

Somehow she managed to free it, and passed the painting to Emily. They were being careful not to damage it, but like all the items in the cupboards upstairs, she would not be taking them with her and if they couldn't find a buyer, they would be junked.

Danielle stepped down to catch her breath. The safe could be seen now. Emily always knew it was there but never had cause to open it. Pete told her he kept private things in there and didn't want her looking, but she was never tempted, even if she could have manhandled the big paintings by herself. In his will, Pete didn't leave the business to her, but to their daughter and so she was hoping the safe contained something of value to tide her over until the house was sold.

Emily flicked through the blue book and found the code. Danielle climbed up again, and turned the dial on the front of the safe based on her promptings. With a cry of 'Ta dah,' from her daughter, the door opened. She reached inside.

'It's nothing but a load of papers and Dad's passport,' she said as she flicked though the pile she had extracted.

'Pass them down.'

Emily looked through the papers and found the divorce papers, deeds for the house and other documents relating to the business.

'Is there anything else in there?'

Danielle dipped her hand inside once again. 'Nope, it's now officially empty. It's a big safe for not a lot of stuff.'

'Are you sure it's empty?'

'Yes, I'm sure. I'm an 'A' level student and not a ten-year-old kid. You look disappointed. What were you expecting, diamonds and gold?'

TWENTY-FIVE

Bristol 1989

Derek Crow tumbled out of bed and fell on the floor with a thump. He loved touring but hated how he couldn't remember which bed he crawled into the previous night and whether it butted up against the wall or not. This one obviously didn't.

He looked at the girl occupying the other side of the bed through bloodshot eyes. She looked fast asleep, just as well as he didn't look or feel his best this morning. God knows how many pints of ale and vodkas and coke he'd downed, and then they smoked some weed Eric brought back from Germany.

The gig they did last night at the Colston Hall in Bristol was up there in the top five of Crazy Crow gigs, but borne out of yet another big argument between Eric and Danny. Their constant bickering got on his nerves but if it ever had a positive side, last night was it. They played many songs from the new album and while sometimes playing new material often went down like a lead balloon, as the fans came to hear the old favourites, last night they loved it. They shouted and screamed out the lyrics, giving Danny a special thrill as he'd penned a couple of them.

He left sleeping beauty to her slumber and wandered down to the restaurant to satisfy his strong craving for food. Unlike the other members of the band, Barry possessed an iron constitution and no matter what he got up to the previous evening, he could always make it down for breakfast. Sure enough, when he walked through the reception area, he found Barry in a quiet corner, enjoying a cup of post-breakfast coffee and reading a newspaper.

'Morning bro,' Barry said looking up as he approached.

'Morning Barry, how are you?' he said slumping into the seat. 'In fact, don't answer that as I saw you neck down a couple of pints before you headed upstairs with a gorgeous bird with long black hair.'

'I'd rather spend the night shagging a lass like her than getting drunk like you lot. Plus, it means I feel a lot better for it in the morning.'

'I can't argue with you there.'

Derek called over a passing member of the hotel staff. She was aged around nineteen with her hair scraped back in a severe pony-tail revealing a pretty, unblemished face. It was a good job Barry was stuck behind a table, as she looked his type.

'Can I order a coffee tray like his, and is there any breakfast food left?'

'Oh my God. You're the singer from the band I saw last night, the Crazy Crows. Can I just say, you guys are bloody brilliant? My friend Melissa and me had the best night watching a band we've had in years. She'll be thrilled and jealous as hell when she finds out I've met you.'

For the last five years, he could stand naked like a mannequin in a shop window in Oxford Street and nobody would bat an eyelid. A combination of releasing a well-received album, their fourth, and playing as many gigs as their promoter could book, had elevated them onto a whole new plane.

'I'm glad you enjoyed it. You'll need proof to show to your friend.'

She nodded with enthusiasm. 'You could use my notebook.'

'Nah, you want something more personal.' He looked over at his brother. 'C'mon Barry, sign that clean napkin.' He signed it and passed it over and Derek did the same. In seconds, it disappeared into a pocket of her apron.

'Thanks a lot. Now what would you like? I could get you a sandwich.'

'How about a toasted sandwich?'

'Can do. Would you like bacon, ham or fried egg?'

'One bacon and one egg and a couple of rounds of toast as well, I'm starving.'

'Coming up,' she said as she turned away and rushed off, not so much to assuage his ravenous hunger but to alert the other restaurant staff as to their presence, and to hide the napkin in her locker.

'I fear the days of sitting unnoticed in the corner of a place like this are coming to an end,' Barry said. 'Are you ready for it?'

'I don't think so,' he said as he helped himself to the remaining nuts in Barry's little bowl. 'Is anybody?'

'I like not being recognised, not being pestered by autograph hunters and folks with their bloody flashing cameras.'

He crunched the nuts. The first few bites tasted of toothpaste, his earlier attempt to get rid of the shitty quagmire in his mouth, and like a slow intro, the sharp, salty flavour came crashing through.

'I guess we'll all need to get used to it. In a way, it's what we've all signed up for.'

'Aye, maybe you're right. Can I talk to you about last night?'

'What, was your performance in the sack not up to its usual high standard? Has she made a complaint about you to hotel management?'

'Don't be daft, there's fuck all wrong wi' me or my tackle. I'm talking about the concert.'

Here we go again. Barry could be a bit of an old woman and at times Derek thought him unsuited to playing in a rock band and touring, as he wanted to nit-pick every performance, reminding him too much of the production manager in the meat packing factory where he used to work. Derek, you sang out of tune there; Eric never plays the same riff twice; Pete hits the snare too hard. It sounded like a scratched record, the needle jumping back, time after time to the same part of the song.

Relief came ten minutes later when the food arrived, as he didn't need to look at his brother and feign interest. Fame did have its compensations as the plate was crammed with food. Between two slices of thick, toasted bread he could see numerous rashers of bacon, a fried egg between two more, and at the side, a couple of sausages, hash browns and dollop of baked beans. To crown it all, a little bowl of tomato sauce.

'That stuff will set you up for the day,' Barry said, 'or give you a bloody coronary.'

'I'm too young to die,' he said tucking in. 'I'll take the first one.'

*

Sometime after midday, the rest of the band appeared and shuffled towards a large people carrier. Last night, the roadies had packed all the equipment and taken it to a

166

storage facility in South London. Now, with a four-day gap in the touring schedule, they headed to a house in Dorset rented by their manager Frannie Copeland, in the hope they could come up with some ideas for the next album, and to indulge in some much needed R&R.

It was a peaceful journey, with those who hadn't made breakfast dozing, only capable of making stupid comments, and those with food in their bellies awake and enjoying the green, rolling countryside. The house wasn't far, seventy-odd miles, and Derek took the wheel. Barry offered to do it but he had a well-deserved reputation for lapses in concentration, his mind elsewhere, compiling a list of all the women he'd rogered in the last week or thinking up another entry for his 'on the road' rock diary.

They arrived at the holiday house around three o'clock in the afternoon, and in tribute to Frannie's organisational abilities and his largesse with their money, a local shop had delivered four boxes of groceries, including loads of booze.

It was only a short break, not enough time to go home, although only Pete was married, but plenty of time to catch up on sleep and to do some song writing. At the back of Frannie's mind, it was an attempt to try and cool the animosity between Eric and Danny, free from the pressures of concerts and away from easy access to coke and weed, drugs that were making Eric paranoid and unpredictable.

The house lay a couple of miles outside Weymouth at Osmington Mills, a large family place with six bedrooms and a massive country kitchen. They used the spare bedroom to store all the equipment they'd brought with them: three acoustic guitars, a couple of practice amps, and bongo drums so Pete could play without sticks.

If he asked one of their fans to use one word to describe Barry, they would call him, 'solid' or 'dependable', or if he asked Eric, 'boring.' In his mind, Barry was 'cohesive.' He acted as the band's peacemaker, a man who did what he could to keep things together, and while everyone else went off for a kip, he cooked the evening meal.

By eight, everyone was milling around, drinking beers and chatting. Thirty minutes later and around the big table in the spacious kitchen, they all tucked into the cook's speciality, Spag Bol with a little twist. It contained chilli and peppers, plenty of each.

'Fuck me it's hot,' Eric said after incautiously scooping a large dollop into his mouth. 'Pass me the water. I think I'm gonna melt.'

Derek raised a wine glass. 'Fellas, a toast.'

'What are we celebrating?' Eric said. 'You making your way through a full concert after playing all the right chords?'

'Listen to you, Mr ad-libber over there,' Pete said. 'The amount of times I have to pull you out of a hole when you lose your place in a song.'

'Listen fellas,' Derek said, still holding his glass aloft and banging a knife on the table to quieten them. 'I spoke to Frannie while you lot were still in bed...' He paused.

'He told me he's seen the latest NME album chart.'

He looked around at each of the expectant faces.

'Our new album, number four if anyone's counting...'

'Get on with it, Crow,' Eric shouted.

'Our new album, *Black Saturday* has shot into the album charts...'

They banged their cutlery and glasses on the table and whooped.

'Wait for it, boys, at number seventeen.'

A big cheer rang through the rafters.

'Fuck me,' Eric said, 'we've made it at last.'

'The trick now,' Danny said, 'is to find a way to stay there.'

'What do you know rookie? You've only played with a couple of two-bit outfits who were lucky to get a gig above a pub.'

Derek could sense an argument brewing so he said, 'Does anybody know if Fast Eddie got hold of the new kit we ordered?'

'I'm still waiting for a new hi-hat,' Pete said. 'The last one got bent at the gig in London.'

'I need a new phaser pedal,' Eric said, 'as that new roadie, Bill whatshisname broke my old one. I don't think I've seen a replacement yet.'

'You could still play with the broken one, Eric,' Barry said, 'no one would know the difference.'

'Fellas, fellas,' Derek said. 'Knock it off. It's the first night, let's see if we can behave for once.'

'I'll get you back later, young Crow,' Eric said, an evil glint in his eye.

They talked equipment for a few minutes when Pete, who often didn't say much in these get-togethers as they were loud and raucous said, 'I've written a new song.'

'Great news, Pete,' Derek said. 'Where is it? Did you bring it with you?'

'Yep.'

'Let's get the gear,' Eric said, 'and give it a try out.'

'Maybe we should tidy up first,' Barry said, 'if you all

169

wanna eat in here in the morning.'

'Fuck that for a game of soldiers,' Eric said, 'I'm getting my guitar.'

They brought the gear into the living room, a large space which occupied about a third of the ground floor, but the acoustics were crap, the soft furnishings soaking up the sound, deadening it. It was a surprise to hear Pete had written a song, but he shocked them all by playing the melody on the baby grand piano, kindly left by the owners for their use. His playing was basic but he did enough for them to hear the tune, and once Danny had listened to it a few times, he took over.

Somebody picked up the wine bottles from the table and brought them over and with glasses re-filled, they got down to the serious business of adapting the song for the band, as it was a good song and fitted well into their existing repertoire. There were plenty of examples of drummer-singers, like Ringo, who did the occasional turn for the Beatles, and Don Henley, who sang on most of the Eagles' big hits, but Pete was a lousy singer and didn't sound good, even in his own bathroom, so Derek didn't ask him.

They worked until two in the morning, alternating between Pete's new song and one Derek had brought with him. It ended up being a terrific session, as everyone concentrated on their work and nobody sniped at one another or zoned out due to drugs. The number of empty beer cans and wine bottles lying around the lounge suggested booze played a large part in the creativity, and when someone suggested a walk on the beach to clear their heads, they all trooped outside.

The narrow route to the beach took them past several

houses set back from the road, all shrouded in darkness, the occupants safely tucked up in bed. It ended at a car park overlooking the cliff, and beside it stood a quaint old pub, The Smugglers Inn.

The path down to the shore felt steep and loose rocks made it slippery underfoot, but they were all so pissed it wouldn't hurt even if they did fall. With only the glow of the moon the beach looked spectacular, with a long line of golden sand, the cliffs towering above, dark and mysterious, and the sea twinkling and moving with the restlessness of the planets, making a leisurely plopping noise, increasing in volume the lower they went.

'I'm glad I don't live around here, Pete,' Derek said after they removed shoes and socks and walked barefoot across the sand.

'Why? Don't you like the country and all this peace and quiet?'

'I like it fine, but my songs would start to sound like Victorian love poems; I keep thinking of lines like 'The majestic power of the sea' and the 'Foreboding shadow of the cliffs."

'Hey fellas,' Eric shouted from a distance away, 'there's a boat over there. Who fancies a sail?'

'Not me, I hate the bloody water,' Derek shouted back.

'Pete, how about you?'

'No, I'm staying here. I don't fancy getting wet.'

'See ya, you couple of sissies.'

Derek sat down in the sand and Pete dropped down beside him. He dipped into the bag he'd carried down from the house and handed Pete a beer, taking one for himself. He sipped the beer while chatting to Pete and watching the three stooges walk along a small stone pier.

Close to the end and impossible to see clearly against the dark shadow of the pier, they tottered down steps, which from their position looked as if they were walking on air; beer fumes maybe, but air? No way. At the bottom of the steps, they faffed around with the boat for a couple of minutes before Eric and Danny climbed in. Barry loosened the rope, jumped in beside them, and with much shouting and giggling the three men in a boat set off.

Derek didn't know if Eric was a keen sailor, as he couldn't recall him ever mentioning it, but if the way he handled the oar was any indication, his nautical knowledge had long been forgotten or was buried under too many dead brain cells. The strain of concentrating and peering into a murky seascape with a beer-sizzled brain left him tired. He screwed the beer can into the sand to make sure it didn't fall over, laid back and shut his eyes. It felt so peaceful lying there, the warm breeze wafting his face with the gentleness of silk, the somnolent effect of the lapping waves and the comfortable feel of the sand, slowly moulding to his shape.

He dozed off and it took a couple of prods from Pete to rouse him.

'Yeah?' he said sitting up and rubbing his eyes. 'What is it? Are we going back to the house?'

'I think something's wrong.'

'What? Where?'

Pete nodded towards the water. 'Out there, the lads in the boat. I heard a lot of shouting and screeching.'

Derek found it hard to focus; the booze, the poor light, and his fuzzy brain conspiring against logical thought. A few minutes later he saw the boat, Barry rowing and Eric sitting at the bow. Gone was the boisterousness of earlier, and the lack of activity inside the boat spoke volumes.

Derek got up and headed towards the little pier, ran down its length and climbed down the worn, stone stairs. Five, maybe ten minutes later, Barry rowed towards him.

Barry and Eric sat there, but Danny was nowhere to be seen.

TWENTY-SIX

Ms Jenner,' Henderson said, 'I would like you to go over your story once again if you can, but slowly this time.'

DI Henderson was sitting in an interview room alongside DS Gerry Hobbs, and facing them, Nicola Jenner, a witness from yesterday's jewellery robbery in the Lanes. She was alone as this wasn't a formal interview and she wasn't under arrest.

'I popped into the shop, Davis and Sons in the Lanes, to see if I could get my mum's old wedding ring valued. She gave it to me when she died,' she said looking down, 'and now I need the money.'

'I see. How long were you inside the shop?'

'Ten minutes. No more.'

'Go on with your story.'

'I was standing in front of the counter talking to Mr Roberts who told me what he thought it might be worth and he offered to sell it for me. We started talking about his commission and all that sort of stuff when the...the robbers burst in.' She stopped as she snivelled into a hanky.

'In your own time,' Hobbs said, 'take it nice and slow.'

Nicola Jenner was their only witness to the jewel robbery. The Lanes in Brighton was one of the town's most popular tourist destinations. The narrow passageways would be busy, even on a Tuesday afternoon in March, but with metal grilles on the window and the windows chock-full of merchandise, it came as no surprise when a request for witnesses didn't produce anyone else.

Nicola was aged twenty-six, lived with her father in Patcham and worked as a dental receptionist. She had unsightly peroxide-dyed hair with red and pink strands, several rings on both hands, a face covered in too much makeup and perfectly shaped, gleaming white teeth. Now that her employer had sorted out her dental situation, she needed to change jobs and work for a beautician or a hairdresser.

'They shouted at Mr Roberts,' Nicola said, 'to lie on the floor but I think he did something to upset them, as they fired a shotgun above his head. It practically deafened me as they fired it close to my ear.'

'They fired it to knock-out the CCTV camera behind Mr Roberts.'

'Oh, I see. Next thing, one of the robbers bashes me with the handle of the shotgun, that's how I got this,' she said touching the large bruise on her face, 'and I fell on the floor.'

'What sort of shotgun did they use?' asked DS Hobbs, a keen student of guns.

'I dunno.'

'Was it this long?' he said, spreading his arms wide.

'God, no. He pulled the thing out from the inside of his jacket. It was a small stubby thing.'

'Ok. Did it have one or two barrels?'

'I'm not sure I know what you mean.'

'Was it this wide,' he said, opening his fingers, 'or,' separating them some more, 'this wide?'

'The second one. It was definitely the second one.'

'Well done, thanks.'

Henderson had received his introduction to shotguns while assisting ghillies on the Ardgour Estate in Scotland as a youth. In grouse and deer shooting, the length of the barrel is important, a short barrel length for hitting close range targets and a longer length for stalking deer or flying birds. A sawn-off shotgun is a commercially purchased shotgun with part of the barrel removed and beloved by many classes of criminal, as it could easily be concealed under a jacket, noisy when fired in a confined space, capable of causing widespread damage, and frightening to those in the line of fire.

'Did you see anything more?' Henderson asked.

'No, as I told you before, a few minutes later they stepped over me and left the shop.'

'You must have heard something.'

'I suppose I did hear ring trays being emptied into a bag, muffled voices between the robbers, that sort of thing.'

'What did they say?'

'I...I couldn't hear anything specific.'

'You couldn't tell from the voices if they were black or white, British or foreign, or if they spoke with local or regional accents?'

'Like I say, I didn't hear too much.'

'Ms Jenner,' Henderson said, 'I'd like to show you something,'

From a folder he removed three CCTV pictures and placed the first in front of her.

'It's me,' she said looking down, 'where did you get this?'

'This is a picture taken as the two raiders came into the

shop and before the CCTV was smashed. This is you talking to Mr Roberts, yes?'

'Yes, it is.'

'Look closely at your face, what do you see?'

She stared at the photograph. 'I dunno, nothing much.'

'Look here,' he said pointing at the side of her face in the picture. 'I can see a slight shadow. Can you see it?'

'Yeah, sort of, but everything looks different in black and white, doesn't it?'

Henderson knew that if it wasn't for the heavy face makeup, she would be blushing now.

'We looked through the pictures until we got a good side view of your face and blew it up.'

He placed another picture in front of her

Her face reddened. 'The picture's not right. My foundation must be smudged or something. You've doctored it or something.'

Henderson picked up the picture and held it high, comparing it to the face in front of him. 'I would say the shadow on the picture corresponds almost exactly to the big bruise on your face. What do you think, Sergeant Hobbs?'

'I agree.'

'Don't be daft. I told you, the robbers did it.'

'That's not all,' he said producing the third picture. 'You can see in this picture, the two men are standing on your left. If they hit you with the shotgun, as you told us in your story, the bruise would be on the left side of your face, not the right.'

'I dunno, I dunno.'

He slapped the picture down on the table, making her jump. 'Don't give me the innocent victim story, Nicola.

177

You had a bruise on your face when you walked into the jewellery shop. I think the robbers did it before the raid. I think you know them, don't you?'

She started crying. A few minutes later a sorry face looked up at them.

'I want a lawyer.'

'We'll get you a lawyer, you're going to need one,' Henderson said. 'You will be charged with aiding and abetting an armed robbery. Do you know what sentence you'll receive for a charge like this?'

'No.'

'Fifteen years, and if you're lucky and come before a lenient judge, twelve. Nicola, you'll be touching forty when you come out.'

The sobs turned to wails. Three or four minutes later she looked up.

'What will I get if I help you?'

*

Henderson didn't like driving while wearing a bullet-proof vest as it restricted movement and made him feel hot, but he knew when they reached the destination there wouldn't be much time to spare, so he put it on in the office before coming out. At least it was dark and any driving mistakes he made on the way to Springfield Road wouldn't be a problem as there wasn't much traffic around.

The name of Nicola's boyfriend, Des Hamlin, rang several bells in the minds of Henderson and Hobbs. A career criminal in the truest sense of the word, he'd started committing offences while still at school and when he left, joined a criminal gang straight away. They believed he now worked for Trevor Frank as one of his many enforcers. Frank was one of Brighton's biggest drug dealers and the man who took Henderson's nark Davy Cairns under his wing when he'd found a bag of money belonging to Frank, the proceeds of a drug deal that ended in a shoot-out.

'You don't think he's got rid of the shotgun, do you Angus?' Hobbs asked.

'Plan for the worst and hope for the best is what I told Sergeant Briggs. Are they still behind? I can't see the van.'

Hobbs turned, not easy to do while wearing a stab-proof vest. 'Yep it's still there, about three cars back.'

'Good. No, I don't think he's got rid of it yet, as the robbery only happened yesterday and with no witnesses or forensics, we can't connect it to the robbery or the villains because as you know, one shotgun pellet is like any other shotgun pellet.'

'You're right, he wouldn't get rid of it because if he sold it to someone else and we nicked them, we've got a better chance of connecting the gun to him.'

'Yep, plus if this pair did the job because Franks ordered it, maybe he supplied the tools and wants them back.'

'Rob and Return, I could start a new business. It would be nice though, to nab that bastard.'

'It's not going to happen tonight, my friend,' Henderson said. 'Frank is too wily an operator to get so close. If he is behind the raid, he won't be bothered if we arrest Nicola's boyfriend and his mate, Ros Vincent, as long as Frank's name is kept some distance away from it.'

'Do you think Frank is behind it? What would he gain from it?'

'Good question, maybe his mother fancied a ring and he didn't want to pay for it.'

'Ha, maybe the Police and Crime Commissioner's brother turned all self-righteous when his brother started hobnobbing with the Chief Constable and refused to pay protection.'

'Frank is more into drugs than protection. Maybe he snatched the merchandise in payment for goods supplied.'

'Perhaps we need to take a closer look at the shop owner.'

'I'm thinking the same thing. Right, this is Springfield Road. Number thirty-seven isn't it?'

Hobbs looked down at his notes. 'Yes, sir.'

Henderson watched in the rear view mirror as the black transit van pulled up behind him. They exited the vehicles and walked towards the house. One officer ran around to the back of the terraced house and the rest approached the front door. The banger moved into position and seconds later the front door flew back. Henderson followed three officers as they swept the downstairs rooms while Hobbs and two others clumped upstairs.

An officer pushed open the kitchen door and inside, Ros Vincent, Nicola Jenner's cousin, was standing at a worktop buttering a slice of toast. Vincent looked up, and on seeing the officers, reached over for a carving knife lying close by. His fingers barely touched the handle when a large gloved hand smacked him in the face. His head bounced off the edge of the worktop and he fell to the floor in a heap.

'Good work sergeant,' Henderson said to Sergeant Briggs as he flipped the prisoner over and applied the cuffs. 'Check he's still breathing as the crack when he smacked his head was loud enough to be heard next door.'

'It would serve the little bastard right, he was reaching for a lethal looking blade. Only last week this guy came at me—'

BOOM!

Henderson turned and ran upstairs. He did a quick count as he passed several prostrate officers. 'Gerry, is anyone hurt?'

'No,' Hobbs said from his crouched position in the security of the bathroom. 'As soon as we tried opening the door he let loose with the shotgun; both barrels. If he'd waited a few seconds, one of us would have been a goner.'

It was an old terraced house near Preston Circus, renovated no more than four or five years ago, judging by the light scuff marks on the walls. To save money, people often used cheaper, moulded doors and one of them wouldn't stop a child's baseball bat, never mind a shotgun, but the lack of holes on their side of the door made him think it was made of solid wood. It was comforting to know he couldn't shoot them through it.

Henderson pressed himself against the wall beside the closed bedroom door, first checking it was made of stone and not plasterboard, important considerations with an agitated gunman on the other side.

'Des, are you in there?' he shouted.

'Course I'm fucking in here. Who else do you think it is, the tooth fairy?'

'Des, this is Detective Inspector Angus Henderson of Sussex Police. Put the gun down and come out, what you're doing is stupid.'

'Fuck off.'

'If you don't come out now, every armed officer in Sussex will turn up at this house and I think you know how that story is going to end.'

'I'll take my chances.'

'We know you did the jewel robbery with Ros Vincent, but you don't want a murder charge added to it as well, do you?'

'I don't give a fuck.'

'You might not, but I bet Nicola does.'

'She didn't have anything to do with this.'

'Oh, I think you're telling porkies, my friend, because I think she did. In fact, I'm going to charge her with helping you guys. She'll be lucky to get less than fifteen years.'

'You fucking bastard, Henderson.'

'Boss, what are you doing,' Hobbs hissed. 'You're winding him up.'

Henderson held his index finger to his lips.

'She'll be in a different jail from you, Des,' Henderson said to the blank door. 'She'll be in Lewes and you'll be in Wakefield or some God-forsaken place. Fifteen years is a long time, she'll forget what you look like.'

'You fucking bastard.'

BOOM!

Two barrels. Henderson heard the tell-tale click of the barrel snapping, reload. He kicked the door open. Hamlin was on the bed, trembling fingers trying to put a cartridge into a shaking gun.

Henderson dived on top of him. They rolled on the floor, Henderson landing a fist in his face but when he tried to do it again, the butt of the shotgun smashed into his. His lights went out for a few seconds but before Hamlin could take advantage and pound him into a pulp or pull the trigger, other bodies piled into him.

A few minutes later, they bundled Hamlin out of the

room, the shotgun and cartridges all bagged, ready for forensic analysis which hopefully would prove it was used in the jewellery heist. Henderson sat on the edge of the bed, Hobbs beside him.

'You're going to have some bruise on your face in the morning, Angus.'

'It's not harming my good looks I'm worried about, I feel drunk.'

A phone started to ring. It didn't belong to Henderson, or by the look on his face, Hobbs. Henderson spotted the glow on top of the dresser. He reached over, picked it up and handed it to Hobbs.

'It's Trevor Frank. You know what Hamlin sounds like. You can do a Brighton accent better than me.'

Hobbs held the phone to his ear, Henderson close by.

'Yeah?' Hobbs said.

'Des, it's Trevor Frank.'

'Hi, Trevor.'

'You get the stuff like I asked you to?'

'Yeah.'

'Good boy. No problems?'

'Nope.'

'Bring it all to me tomorrow night and make sure you're not followed. Y'hear?'

'Yeah.

'Bring it to my house in Orpen Road in Hove, you know it?'

'Nope'

'Now I think about it, you've never been here before. Halfway along. It's called Standen House. See you at eight.'

183

TWENTY-SEVEN

The car park at Sainsbury's was busy, but it meant no one would take a blind bit of notice of him. He soon spotted the target's car, older and shabbier than anything around it. He flicked the toothpick over with his tongue in one movement; five minutes one way, five minutes the other.

He approached it and bent down beside one of the wheel arches. He put gloves on as he didn't want any of this stuff on his hands, reached underneath and felt for the brake cable. Good, it hadn't been touched since last night when he'd cut the cable, drained some of the brake fluid and made a temporary repair.

He stood and stretched, as if the car seat had made his back ache, but still no one took any notice of the handsome stranger. He took a little walk, enjoying the early morning sunshine but hating the sea of concrete and metal all around him, swarming with hordes of greedy shoppers who thought of little else but what could be dumped into their trolleys or rammed into their fat faces.

Five minutes later he saw Eric Hannah, his eyes greedily ogling the pretty girls as he wheeled his trolley full of booze for his not-so-secret stash, destined for his shed. Today, while his wife took the little one swimming and the older girl to hockey, he'd fill the fridge in the shed, a regular weekend ritual which the stupid fool probably believed she didn't know anything about. After closing the boot, he ambled towards the driver's door. When the target eased himself inside, he slid into the passenger seat.

'What the fuck's this?'

He pulled out a gun, a child's toy but what did this prick know about guns? 'Shut the door.'

'Bloody hell, a gun! Take it easy, mate!'

'Stop talking shithead. Now drive slowly and easily.'

Away from the car park and the prying eyes of the CCTV cameras he relaxed, but Hannah, perspiring greatly and gripping the steering wheel with white knuckles, didn't.

'Where are we going?'

'Just shut your face and drive, slow and careful. No sudden movements or this gun might go off.'

He poked the gun into Hannah's gut, causing him to sit bolt upright, and as he did so, removed his wallet and house keys from his jacket pocket.

'Turn left into the next road.'

A few minutes later, he directed his pale driver into a petrol station on the A31 and instructed him to park the BMW close to his van, parked well away from the main building. He poked the gun again into Hannah's ribs. 'I'm out of here but I'm going to follow you back to your place where we're going to have a nice little chat. Understand?'

Hannah nodded.

He leaned over towards him. 'Listen to me mate, I want no heroics. Drive like normal and you'll be fine. Don't forget, I know where you live.' The dumb fucker nodded up and down, up and down like a parcel shelf dog.

He got out, tucked the gun into his trousers and ambled towards the van, whistling. Any rational man would now take off and put as much distance between himself and a gunman as he could, and hallelujah, his mark did just that. He climbed into the van and set off after him, but there would be no screaming tyres or the smell of burning rubber; it didn't do to attract attention. In any case, he wouldn't get far.

On the fast dual carriageway, he soon caught up with him as the van was fitted with a four-litre engine and powerful enough to overtake if he wanted to, but that wasn't part of the plan. It took a while for the target to realise he couldn't lose the van no matter what he tried to do in his crappy old BMW. Where did he think he could run to on this road, Winchester?

If his assumptions were correct, he would turn off as soon as possible and try and find the nearest police station. With the next major junction less than a mile ahead, one so important it needed its own name, the Coxbridge Roundabout, he was confident he would turn off there. He increased speed, causing the BMW in front of him to drive faster.

Like a couple of boy racers, they hit the slip-road at eighty-five miles an hour and immediately he stamped on the brakes of the van. Big carbon discs gripped the wheels, slowing the van rapidly, but when the brake lights of the BMW glowed, the car didn't slow. It rocketed towards the roundabout, shot across the road, and with the inside lane temporarily blocked by cars taking the left turn, slammed into the back of a lorry edging its way round.

In the rear view mirror, he could see the blazing BMW lighting up the morning sky, thanks to all the extra fuel he'd bought at the supermarket before loading the booze. If the crash didn't kill him, the fire would. Humming his favourite song, he pointed the van in the direction of London and turned up the radio.

TWENTY-EIGHT

GrooveTime Music Studios occupied one half of a converted Victorian warehouse in Narrow Street in the Limehouse district of East London. Once the home of rope makers, tea merchants and even earlier, lime kilns that gave the area its name, most of the old warehouses were now apartments and large living spaces for urban professionals, or light commerce for new, lighter industries, such as music, television programming, software and PR.

DI Henderson pressed the buzzer on the door and waited outside with DS Walters for a couple of minutes as a bitter wind whipped around the buildings, lifting litter and blowing leaves towards them at head-height.

Back in Sussex, Henderson had left DS Gerry Hobbs in charge of the Lanes jewellery heist. Following Eric Hannah's death in a car fire at the weekend even the ACC was persuaded that something more than coincidence had killed three former members of the Crazy Crows. He was no doubt influenced by sensational newspaper stories suggesting the Prime Minister's 'favourite businessman' was now in mortal danger and demanded a result.

Feeling vindictive for whacking him with a shotgun butt, Henderson wouldn't let Des Hamlin see his girlfriend, Nicola Jenner, until he agreed to appear at the rendezvous with Frank. In the end, he valued his organs more than the jail time he would lose for helping the police, but his mate Ros Vincent didn't have such scruples. They concocted some story about Hamlin being arrested for drunk and disorderly and Vincent stepped happily into the breech. They fitted him with a wire, and five minutes into the meeting with Frank, they'd heard enough to enter the house and arrest him and two of his associates. Vincent was now under police protection and would soon be moving to the West Country.

Above the roar of London traffic, Henderson heard a noise inside the building, and a few seconds later the door opened. A sultry teenager called Marlene took them upstairs to the top floor and directed them into the control room at the side of Studio 2.

'Detective Henderson, good to meet you man, and you too Sergeant Walters. I'm Sam Schweinsteiger,' the older guy sitting behind the mixing desk said, after spinning around in his chair to shake hands. 'This is Steve, my sound engineer.' Henderson looked towards the guy sitting next to Sam, a hairy head clad in headphones, but received no more than an almost imperceptible nod.

'If you sit over there,' Sam said, indicating a small settee pushed back against the wall, 'you can watch how it's done, providing you keep quiet. I'll only be about another ten minutes.'

According to Wikipedia, record producer Sam Schweinsteiger was forty-nine and the producer of the third and fourth albums for the Crazy Crows, *Tropical Storm* and *Black Saturday*,. Henderson could see he made strident efforts to look younger, or at least hipper, in keeping with the industry he worked within, wearing a zany-patterned t-shirt, faded and ripped jeans, and with his long hair pulled back into a pony-tail, streaked in grey. His chubby, jovial face, however, spoiled the effect as it was wrinkled from too much sun, or casting his mind back to the overcast and dismal weather outside, the overuse of sun beds.

Henderson was disappointed to discover Studio 2 was not showcasing some new indie band with a unique and interesting sound, or some old stagers hoping a new producer would sprinkle some fairy dust on their music and give them a hit single. Instead, they were recording the voice-over for a television or radio advert.

On the other side of the glass sat a Scottish comedian he recognised, but whose name he couldn't recall without confusing him with an actor jailed for buggering young boys, or the host of an early evening quiz show. He was attempting to do the voice-over for a well-known make of car, but was having trouble saying the curt, German strap line. Every time it came out of his mouth it sounded like Joseph Goebbels exhorting a mass rally of brown shirts.

The over-wrought Jock took a deep breath and started once again at the beginning of the script, causing Sam to utter to no one in particular, 'Fucking hell, you would think Robert the Bruce here was doing this for the first time, the wanker.'

As if by magic, three attempts later, 'The appliance of innovative technology,' came trotting out of his mouth in flawless diction. Sam blew a long blast of frustration and angst at the ceiling, muttering, 'Thank fuck for small mercies' and pushed his chair away from the control desk.

The comedian removed his headphones with an exaggerated expression of exhaustion, as if talking into a microphone for an hour was as taxing as dragging coal from the bottom of a pit, or loading boxes on the back of a lorry, and Sam stepped into the corridor to greet him. Through the open door he could hear and feel the bonhomie as mutual back-slapping and hearty congratulations filled the air, including such flattering comments as, 'Sterling performance' and 'You knocked my socks off', a touch ironic as the old hippy wasn't wearing any.

A few minutes later, Sam ducked his head back into the control room. 'Let's go upstairs and grab ourselves a cuppa, we can talk there.'

The top floor of the building, a large airy room overlooking the street, was set out as a canteen. Henderson could see half a dozen tables, a hot water urn, a variety of multi-coloured mugs and cups and much of the debris of a round-the-clock eating place: an overflowing bin, stained work surfaces and a dishwasher with more dirty dishes sitting outside than in.

Two people seated on opposite sides of a table were having an animated discussion, but to a more sensitive soul, it might be considered an argument. Beneath the grubby windows and overlooking the street, long cushions were laid out to create a sociable seating area with good natural lighting for reading or watching the world go by, but today it was occupied by a couple of worn-out musicians enjoying some shut-eye.

Sam made coffee in clean mugs using boiling water from the urn and a large teaspoonful of Nescafe from a canteen-sized tin. Henderson, more used to over-stewed Sussex House coffee and curdled milk, wasn't complaining.

'So, Inspector Henderson,' Sam said as he took a seat

across from the two detectives at one of the tables, 'you said you wanted to talk to me about the Crazy Crows.'

Henderson gave Sam a summary of the deaths of Barry Crow and Peter Grant, to which Sam nodded in sombre fashion, but looked surprised when the name of Eric Hannah was mentioned.

'Bloody hell, Eric Hannah? Christ, I forgot about him. I assumed he'd popped his clogs a long time back, he was such a coke-head. The worst sort in my book, he could never seem to get enough.'

'Eric died in a car accident at the weekend, and with the other two deaths you know about, you can understand why we think something in their past must be triggering it.'

Eric's death on Sunday morning had made many of the nationals as the crash not only disrupted traffic for hours, but the death of three musicians in the same band was now starting to interest them. His reputation for drink and drugs, and the fact he'd bought lots of booze in Sainsbury's before the crash, only fuelled speculation that he was high on drugs or booze at the time, or that he wanted to shuffle off his mortal coil in spectacular fashion.

'Yeah, I can see where you guys are coming from. I mean, I didn't work with the Crows all through their career, but I'll try and help where I can. I liked the band, especially Barry and Derek.'

'When did you first come into contact with them?'

'Let me think...early '90 it would be. I first met them during the recording sessions for their third album, *Tropical Storm*. The record company kind of tolerated all the goings on in the studio, you know, the women and the drugs and booze, all while the new album was on schedule, but as soon as it fell behind they lost their rag. They sacked their producer, Dave Stevens, and brought me in. D'you know Dave?'

Henderson shook his head.

'Great guy, bloody good producer and a wizard with a synthesiser, which saves bands a fortune on studio time as they don't need strings and orchestras. This is where Derek got the idea of bringing in Danny Winter.' He tapped the side of his head. 'Smart bloke Derek. When Dave got kicked off the Crows, he went on to work with Bon Jovi and Texas, so it didn't do his career any harm, but he lacks the strength of character to kick arse; he's a musician's producer, if you know what I mean.'

Henderson nodded and tried the coffee again, it tasted cooler this time and he dared take a sip.

'It's great if a band are hard working and serious, but when they're a bunch of lazy bastards like the Crows, it was like shitting in the dark with no toilet paper; no bloody fun at all. They hired me because of my reputation for knocking bands into shape, which I can do if I'm handed a clear brief, either by the band if they know what they're doing, or by the record company if they know what they want. I've calmed down a lot since then,' he said with a smile, 'but not much.'

'What did you find when you took them over?' Walters asked. 'Did you have a mess to clear up?'

'Once they toed the line and did things my way, it all started to improve. They were good musicians, make no mistake, but up until then, they were coasting.'

'How did you find them to work with? Were they difficult?'

He sat back and sighed. 'It's a bastard not being able to

smoke in this place. Times like this, I could do with a little nicotine boost, but it's too bloody cold to stand outside. Let me think. Yeah, Eric and Pete were the best musicians by a long chalk. I think Barry only did it to pull skirt and Derek to get away from a shitty home life. He didn't get on with his dad.'

'Did they have any enemies?' Henderson asked.

He laughed. 'How much time have you got?'

'Try me.'

'Derek has a direct manner of speaking, and that's putting it lightly. He winds people up. He tried it on with me, but I told him in no uncertain terms to take a hike. I mean, he pissed off roadies, stage managers, fans even, but the lot he wound up most was the record company.'

'For the bad boy behaviour?'

'Nah, for walking away when *Black Saturday* started to receive great reviews in the music press and racking up big sales in the shops. I knew the album would do well just as soon as I heard the first three or four tracks, you know, and I think the record company did too.'

'Maybe they packed it in,' Walters said, 'because they'd all made so much money.'

Schweinsteiger shook his head, 'nah.'

'Really? I'm surprised to hear it, as each of them started a business not long after leaving the band. You need money for that.'

'I don't know where they got it from, but I do know they made bugger-all in the band.'

'How come?'

'The first two albums didn't make much and covered more or less what they borrowed to buy instruments and such. The third did well, but by then, tours were international and getting costlier and they were spending more time in the studio, and don't forget, they partied like it was going out of fashion. Nah, if they had more than their bus fare home in their pockets, I would be very surprised.'

TWENTY-NINE

The kettle clicked off and a tired Suzy Hannah rose from her chair to make tea, wondering why her lazy bitch of a sister couldn't do it herself.

'So what are you going to do now?' Lorna asked.

She sighed. This conversation seemed to have gone on for most of the morning as she'd insisted on dissecting Eric's car accident in minute detail. It ranged from the 'official' version as it appeared in the local paper, to the laughable conspiracy rumours popping up on the web like fairground 'knock 'em downs.' One suggested it was a drug hit and another said a rival fan had taken his revenge. Suzy didn't have anything else to add, but Lorna could always find something.

'I'm not sure,' Suzy said as she poured the tea. She placed the mugs on the kitchen table, and with her mind elsewhere as if in a dream, she returned to her seat.

'Ahem, I take two sugars and milk,' the snotty cow said. She sounded like the strict headmistress she might have become if a promising teaching career hadn't been thrown out of the window like a half-chewed apple after she'd married a useless shit like Dave, and if she'd kept her legs closed when the number of kids reached two.

At forty-one, she was nine years older than Suzy and sometimes when they went out together Lorna would be mistaken for her mother, making Suzy laugh and Lorna mad. It didn't help that her sister never put on makeup, her hair was cut in the same old way, and her frumpy clothes did nothing to disguise an overweight frame.

Suzy rose from her seat, tipped in a little milk and searched in the cupboard for the sugar container, something she and Eric didn't use. It would serve her sister right for winding her up if she picked up a packet of Eric's constipation tablets or the garlic powder by mistake.

'The house is paid for,' Suzy said, after resuming her seat, 'and I earn enough at the salon to keep the kids in shoes, but no more holidays for a while.'

Lorna sipped her tea, a look of disgust crinkling her eyes, suggesting too much sugar, not enough milk, too much tannin from a pot sitting on the hob, or her mug handle didn't face Mecca. Whatever the problem, she wasn't moving.

'Don't be daft girl, there's the Jeans & Co business. It must be worth something?'

'According to Eric it hasn't made any money for years.'

'He was lying to you, same as he lied about everything else. Sell it girl, I'll help you.'

Oh my Lord. The word 'help' from her sister's lips was like hearing 'fuck' from a priest or 'free sample' from a drug dealer; seldom spoken and only in the most extreme of circumstances. The same sister who'd refused to give her refuge when Eric was off his rocker and away on another of his wild and drunken phases. When his paranoid mind believed the world was conspiring against him and he thought nothing of punching her in the face or kicking her in the stomach when he thought she was pregnant. Lorna had refused to lend her any money when Suzy didn't possess more than five pounds in her purse after her prick of a husband spent the housekeeping on a 'must have' and 'not to be missed' dope deal.

Eric had been an immature and self-centred sod who'd liked to think himself as sly as a fox, but he could be as open and readable as one of her kids' comics. He was convinced she didn't know about the drugs in the shed or the booze in the fridge, but she did, and she also knew the only reason he went down there was to smoke weed and drink, a fact he would not admit to himself.

He'd believed his real purpose in religiously heading into the 'studio' was to keep his guitar playing up to speed, in case the band reformed and decided to tour again. Eric couldn't see it, but the delusional sap smoked so much dope that even a music novice such as herself could hear he sounded crap. No way could he could remember the riffs, notes and words of one song, never mind the full twenty-song repertoire of a performing band.

'No, I'm not going to sell it, not yet.'

'You should girl, you'll need the money.'

'I don't know enough about it, I need to take advice.'

'What about all his gear in the shed? Some of the guitars in there are worth thousands.'

'Which ones?'

'The blue Rickenbacker and the signed Fender Stratocaster Eric Clapton used to play.'

'How come you know so much about his guitars, then?'

'You told me.'

'No, I didn't; I didn't know.'

'It must have been him then.'

'How often did you go in the shed?'

'I don't know, once or twice.'

'Funny how he would let you go in, but he never allowed me.'

Suzy could read her like a book, always could. She knew when she was telling lies and knew when she was trying to hide something.

'You were screwing him, weren't you?'

'Suzy that's outrageous, even for you. You're upset about Eric's death and not thinking straight but I'm trying my best to help you.'

'I'm thinking straight all right and it's coming back to me now. The sly looks you gave him when you thought I wasn't looking, the times he disappeared upstairs to help you with the kids when he did bugger-all for his own, and the days he went around to your place, while moaning to me he couldn't stand Dave. I could never work it out then, but I can now.'

'Calm down Suze, we can talk about it.'

'Talk about what Lorna? The size of his dick or the sexual positions he liked best?'

'Suze stop shouting, it wasn't serious, just a casual fling.'

'Well, you won't mind if I casually fling you out of my bloody house! Go on, get the hell out!'

Lorna stood, unsure what to do, how to react to this crazy outburst from her underling. The servants sure didn't behave like this at Downton Abbey.

'Look Suze I'm sorry for your loss. Don't let us fall out. I can help you sell his things and the business, we can work together.'

'Yeah, so you can take a big cut out of the proceeds? No thanks. I know you too well, all you want to do is take, take, take and give nothing back. You haven't changed one bit. Now get the hell out of my house and don't come back.'

'Suze...'

'Out I said!'

The front door slammed shut and Suzy returned to her seat in the kitchen, where she buried her head in her hands and cried. She cried, not for her dead husband, the moribund relationship with her sister, or for her mother who'd died last year, but for herself.

How could she have been so stupid to marry Eric Hannah and stay married to him for so long? She knew about his affairs, perhaps not every one of them, but enough to realise he could never be a faithful husband. He'd possessed all the traits her mother warned her about: no ambition, no morals and no love for anyone other than himself.

She wiped away the tears and began to clear away the mess left by her sister, who made more crumbs than her kids. They were at a young age and didn't feel death in the same way as teenagers or adults. They would miss Eric as their love was unconditional and unencumbered by an understanding of what had happened, and in any case, most of the shit in their relationship was directed at her.

She walked into the bedroom, determined to start again. Once Eric was buried, she would make an effort to enjoy life, but right now what she needed was money; money to bury him, money to keep the kids lives as normal as possible, and money to buy her some time until she could get her head straight.

At the top of the wardrobe sat a suitcase she had been warned never to open. She felt sure it contained something valuable, as any time she went near it he'd make such a fuss. She placed a chair close to the wardrobe, stretched up and pulled the case down. A smile creased her face at a taboo now smashed, but it died on her lips when she noticed the lock was broken. With a keen sense of apprehension and anticipation she threw the lid open, but was crestfallen to discover it was filled with old stage clothes giving off a rancid and mouldy smell, as if none of them had ever been washed.

Tears of frustration rolled down her cheeks. Like everything else in Eric Hannah's life, it was all smoke and mirrors. There would be no world tour, no new five-album deal, no big pension pot to see him comfortable into his old age and bury him in fine style, or to pay a builder to smarten their tatty house.

She wiped her face and stood close to the wardrobe door and swung the suitcase back in place, but it wouldn't sit right. She didn't suffer from OCD but if something in her line of sight wasn't straight, be it a picture on the wall, cushions on the settee or magazines under the coffee table, she would correct it. The problem was one of height. At five-foot four she couldn't reach the top of the wardrobe, and in order to shift the item blocking the case, she needed to climb higher.

She returned to the kitchen and reached for the shed keys, but hesitated, borne of a thousand warnings to desist from progressing further. She grabbed the keys in triumph and headed into the garden. What Eric called the 'shed' was his fantasy house where he indulged himself like the rock musician he aspired to be. Behind it, and under a tree, stood a run-of-the-mill garden shed where all the tools and ladders were stored.

She opened Eric's musical playhouse first. If she didn't know what went on in there, it wouldn't take the skills of a seasoned detective to find out; the air was seasoned with the sweet, fragrant aroma of cannabis. On the table beside the settee sat a packet of cigarette papers and his stash from the Lebanon or Afghanistan, bought at great expense when she didn't have enough money in her purse to buy the kids sweets.

She knew little about guitars, but even she had to admit seeing them lined up on the wall was impressive and gave the place the look of an arty music shop, but she vowed not to touch anything until after the funeral. By then, she could be sure this little dream wasn't part of some elaborate insurance scam to remove him from financial difficulty and jettison her out of his life, and only then would she take them down to an auction house and sell them.

She knew it was stupid to think he could come back, as she'd seen pictures of the burnt-out car and knew no one could have survived such carnage. The undertakers were coming in the morning to discuss arrangements but there wouldn't be much to bury. She was tempted to tell them he was an eco-warrior and insist on a bio-degradable coffin made of cardboard, however, his old mother was a religious zealot, making the Taliban look like intelligent moderates, and would demand only the best for her boy. Woe betide her if he was interred in anything less than polished mahogany or walnut.

She shut the dope house, opened the garden shed and lugged the step-ladder back to the house. The problem throughout their marriage was money, the lack of it. On paper, they were well-off with a multi-site retail business, two cars and a big detached house, but in short supply was the green, folding stuff. Eric was, in his own words, a hand-to-mouth kind of guy. He didn't trust banks, stock brokers or insurance companies and she knew there was no point in searching for a well-loaded bank account or an insurance policy to cash in.

She climbed the ladder and could now see the suitcase she had been trying to put up was being blocked by another, smaller case. It was the size of a large camera bag, but when she tried to move it out of the way, found it heavy and bulked out, as if something inside was putting a severe strain on the seams. She carried it to the bed but it took her several minutes to open, as the zip was stiff and proved difficult to move.

To her utter amazement, the bag was stuffed full of money; fifties and twenties. She picked up one of the notes and took a good look to make sure it wasn't counterfeit or discontinued twenty years ago, before holding it up to the light and checking for watermarks.

Satisfied of its authenticity, she fished out handful after handful and laid them on the bed, and for a moment, had the urge to remove her clothes and wallow in the stuff like a decadent film star. Near the bottom of the bag, her hand touched something cold and metallic and slowly, slowly, she extracted two shiny gold bars.

THIRTY

Frannie Copeland had been the manager of the Crazy Crows throughout their career. However, it wasn't the Crows' limited success that fuelled his well documented cigar-chomping, jet-set and champagne-guzzling lifestyle, but way-more successful outfits from his stable such as Big Door, Tree House and pop sensation, the Indies.

The Docklands riverside penthouse was long gone, and home for Frannie now was Fairfield House, a large and elegant Georgian-style house set in several acres of ground, tucked behind the village of Ide Hill in Kent. Frannie's wife, Mary, opened the door and welcomed him inside, before guiding him into a room overlooking the front lawn where Henderson found her husband sitting in a chair, reading a newspaper.

'Good afternoon Mr Copeland, I'm Detective Inspector Angus Henderson. We spoke on the phone.' The DI was on his own today, not ideal as a second officer often noticed things the first one didn't and could corroborate any statements made, but Frannie wasn't big on visitors or the police, so he kept it simple.

Frannie took off his glasses, put down the newspaper and in a slow, deliberate movement which was hard to watch, he got out of the chair. The wheeze of his breathing and the rattle in his chest indicated he was not a well man, and the pasty complexion and red, deep-set eyes did nothing to detract from Henderson's amateur prognosis.

'Hello,' Frannie said shaking his hand, 'good to meet you. Take a seat.'

He was smaller than Henderson by at least six inches, and portly around the middle, giving his body a Teletubby shape. His face was angular, as if all parts pointed towards an area between nose and mouth, leaving him with a permanent scowl. It was disconcerting at first, but he could see it would be a valuable weapon in dealing with diva-infused rock stars and in terse contract negotiations with obdurate record companies.

Frannie sat down, movements just as slow, giving Henderson an opportunity to take a look round. At first glance, he assumed the dark wooden bookshelves behind him were full of books, but on closer inspection he could see it wasn't books but hundreds of LPs, CDs and DVDs, all segregated and neatly lined up.

With Frannie settled in the chair, Henderson began the same spiel he'd given Sam Schweinsteiger, and as he did so, the man's face crumpled.

'What a bloody shame, I liked those boys. I mean, Derek was all right but he could be a handful and liked to throw his weight around, but I was no pushover either.'

'What about the others?'

'Barry was quiet and thoughtful and just got on with things, Pete's the same but always trying new things, trying improve his playing.'

'Eric Hannah?'

'Hannah was a sparky, lively character, life and soul of the party but he gave me nothing but grief.'

'Was he as good a guitarist as everyone says?'

'He had a brilliant, raw talent. You see, good guitar players don't just learn their craft and become rock-gods, they refine it week-by-week by discovering new chords and riffs, they experiment and jam with different musicians and bring in sound effects boxes and amplifiers and try out new sounds. Eric didn't do any of this, he was too busy having a good time. I mean, we all liked to party, who didn't, but he couldn't drink alone. Oh no, he needed to take everyone else along with him and it didn't take long before the whole band were pissed out of their heads on stage and wasting valuable time in recording studios and hacking people off in radio interviews with stupid antics.'

'I suppose you must have had similar experiences with a lot of bands at the time.'

'Sure I did, but when it came to the crunch, they got down and did the business, but the Crows needed a good boot up the arse before they'd start working.' He started to cough, a thick, lung-wrenching hack that brought colour to his cheeks, but probably knocked weeks off his life expectancy. 'Let's take a walk in the garden,' Frannie said in a strangled voice, 'I can't breathe in this bloody house.'

It was a warm afternoon after a chilly start, and in driving over here, he'd found many of the dips and valley bottoms still with a residual layer of fog and frost. Out of sight of the house and shielded by a high hedge, Frannie took out a fat cigar and sparked up.

'It helps my breathing, but her indoors says I'm talking crap,' he said as he chugged it alight. 'Sod it,' he said behind a cloud of not unpleasant-smelling smoke, 'we've all got to die of something.'

'True enough.' However, some deaths were less awful than others, and gasping for air at the slightest hint of anxiety and sucking on an oxygen mask on the way to bed would come close to the bottom of Henderson's 'Ways to Die' bucket list.

'As I was saying back in the house, the band were going nowhere musically until the record company drafted in Big Sam Schweinsteiger to try and salvage something.'

'Did it bother you to have a producer shoe-horned in?'

'I recommended him. Have you met him yet?'

He nodded.

'He's a good man; doesn't take shit from anybody. If you can't play or you can't be bothered, he doesn't care one bit, just piss off out of his face. He's a man after my own heart.'

'He hasn't changed much.'

He laughed. 'I'm pleased to hear it. When Sam came on board and started knocking them into shape, it didn't take long to see the signs of what was to come on their third album.'

There followed a short bout of coughing, but after a few puffs on the cigar, he was back in the land of mortals once again. They resumed walking.

'They had a strong following in Germany, Holland and Belgium, much better than in England where fans were getting a bit pissed off with the heavy rock scene, but out there, the Krauts couldn't get enough. I put together a tour, the biggest for them, and to their credit they knuckled down and rehearsed and played. Derek wrote a load of new material and gradually introduced it to the shows and the fans seemed to like it.'

'It sounds as though things were moving in the right direction.'

'They were, but I knew it wouldn't last; it never does. After the tour and playing a few gigs in Scandinavia, they were ready to make a new album. When the boys finished writing, I persuaded the record company to book us into one of the best recording studios in London, and there Big Sam worked his magic.'

'*Black Saturday*?'

'Yeah, and black it sounded as the lyrics were bleak and dark. It had a lot to do with the influence of Danny Winter in song writing and keyboard playing, as he'd had a troubled childhood.'

'Were you pleased with it?'

'We all were. It was a huge improvement over the previous stuff, and something to shut the critics and naysayers up. Miracle of miracles, the phone started ringing with offers of tours and interviews in the UK and I thought, at last I can do something with this bunch. Like I said, it didn't last as one day out of the blue, Derek announced he wanted out.'

'It must have come as a shock.'

'Shock? I could have wrung his fucking neck.'

Frannie was away in a daze for a moment, shaking his head like a dog.

'This happened after the death of Danny Winter?' Henderson said, trying to nudge the needle back onto the record.

'Yeah, right, the death of Danny. Derek said he was so upset about losing the boy he couldn't go on, but it was bullshit. Derek was a hard-hearted bastard, he still is from what I read in the papers, and he didn't give a shit about anybody, not even his own brother.'

'Why do you think that?'

'If Barry ever got into trouble with someone and providing it didn't affect him or the band, he'd let him get on with it and he got beaten up a few times by skinheads and punks. Derek could have replaced Danny like this,' he said, clicking thumb and middle finger together, 'if he really wanted to.'

'So why didn't he?'

'He wanted out.'

'Why?'

'I don't know the answer to that one. I asked around at the time and some said Derek wanted to start the tanker business with his uncle, others said he thought the record company were chivvying too much. If you can believe it, he even said to me I was charging them too much.' A rare smile parted his lips. 'Derek could be a pig-headed bastard when he set his mind to it, and so when the wheels started rolling there was nothing much I, or anyone else, could do to stop the bus.'

He coughed again, this time not a mighty phlegm shifter but a mini throat clearer.

'You see, the band signed a contract to deliver four albums and at the end of the day, they gave us four albums. It also said something about promotion and advertising, the bit the Crows didn't do and the main point of contention between me and the record company in subsequent negotiations. Of course, I'd seen it all before with an American band called Pale Rider...'

Henderson wasn't too fussed to hear about Frannie's nostalgic sojourn down Tin Pan Alley and wanted him back on the song-sheet as soon as, but he didn't seem the sort of man who appreciated being told what to do. Instead he nodded at various points in his dialogue and admired the garden.

A section close to the back of the house looked recently

dug-over, as he could see a succession of little plants struggling to push their faces closer to the sun, although he thought it unlikely the handiwork of Mr Wheeze beside him as it was a sizeable plot.

Frannie finished his monologue and quietly enjoyed an elongated puff.

'Is there anyone from the time,' Henderson said, 'who became, at the risk of sounding too melodramatic, an enemy of the band, or warned them he would take revenge for something they'd done?'

Frannie thought about it for a moment or two. 'A couple of promoters threatened to break my legs,' he said smiling, 'but I guess I did stitch them up at the time.' He puffed at the cigar, thinking. 'Revenge, enemy; yeah I guess it sums up this guy.'

'Who?'

'Close to the release of their third album, the band were doing bigger gigs, and while there was a nucleus of roadies like Fast Eddie and Smelly Dave, we brought in contract guys for the larger tours. This one guy worked for them on and off for a number of years, a little geezer, strong as an elephant and a good man to have around, but rumoured to be a serious criminal with jail time behind him.'

'Really?'

'Yeah, he knew loads of crooks who were involved in knocking off warehouses and delivery vans and could bring us anything, like clothes, radios, food, you name it. Derek liked reading some American gun magazines and joke magazines he couldn't get over here, and Eric would hang around with him at his gaff, saying he liked courting with danger or some crap like that.'

He stopped and looked into the distance as if searching

for a long, lost memory. 'Yeah, he knew Danny. When Derek started the search for a keyboard player, he told Derek to take a look at this boy Danny Winter as he'd seen him in some East End pub and thought he was good. He might have been a relative or something, I don't know.'

'Can you remember the man's name?' Henderson asked.

'I can see his face. A little guy with a serious, weather beaten face and eyes like a cornered ferret. I would imagine he's dead now, I know I should be.'

He stopped walking and puffed the cigar in the still air, sending a large plume spiralling skywards, like Indian smoke signals warning of the approach of a neighbouring tribe. If his wife didn't know he was still smoking, she was either turning the proverbial blind eye of Nelson, or had to be as thick as a plank.

'His name will come back to me in a mo.'

They started walking again. 'Don't you think it's great,' Frannie said, 'rock music is still being played today on those new digital radio stations like Planet Rock? I love hearing all the old stuff.'

There came a shout from the house which either Frannie didn't hear or chose to ignore.

'I think your wife is calling,' Henderson said. 'She says you need to go back inside and take your medicine.'

'Did she? I'm a bit Mutt and Jeff. Perhaps I better go in as I've been feeling like crap today and the medicine does give me a lift.'

They turned and walked towards the house. 'Her indoors does great work out here, don't you think? She's planted beetroot,' he said pointing, 'celeriac, onions, potatoes, celery and loads of other stuff like peas, rhubarb...Mattie Street. I'm sure that's it.'

'If that's a vegetable, I've never heard of it.'

'Ha, ha it's not a bloody vegetable, detective. It's the name of Eric Hannah's favourite little criminal. I remember him now, it was Mathew Street.'

THIRTY-ONE

Dorchester, Dorset 1989

The inquest into Danny Winter's death was held on 25th September 1989 at County Hall in Dorchester, Her Majesty's Coroner for Dorset, Henry Faraday, presiding. The coroner, a genial-looking man with wispy grey hair, gold-rimmed glasses and the bedside manner of an experienced doctor, explained to those in attendance that an inquest was not a trial but an opportunity to lay out all the facts and assess them. The police had already concluded that the death of Danny Winter had been an accident.

In turn, each of the four remaining Crazy Crows gave their account of the day's events. Derek said he saw no more than the boat leaving with three high-spirited occupants and returning about forty minutes later with only two. He didn't hear if an altercation took place on board, as he fell asleep on the sand, but reiterated Peter's statement that he didn't hear anything either, and he would have woken Derek if he had.

Eric told the inquest that Danny started fooling around, stood up and fell in. Eric was not a confident swimmer and if he'd also gone into the water, they would be talking about two deaths today and not one. In any case, it was dark and he'd quickly lost sight of him. He woke Barry. He was a good swimmer and would have dived in, but they couldn't see sign of Danny anywhere.

They were unaware at the time, but Danny couldn't swim, a fact brought to light first thing that morning when they were confronted by his mother outside the hall, who launched a hostile attack, blaming drugs, booze and their recklessness for her son's death.

Barry told the inquest he believed all was amiable between the three men when they set out from the pier, and that little changed during the sail. He told Derek afterwards he'd noticed a strange glint in Eric's eye and at the time he'd put it down to drugs, but now he was not so sure. He informed the inquest that due to a combination of a late night the day before, when they drove down from Birmingham to Bristol after a gig, and the amount of alcohol he'd consumed on the night in question, he laid down in the bottom of the boat and fell sound asleep.

The evidence that turned out to be the most interesting of the day did not come from Eric Hannah but from a guy called Graham Radcliffe. Graham, a resident of Osmington Mills, suffered from a recurrent nightmare relating to the death of his father, who died four weeks before from cancer. Each time a nightmare occurred, rather than try to fall asleep and risk it happening again, he got dressed and took his dog for a late-night walk.

He often walked along the beach, but when he heard voices, he thought they belonged to a group of rough local lads who would lark about and fight after consuming cans of strong lager. Instead, he followed the path on top of the cliffs. It was a warm, summer's night with clear skies and a three-quarter moon. He could see two men lying on the sand, and out in the water he could make out the shape of a rowing boat, one he knew belonged to another local man, Harry Langham.

The boat pulled away from the pier and soon became indistinct, but he could still hear voices. Unlike Barry, he didn't think all was well aboard the boat as he could hear two men talking loud as if arguing. He couldn't make out what they were saying but by the pitch and the tone of their speech, it didn't sound like a friendly or animated discussion. It ended with a short, sharp increase in voices and then a loud splash and nothing for a minute or two before he heard two voices again, but this time one of the voices was different. He knew now, the additional voice belonged to Barry after being woken by Eric.

The verdict was predictable enough, accidental death, and Derek wouldn't want it any other way. There remained a niggling doubt about the part played by the animosity between Eric and Danny, but he didn't want these misgivings appearing in the coroner's report or in the press in case his fear was groundless. He couldn't believe Eric would go as far as to shove Danny overboard, but did anyone know how he would react in the heat of the moment, or if he felt threatened? If his misgivings didn't disappear, it would be something he would raise with Eric at a later date in private.

Following the delivery of the Coroner's verdict, they walked outside into the warm Dorset sunshine. As he waited for the others, he could see Danny's distraught mother being led to a car by her daughter. He wanted to tell her how much he'd liked Danny and what a burgeoning talent he was, but the words wouldn't come out when he first met her and now didn't seem like the best time.

They left the cars they used to travel down to Dorset in the Council car park and walked into town. They came across a smart-looking pub but ignored it as Eric could not be trusted not to get rat-arsed and speak ill of the dead, leading them all into a fight. Instead, they headed for Luigi's, a small family-run Italian restaurant where the four remaining Crows plus manager Frannie Copeland sat down at a table.

Frannie, uncharacteristically taciturn throughout the morning's unhappy proceedings, rallied when a glass of brandy appeared in front of him.

'Here's to Danny,' he said holding up his glass. 'A fine keyboard player, now immortalised on vinyl.'

'To Danny,' they all said.

He didn't trust many things coming out of Frannie Copeland's mouth, but yes, Danny would be remembered for as long as people listened to their music. A fitting memorial for a fine young man and heaps better than a cold tombstone.

'I've never attended an inquest until today,' Frannie said. 'I've been to plenty of court cases, all civil ones for contract disputes, that kind of thing, but never an inquest.'

'What sorts of cases,' Derek asked. 'Were you being sued or were you suing?'

It sounded an innocent enough question and Frannie answered it as such, but in his mind it was anything but. Like many bands starting out, they'd signed the agreement put in front of them just to get a manager, play a gig and get a recording contract. They didn't read the fine print, and now older, wiser and generating much more money, Derek, was convinced Frannie was ripping them off.

He knew from information supplied to him by the record company what their weekly and monthly sales were, and he knew the price of an album in the shops before tax. If he deducted the cut Frannie and the record company took from the gross profit, they should be left with way more than they were getting now. In fact, the amount of money given to Derek to pay roadies, equipment hire, the guys in the band and all the rest, hadn't increased much over last year, and yet copies of the new album were flying off the shelves.

The food arrived, breaking Derek's morose chain of thought. He realised it would be the first thing he'd eaten all day as he hadn't felt like food first thing this morning, and the large plate of Tagliatelle sitting in front of him was just what he needed, accompanied by a couple of glasses of the house Chianti. The board outside promised the best Italian food in Dorchester, and true to their word, it tasted like it. It was a shame the band weren't as big in Italy as they were in Germany, as he could take or leave Schnitzels, Sauerbraten and Bratwurst, but he couldn't get enough pasta and pizza.

With a couple of glasses of wine inside him, Eric could usually be relied upon to turn his calm exterior into his argumentative but nevertheless sociable self, but not today, as a black mood had taken over. He barely touched his food. The other guys were more stoic, and if asked to play a gig tomorrow, their presence would be assured.

Fifteen minutes later, Frannie put down his knife and fork and lit a cigar. Everyone had finished eating except Pete, who was often last, but it didn't excuse the ignorant sod for his lack of manners.

'Let me tell you first about my meeting with the record company a couple of days ago,' Frannie said in between puffs, 'and then about some plans I'm making for the future. You should know, the suits at the record company are well pleased with *Black Saturday* as it's charted in the UK, Germany, Japan and they think soon in the U.S.'

Barry nudged Eric beside him. 'Did you hear that Eric? Next stop an American tour.'

'I'll believe it when I see it,' he replied.

'I thought you always wanted to go there?'

'I do, but not today, ok?' He pushed his chair away and headed towards the toilets.

Undaunted, Frannie continued. 'They say they'll finance you for the next two albums but if the next one's a flop, you can forget I told you this, ha, ha.'

A similar comment would normally raise a good laugh if they were drunk or high after a concert, but today it fell flat.

'Now, if you can produce another cracker like *Black Saturday* and we all hope you do, it doesn't matter what they think. You'll be telling them what to do, as they'll be afraid of losing you to someone else.'

They batted the subject around for a few minutes, everyone starting to feel more upbeat except Derek. Eric came back from the toilet and slumped down in the seat like an overgrown adolescent. His nose looked devoid of the white tell-tale marks, but it was obvious he had done a line in the loo as his eyes were glazed and red. When did this guy ever stop? On this day of all days, Derek expected a bit more respect for Danny.

'Now for the tours,' Frannie continued, under a pall of cigar smoke, 'we're not talking about the US yet, but once this tour is over, I know a promoter who wants you guys to headline a tour right across Europe, and wait for it, over to Australia and New Zealand.'

Barry, Pete and an invigorated Eric were all for it, but

Derek could foresee insurmountable problems. Firstly, what to do about Danny? The obvious course of action, and one Frannie would be exhorting him to do in a week or so, was to hire a straight replacement.

The question remained, would the new guy be as creative as Danny and would he collaborate with Derek on song writing? As an alternative, they could do without a keyboard player and return to the old days as a guitar band, with Eric playing solos that Danny used to play on his keyboard. No way did he want to do that, as the keyboard gave them a different sound and the first option, filled him with dread.

Problem two, was what to do about Frannie. Sure, he was working hard, lining them up with tours and he had a good relationship with record company bosses, but Derek had no illusions he would drop them like a stone if sales fell or Eric went on a long-term bender. All this would perhaps be workable if the thieving bastard wasn't robbing them left, right and centre. He had proof now, but when he'd taken it to a lawyer, he was told Frannie was doing nothing wrong. It was immoral, greedy and self-serving, yes, but illegal? No.

Last but not least, what could be done with the once mercurial Eric Hannah, now the volatile and unpredictable Eric Hannah? No one, not even Eric, knew what sort of mood he would wake up with in the morning. He took out his ire for a shitty upbringing, an absent father and an alcoholic mother, on Danny, suggesting to all it was about the music, but Derek, knew different. With no Danny, who would his target be, himself or Barry? It wouldn't be Pete as he was a difficult man to provoke, and once roused, he would get a broken nose for his trouble.

'You're not saying much Derek,' Frannie said, after giving him a nudge. 'It's not like you.'

'I've been thinking about what you said.'

'Don't you like it?'

'It sounds great, but you're going to have to do it without me.'

'What do you mean?'

'I quit.'

'You can't fucking quit,' Eric said, 'not now, not when we seem to be moving into the big time.'

'I'm finished with it. Danny's death made my mind up for me. I couldn't carry on even if I wanted to.'

He pushed back his seat, stood and put on his jacket. 'See you around.'

He walked out of the restaurant and retraced his steps towards County Hall where he'd left his car. He'd given Frannie a lift down to Dorchester but he would find room in Barry's car if he could stand some of the jazz music he listened to, or if he couldn't, he could always take a taxi. It would cost him the best part of £200 but the voracious bastard could afford it, he'd made enough out of them.

He was walking along High West Street when a hand pulled him back. He turned to find an out of breath Eric Hannah standing there.

'What the fuck do think you're playing at, Derek?' he said, his eyes wide and wild but not all from his recent exertions.

'What do you mean? I told you in the restaurant, I'm getting out. I've had enough; enough of Frannie, enough of your drug taking, and enough of dead musicians and bloody inquests.'

'The fuck you are. We're on the verge of doing

something great and you wanna fuck it up. I'll stop doing the drugs, honest I will.'

'I've heard it all a thousand times before. Moses could stop the Red Sea, but you can't stop taking dope. You're too weak.'

'You fucking bastard, you only think of yourself.'

Derek continued to walk away but a hand hauled him back. He turned and a fist came flying towards him. He jerked his head to the side and it bounced off his cheekbone. Without hesitation, he punched Eric straight in the face and followed up with a punch in the gut. He collapsed in a heap on the dirty pavement.

'Don't do this to me, Derek,' he said sobbing, tears mingling with blood on his face. 'The band is all I've got.'

'You can start another band, you don't need me.'

'I couldn't. I love the Crows. It's my life.'

'I can't help you there. My decision is made and I'm not changing it.'

'What am I gonna do?'

'Join another band or try your hand at something else.'

'Like what? The only thing I know is playing the guitar.'

'The criminal roadie you're always hanging about with could get you a job as a getaway driver on a bank robbery or something. No, forget it, you'd fall asleep at the wheel.'

'You can laugh all you like,' he said, his bloodied face now firm and resolute, 'but maybe I will. He did a big job a couple of days ago and I know where he hid the loot.'

THIRTY-TWO

CI Bill Paterson (ret) lounged on the leather sofa in Derek Crow's office as if he owned it. In the Met, he'd worked Vice, and at times he'd no doubt felt there wasn't a business, house or shop premises where he couldn't barge in and shake-down the occupants, making him feel like he ruled the world, or at least his small part of it.

Following the deaths of Barry and Pete, Derek Crow had asked Paterson to review both accidents and examine the police investigation, and assess their verdicts. In his report back, Paterson told him he had no issues with the police investigations and considered their judgement sound. Now with the death of Eric Hannah, the reassurance of propriety from Paterson would no longer wash. Something or someone was killing his friends and Derek needed to find out quickly and stop them or he would be next.

Paterson had suggested the compilation of a 'hate' list, the names of anyone with a serious grievance against the band. Paterson had done this as much to line his own pockets as to help him, but he didn't mind as he liked the former copper's direct approach, and Crow never did believe the solution lay with warlocks, curses or karma. In Paterson's mind it was simple. If the lads didn't die in accidents or commit suicide, someone had killed them.

If deciding the way ahead was easy, compiling the list was not, as it had opened a host of old sores and wounds and railed against his philosophy of never looking back. There were many things in his past of which he was proud, and in some cases, worked hard to replicate, but like many people he knew, he'd made mistakes too. The difference between him and others was he refused to dwell there, feeding on former glories and replaying the misery of historical failures like a stuck LP.

Bill Paterson was a fat, serious man with thinning grey hair and a heavy, jowly face. Beneath these undistinguished features lurked a shrewd, analytical mind, coupled with an aggressive streak. He thought nothing of breaking the arms, noses and bollocks of unhelpful suspects. He was dressed in a cheap suit, crumpled shirt frayed at the cuffs and the scruffy tyke couldn't knot a tie.

Paterson lifted his tea, Yorkshire, strong with milk and three sugars, and took a long, loud slurp. He opened his report.

'Are you ready for this Derek? A rake through the old coals of a sordid, self-indulgent past might be a bit of a sobering experience for some.'

'Yeah, go ahead,' he said with a confidence he didn't feel. He wasn't ready for this, he could never be ready, but fear drove him on.

Paterson dealt with what he called the 'easy' ones first. Kingsley Dass, the band's self-proclaimed champion at the record company had been sacked when the Crows split up. He didn't find a new job for two years and during this time his wife sued him for divorce, resulting in an acrimonious court battle, played out in the tabloids. Boz Strider, a session guitarist, had been hospitalised after taking a pop at Eric. Simon Rother, religious zealot, had not been best pleased when Derek tipped him and all his pamphlets into a fountain in the centre of Manchester. Lindsay Tremain, a new-age author, had claimed her books were being plagiarised in the lyrics of their songs. After each name, Paterson replied 'forgotten about', 'no problem' or 'annoyed at the time but they're over it.'

To Derek's knowledge, two on the list still bore a grudge and said as much whenever reporters asked them about him, but Paterson was emphatic, there was nothing to worry about. The 'easy' ones took an hour and depleted his store of emotional capital, but alas, it was but the warm-up for the 'difficult' pile. He ordered a fresh pot of coffee and biscuits and after the tray arrived, Paterson opened the first file.

'Dave Manson, a former roadie for the Crows.'

'Ok.'

Known to all as Smelly Dave, Derek tried to picture him. An image came into his mind of a big, grizzly bloke with long black hair, pock-marked face, four days' growth, toothy smile and a fat gut. As a consequence of his copious beer and curry consumption, he was a contaminated individual to sit beside in the confines of a Transit van or a bus. His continual farting, burping and rancid body odour made the journey from London to Dusseldorf, and even shorter hops like London to Northampton, unbearable.

'He was sacked from the band in 1987,' Paterson said, 'for stealing two amps and a speaker cabinet. He denied the charges at the time but in his defence, admitted he couldn't remember much about the incident as he was drunk.'

'Yeah, sounds about right. He was forever pissed.'

'When I met him he was living in a refuge for

recovering addicts. He weighs about eight stone now and looks well, if a bit frail, but the light that still shines bright is he hates your guts. He says he never recovered from his sacking from the band, which was his dream job, and hasn't held down a proper job since. This led him into a cycle of drug taking and stealing, he lost his house, his wife, and doesn't see his kids. He blames the band, you in particular, for sacking him, and Eric for starting him on the sauce.'

'Bollocks, he took drugs before he joined the band. Bloody hell, he still remembers this after all those years? There's fuck-all wrong with his brain cells.'

'As I said, he's in this recovery place and says he's feeling healthier and fitter than he's done for a while, but he could have fooled me. I've seen dead people in better shape.'

'Could it be him?'

'Possible, as he's mobile, he's got access to a car belonging to one of the aids, he seems to have a lot of mates in the place and his hate burns bright as the sunshine.'

'That might account for the twenty-plus-years delay, him just getting back on his feet.'

Paterson nodded. 'I think so too. It's been a long downward spiral, but he's past the worst, in my opinion.'

Derek thought for a moment. It was one thing to talk about airy-fairy things like curses and hoodoos, but it was another to hear a name and see the face of the person who might have killed his friends. A man who might soon be coming after him. It shook him.

'Are you all right, Derek? You look like you've seen a ghost.'

'No, I'm fine. This stuff is getting to me, that's all.'

'What I suggest we do, is put the ones we think have a valid grudge, and we can see reason why they might wait twenty-plus years to take revenge, into a 'possible' pile. Later on we can decide what to do about them.'

'Yeah, good idea. Who do we have next?'

'Annaleise Quinlan.'

'Shit.' He'd been caught in two minds about even including this one, as the memory still made him squirm, like peeling a sticking plaster back from an aching sore. If the story had any foundation, re-opening it could give the press a field day and wreck his newly acquired public persona and the groundwork done on his political ambitions, but he could see no other option.

He'd met Annaleise in a hotel corridor in Leeds just after a gig, he high on adrenaline and she high on drink or drugs. Soon, she was all over him like a rash. Rather than go back to his room as the others were congregating there, he'd pulled her into a laundry cupboard where they'd had raw, hungry sex. If his memory served him right, it included a liberal dose of biting, slapping and scratching.

'She's a primary teacher at a school in Cambridge. By all accounts she's good at her job and well-liked by her pupils.'

'Maybe, but back then she was a groupie.'

'I'm sure you're right but cries of rape were treated very different in 1986 to how they are now. You said you weren't charged?'

'Nope, it didn't go so far, just an interview with a spotty oik of a sergeant in Leeds Central and nothing was put in a file. Her word against mine, the copper said.'

'Mind you, in a crowd it would be hard to differentiate

those who were groupies, itching for a screw with a rock star, and those who were star-struck teenagers looking for nothing more serious than a flash of your pen.'

'Too true, especially when you've just come off stage and feeling like you could walk on air. We'd grab the nearest couple of birds and head upstairs.' He paused for a moment, a part of his mind awakened by a number of memories of the time, most of which were good.

'So what are you thinking, Bill? Why are you thinking she's a difficult case if it was done and dusted all those years ago?'

'At first she looked like any other settled middle-aged teacher who does a side-line in tutoring seven-year-olds in the rudiments of dance, but then I met her husband. He's a big brute of a bloke, a lorry driver with arms twice the size of mine, and when she was back in the kitchen making tea, he told me she suffers from uncontrollable bouts of crying, anger outbursts and bad headaches because of it.'

'How is he taking it?'

'He's very angry, like a bull at the gate.'

'I see. Why would he leave such a long time before attacking us?'

'He hasn't been on the scene long. They married nine months ago and he only met her four months before.'

'Oh. Why is the band being targeted and not just me?'

'Maybe he blames the band for the lifestyle, or maybe he's saving you for last, hoping you'll suffer.'

Derek shot him a look, daring him to smile, but the expression was the same, impassive and ugly, a face only a mother could love. 'I'm suffering all right. She and her husband belong on the same pile as Smelly Dave.'

'I think so too. Don't look so down Derek, there's only one more to go. It's your old mate Mathew Street.'

Mathew Street; he toyed with the memory. Street was like Paterson, a man who never smiled but he could lay his hands on anything, magazines, a little flick knife he carried in his trouser pocket, cartons of cigarettes, bottles of booze, clothes, all manner of stuff, all knocked off with no questions asked.

'He's an easy man to find as he's got plenty of form, but a hard man to see. I needed to put on my 'Paterson from the Met' hat to get in the door.'

He then trotted out a long list of thefts, assaults, robberies and jail-time stretching from detention centres as a teenager to his release from prison only six months previously.

'Give me the last one again.'

'Street was sent away for twelve for a post office robbery. While he was inside, they found new evidence linking him to the AeroSwiss robbery at Gatwick Airport in 1989. He was given another fifteen to add to his sentence. He's been inside over twenty-five-years.'

'It's still a big whack for stealing some money.'

'It is, but like the Great Train Robbers way back then, the judge wanted to make an example of them because they came tooled up and they shot and wounded a security guard. It wasn't only Street, the whole gang copped it. Plus, when inside, he was involved in the stabbing of some guy and it wiped out any parole he had coming.'

'What did he say when you spoke to him?'

'Not much, in fact it was a bloody waste of time. It was more the things he didn't say that interested me. He told me the fall-out with you was all a misunderstanding. How come you were hanging about with scum-bags like him?'

'He was useful to have around, he could get us all sorts of things and fix broken gear, but as you said, he's a man who robs security vans for a living. He's not likely to take the loss of cash, no matter how small, lightly.'

'What was the story, you guys wanted all this stuff and when he came up with the goods you couldn't pay him?'

'We were temporarily strapped for cash. Frannie Copeland, our manager kept us on a tight leash, to keep the band lean and hungry, according to him. Meanwhile, you could find him swanning around London in a smart car and chomping on those bloody fat cigars he liked to smoke. We told Street we would pay him when Frannie gave us some more money, but he got the hump and refused to leave the goods. He tried to get rid them but couldn't as they were hot and in the end, he dumped the whole lot in a skip, the pig-headed sod. I think he lost a couple of grand.'

'When I talked to him,' Paterson said, 'he laughed the incident off as one of the pitfalls of selling knocked-off gear. Like I said, it wasn't what he said I didn't like, it's what he didn't say. When he told me he still liked you guys and didn't bear a grudge, his body language and the tight expression on his face expressed something else. Derek, I was in the force for thirty years and I can spot a liar at fifty feet. He was boiling inside, but could I get the old fucker to say anything about what was bothering him? No sodding way.'

'Pity.'

'Is there something you're not telling me? Did something else go down between you guys and him, other than the loss of a couple of grand? He might be a criminal and willing to do anything for money, but I don't see him holding a grudge for over twenty years about a measly two grand.'

'I suppose not.' He sat back, thinking. 'No, there's nothing else I can think of. You didn't find out if he was maybe the uncle or godfather of Danny Winter, a relative still grieving over the death of his favourite boy?'

'I didn't explore the point and Street didn't say anything about him, plus I didn't see any pictures around his house of a young lad in his first school uniform or a guy playing keyboards in a band. Is there any significance in Street being put away for his long stretch only a few months after the Crazy Crows split up?'

'Not that I can think of. What's on your mind?'

'I don't know Derek, I'm fishing. It's what we cops, or should I say what we ex-cops do.'

'There was no official connection between Street and the band. We knew him as a contract roadie, a guy who joined up for the big tours and buggered off when they were finished.'

'I understand, Derek, but were you or the other guys responsible in some way for sending him back to prison for twenty-odd years? I know if someone did that to me, it wouldn't be a serious fucking grudge I would hold, I wouldn't be happy until I had their bollocks locked in a vice and my hand on a blazing-hot blowtorch.'

THIRTY-THREE

DI Henderson turned off the A27 and headed towards Eastbourne. It was a fine sunny day with clear views across the Channel, but the biting wind was forcing dog-owners to walk with their heads down and jackets fastened. Shame, the dogs seemed happy enough to be out.

'There it is,' DS Walters said from the passenger seat, looking out of the window at the tops of buildings and over to a murky sea, 'God's Waiting Room.'

'You and your cynical brethren might not be aware, but the number of elderly people in Brighton is much higher than here in Eastbourne.'

'You're kidding me. All I see outside Churchill Square are gangs of young girls, and groups of young lads hanging around the pubs in the Lanes. Any time I go to Eastbourne, the only gangs I see are made up of old folk heading down to the seafront for a snooze on one of the benches along the esplanade.'

'It's true. Brighton has nearly three times the number of over-eighties as Eastbourne, but because it's bigger, there are more places for them to go, and with all the universities and numerous language schools around the place, the youngsters keep the town looking young.'

Derek Crow's friend from the criminal side of life, Mathew Street, lived in Belmore Road, a street not gifted with much greenery, except a skimpy smattering of small privet hedges. He proved a hard man to track down, not because he jetted across the country doing important work or led a hectic social life, but because he wouldn't answer the phone. When he did, he made it plain he didn't like the police and proved reluctant to help them. Walters was forced to apply a little pressure by reminding him they were conducting a murder investigation and if he wouldn't see them in Eastbourne they would drag him to Brighton instead.

The house looked comfortably furnished, if a little on the old-fashioned side for Henderson's tastes, but it was tidy and had recently been cleaned. The man himself was ensconced in his favourite chair with a whisky, watching horse racing on television. He had a thin, wiry face with so many lines and crevices an astronomer could mistake it for the surface of a new planet and sparse almost non-existent grey hair. His skin was dull and sallow, a bad reflection on Eastbourne's claim to be one of the sunniest places in the UK.

'I wanna see what happens in this race, ok?'

It was a statement, not a question, and he didn't look around to see if they were put out, which they weren't. In truth, Henderson loathed horse racing and any form of gambling, as in his experience it wasted lives and destroyed marriages, witnessed at first hand with two uncles in Scotland and a couple of coppers he knew on the Sussex force.

The room may have looked neat and tidy but there was no disguising the reek of cigarette smoke, and even though the window was open as it was a bright, sunny day, he was puffing away as if his life depended on it. He was either addicted to the nasty white sticks or watching the gee-gees made him nervous, as no sooner did he finish one than he lit up another.

From a brief introduction, Henderson detected no respiratory problems nor any issue with his mobility, and he didn't see any walking sticks or his pet hate, oxygen cylinders, in the hall. It was a sad reflection on the lottery of life when Frannie Copeland's only guilty pleasure was tugging away on the odd cigar and yet he would spend the rest of his life moving around like a cripple, while the man sitting here, doing a fair impression of the Flying Scotsman emerging from Stowe Hill Tunnel, seemed to be in full possession of his faculties.

In a noisy climax both on the box and in the room, the race ended with his horse, Bonny Lad, falling at the last hurdle. In response, this particular Eastbourne punter leapt from his chair with surprising agility for a man over sixty, and using more force than necessary, switched the television off.

'Fucking nags, they never do what you want,' he said to the room. 'I should pack it in and take up hill walking. Ha, ha, fat chance.' He spoke with a London twang in deep, guttural tones, not surprising if he always smoked his cigarettes in such an enthusiastic fashion.

'As Sergeant Walters said to you on the phone, Mr Street—'

'Call me Mat, everybody else does.'

'Well, Mat, as my sergeant no doubt told you, we are in the process of investigating the deaths of three members of the Crazy Crows rock band.'

'What the hell's it got to do with me?'

'Nothing, as far as we know. Your name has come up in enquiries, that's all. Tell me, how did you first get involved with the band?'

He ran long fingers through wisps of hair, or what was left of it. 'I was doing some joinery work at the Hammersmith Apollo, fixing the broken seating and re-fitting cracked banisters and handrails after the fans of some boy band trashed the place. I got talking to them when they came in for rehearsals. It developed from there and I joined them whenever they went on tour.'

'What was the attraction for you working for them?' Walters asked.

'It wasn't the bloody music that's for sure, the stuff they played was just a load of fucking noise. I like to listen to country and western myself, there's always a nice melody and I can hear the words, not a load of mumbles over a noisy guitar.'

'If not the music, then what?'

'The job involved a lot of traveling and I was getting fed up with London, too much heat, if you know what I mean.'

Henderson did know what he meant. With any new security van robbery, bank heist or payroll stick-up, a man like Street would be one of the first suspects to be wheeled into a police station 'to help them with their enquiries.'

'What did you do for the band?' Henderson asked.

'I started off as a roadie, but because I could do carpentry as well I also got involved in building stands and rigs for the stage, that kind of thing.'

'How did you get along together?'

'I suppose I got on best with Eric Hannah. I come from the East End and he came from south London. I found out he liked gangster movies and guns, so I got him magazines from the US and took him down to my local boozer in Plaistow and introduced him to some people I knew. He was over the moon, star struck. I thought it was meant to be the other way round,' he said, laughing at a joke Henderson was sure he'd cracked many times.

'So you became good mates with the boys in the band?'

'I wouldn't say best mates, but they could always find me when they wanted summat.'

'According to Frannie Copeland you were around quite a lot.'

'Is the old fucker still alive, well blow me? I thought that ignorant bastard would have died a long ago. Weak lungs you see, he got TB as a kid. He hated me being there as he said it undermined his authority or some shite or other. I think it was because I didn't like him and Frannie only likes people who like him. Weird init?'

My, my, the old bugger could be quite the armchair philosopher and psychoanalyst when he put his mind to it, not to mention behaving like a crabby old pensioner.

'I went touring with them in the UK in '85, Germany in '86, Denmark '86 and a couple more I don't remember. When the tour finished, I wouldn't see 'em again for months.'

'What other things did you do for them?' Walters asked.

He looked at her with narrow, weasel eyes. 'Ach, what do I care what I say? I'm outa the game now, I've done my time. I'd get 'em cheap booze, fags, bits of equipment, clothes like jeans and leather jackets. You name it.'

'It sounds to me,' Walters said, 'you got on with them better than you're letting on.'

'Does it? Well, there you go. Thinking back, they didn't make it easy for anyone to get on with them as they were an odd bunch. Crow junior, that's what I called Barry, was a lap-dog to his big brother and did whatever he told him to do. It was pathetic to watch sometimes, the poor sap couldn't take a crap without his brother's say-so.'

'What about Peter?'

'Grant? He was all right, a bit boring but he got his fair share of the birds. I mean Hannah was the dog's bollocks on the skirt score and I've seen him take three or four birds back to his hotel room, but Grant did ok. He said he got the ones Hannah was finished with, ha, ha.'

'How do you feel now,' Walters asked, 'with three members of the band dead?'

Henderson looked at his eyes to make sure his facial expressions matched the words coming out of his mouth, as for the first time he could see the possibility of a motive developing. Here was a hardened criminal who knew the band better than most.

He shrugged. 'I don't give a shit, if I'm being honest,' he said, his intensive stare not wavering from her face.

'Why not? You were friends once.'

'Nah, you've got it all wrong. It was all business but these boys fucked me over big time, so don't expect any sympathy from me.'

'How do you mean they fucked you over?'

He shifted in his seat. 'It's all in the past. I don't want to talk about it. No comment.'

The door opened and a young girl walked in. 'Are you all right Grandad? I heard loud voices.'

She was perhaps twelve or thirteen, slim with lovely curly blonde hair and deep blue eyes. She possessed the makings of a beautiful girl, but the genes of the old codger sitting across from him were working against it.

'No, no I'm fine love, it's just adult talk.'

'Well, you remember, you've got to watch your heart, the doctor told you not to get excited.'

'Pah, what do doctors know? Anyway, there's no chance of that happening. Now off you go Chrissie, there's nothing for you to worry about.'

'Ok,' she said. As she left the room she looked over at Henderson and gave him a scowl.

'She's my granddaughter in case you're wondering. She's staying with me while my stupid son sorts his fucking head out. He needs a new one if you ask me. Him and his wife have gone away for a few days to sort out their problems, so don't you go away thinking I'm a peado. In any case, she's going to her gran's house tomorrow.'

For Chrissie, moving away from a problem with her parents to stay with him must have been like jumping from the frying pan into the fire. What sort of role model was this archetypal career-criminal Street supposed to be for her?

They talked for another ten minutes but Henderson advanced no further forward. Street seemed to be holding something back because when he asked again why he didn't like the Crows, he stonewalled him.

He tried a different tack. 'All four members of the band seemed to have done well after leaving the music business. Where do you think they got the start-up money? Everyone we've spoken to didn't think they'd made much money from being in the band.'

Street's face hardened. 'What the fuck are you asking me that for? I don't know anything about their money. How the fuck would I know? Now get the hell out, this interview's over.'

THIRTY-FOUR

The Anchor Bar in Shepherd's Bush was the sort of boozer Derek Crow would ordinarily walk past. It reeked of faux old-world charm with acres of polished wood on the long bar and walls, windows engraved with the names and logos of brewers long gone, and serving beers from parts of Germany and Holland he and the other punters had never heard of. Tonight, the pub was filled with young city types gulping down a few jars before heading home to face a needy young wife, or imbibing a bit of Dutch courage to stomach another night alone in an empty bed-sit.

There were times in his past when any pub would do and he and the Crows must have been pissed in every large town from Cornwall to Aberdeen. Nowadays, he did most of his drinking at home or away on business, as he'd exorcised the wilder demons of his youth, and now enjoyed spending more time with his family, although at the moment, he didn't venture out at all unless there was a burning necessity; like tonight.

Retired Chief Inspector Bill Paterson placed two drinks down on the table, a glass of the pub's best red for him and a pint of bitter for the former 'tec.

'I hope you don't mind meeting me here Derek, but I didn't think your office was the place for this sort of discussion.'

'Needs must when there's a murderer about, I say.'

Crow lifted his wine glass and took a large drink.

Whoa, big mistake. It tasted sharp, acidic and alcoholic, a chemical taste overpowering any fruit or tannic flavours lurking underneath, giving the impression it was spirit masquerading as wine. It was too young to be drunk and yet another example of over-eager vineyard owners trying to make a buck before their wares were fit for market, selling to large corporations more interested in price and profit than a fine drinking experience.

'What did you want to tell me, Bill?' he said placing the wine glass down on the table with the same distaste he would with a vile bottle of cough mixture.

Paterson took a drink from his pint and made a loud, slurping noise, similar to the way he drank his tea. Perhaps he was drinking Yorkshire Bitter, or maybe he always behaved like a pig. He put the glass down, a good third of it missing, and wiped his mouth with the back of his hand. The only things missing from this idealist peer into a beer-drinker's heaven was a good burp and a noisy fart, but thankfully he passed neither. Instead, he removed papers from a well-worn folder.

'At our last meeting, you asked me to go back and took a closer look at our three suspects, Dave Manson, otherwise known as Smelly Dave, Annaleise Quinlan and Mathew Street. I did surveillance on all three but came up with zilch initially, as Smelly Dave doesn't do much all day and the lorry-driver husband of Annaleise Quinlan spends his time going back and forward to Spain with only a day or two at home. I then adopted a more direct approach with Street, and I think I've got something for you.'

'Well done, Bill. Let's hear it,' he said, his voice full of enthusiasm.

'When I met him the first time, I went softly softly, but

on this occasion I laid down his record of violence in front of him and gave him a long list of his old confederates who'd all done time. I then accused him directly of having the means and the motive to kill your friends.'

'Good. What did he say?'

'He denied it, of course.'

Crow's shoulders slumped at the news. 'No surprises there.'

'He said he was old, and sure he had grudges, but he couldn't do anything about it now. So I said to him, if it's not you doing it, how about one of your mates? He thinks for a bit and then he says, if I tell you I know something, what's it worth?'

'The wily old fox. He does know something!'

'Easy Derek, the pub needs this table and glasses for tomorrow's customers.'

He tried to calm down but couldn't. 'What did you do? I hope you bashed his fucking brains in so he would tell you.'

'There's a time for violence, for sure Derek, and I can't say I didn't feel tempted to land a fist or two on his wrinkled fizzer, but poke the old bugger too hard and we'd get nothing.'

'I suppose you're right.'

'I played it casual and talked money for a while as these guys always like talking about money in my experience. I then tried to find out how good his information is and so on and so forth, and the upshot is this. He wants fifty grand for telling you who's behind it—'

'Whoa! How do we...'

'Hang on Derek, hang on and hear me out. He's asking for fifty gees to tell you who killed the boys, but he'll only do the exchange in person and wants you to come to his gaff because he doesn't like travelling.'

Derek became distracted by a loud noise and looked around, and in his current nervous demeanour he half-expected trouble. A group of lads were laughing at some funny story, their numbers thinner than before now the call of a hot meal and the evening's entertainment in front of the box beckoned.

He thought for a moment. It made sense for Street, a man who knew many criminals in the East End, to know what was going on and who might be responsible. When he'd known him, he would do anything if you crossed his hands with cash, and he wouldn't put it past him to put the feelers out once he learned the Crows were dropping like last week's novelty single.

'Do you think that's wise, to go to his place? I mean if he's the guy behind the killings, I could be walking into the lion's den.'

'I don't think he's the guy, Derek, and give him a break, he's a sixty-seven-year-old man, not a rabid Rottweiler.'

'True.' He mulled it over for a moment. Hell, what was the downside? Were they not friends at one time?

'Sure let's do it.'

'Good man, I'll fix it up. He says he doesn't travel much but in a day or two he's moving to Brighton for a week to house-sit his son's place, so it's likely you'll meet him there.'

'It's better for me as I know where I am in Brighton, but I don't have a bloody clue about Eastbourne.'

'What about the fifty big ones?'

'I'll sort it out. I'd pay double to get my life back.'

He left the pub ten minutes later. His 'minder', Don

Levinson, sat outside in the car, the big Jaguar engine purring hungrily with his hands on the wheel, ready for a quick getaway. Don was once in the Army and now doubled as a bodyguard, although he hoped his sedentary job as a driver these past few years would not count against him if some action suddenly kicked-off.

Despite the iffy surroundings of the pub and Paterson's personal drinking habits, Derek had rather enjoyed his evening out. Maybe he was working too hard and needed to get out more. The pressure of building the business had never stopped since it started, with frequent twelve-hour days, weekend working and three weeks holiday. Now with the end of this terrible business in sight, he wanted to get away and clear his head of all the Crazy Crows stuff, mourn the loss of his friends without the added strain of watching his back. He made a decision. He would book a holiday just as soon as the meeting with Mathew Street was finished and any information he possessed had been handed over to the police.

Derek was born in South London, but from the age of eight grew up in Brighton. To his shame, he hadn't been back there in a while, as the last couple of times he and Peter Grant had gone out on their boys night out, they went to London, and it would be good to see the old stomping grounds again, places where he'd spent the formative years of his youth. He remembered with affection the Hove dog track where he often won and lost his weekly pay check, the seafront where he lost his virginity to a sixteen-year-old girl called Natasha, and the North Laines where he lost his heart to a beautiful girl who worked in the shop where he bought his first guitar.

He tried to relax but his nerves were jangling, eager to

do something, and for a moment he had been tempted to ask Don to stop the car and let him walk, but this part of London was as alien to him as New York or Calcutta, and instead he reached for his briefcase and opened it.

He pulled out a paper written by one of his marketing guys on how the company could use PR to improve the public's perception of tanker drivers, after the bad press received from the recent pay dispute. According to a recent independent poll, the status of tanker drivers had fallen from their previous middling position to a place near the bottom of the heap, wallowing down in a dank basement and roped together with estate agents, tabloid journalists and bankers.

He looked up for a few seconds and recognised Circus Road, a street close to home. It was a wet, miserable night and the lights of oncoming cars were dazzling his eyes before the wipers caught the errant raindrops and brushed them away. The PR paper was still on his lap and for a few minutes he was mesmerised by the slap-slap of the wipers.

He was in a car, not a smart car like this Jaguar, but a Ford Cortina which had enough design clues to suggest its American parentage, but unlike its Yankee cousin, it was noisy, the seats were uncomfortable and for the most part, it was unreliable. He would be in the back with his younger brother, Barry, who was always a quiet kid but who could blame him, as their mother in the front passenger seat could talk for England in the loud booming voice she possessed. They were supposed to be reading, but instead, they were listening to her berating his weak and ineffectual father for something he'd done or more likely, failed to do.

The purpose of the trip was to see Aunt Beth and Uncle

Harry, and just like his mother, her sister Beth could also talk the hind legs off a donkey. How they understood one another was a mystery, a spectacle he and Barry could only marvel at, as they both talked as fast as he could run and often at the same time

They were forced to sit in the front room and listen to the women go on about bunions, varicose veins, neighbours, useless husbands, cheeky children and the other banal minutiae of their lives, as they didn't want to be alone with Uncle Harry. If they were sent outside to play, he would try to lure them into the shed with the promise of sweets and cake, but his big touchy hands made frequent grabs for your bum and balls while puffing heavy gusts of pipe tobacco into your face.

From the corner of his eye he spotted a car on the left coming towards them from a side street, but to his utter horror, it didn't stop and rammed into the front of the Jaguar. He was jerked to one side, but instantly the seatbelt tensioned and half a dozen airbags came scooting out of the side panels to cushion the impact. When the car stopped rocking a few seconds later, he was amazed to find no broken bones or cuts; dazed and a bit confused but otherwise uninjured.

He leaned forward to ask Don if he was ok, when he shot out of the car and started berating the errant driver, a tall Middle Eastern bloke who wasn't taking any crap in return. He could see where this might lead as Don was ex-Special Forces and didn't take any prisoners, either here or in Afghanistan. He made a move to get out of the car and stop any needless bloodshed, in case Don suffered a PTSD flashback and mistook his antagonist for one of the mop-heads he used to bully and assault. All of a sudden, a strange face appeared at the passenger window.

God, he'd been stupid! This was it! Someone had staged this accident, and while everyone else was distracted by the fracas going on outside, the killer would sneak in here and bash his brains in. This would lead the police to think it had happened when he smacked his head on the back of the seat or something, but no, it wasn't going to happen to him.

He reached into his pockets and then the side storage compartments of the car, but for what? He wasn't carrying a gun or a knife so how was he supposed to protect himself from this madman; hit him with the London A-Z or an AA Routeplanner? The killer tried the rear passenger door but it seemed to be stuck, and the more it wouldn't budge, the more the guy hauled at it. He needed to do something and quick!

He undid the seatbelt, pushed away the spent airbags and tried to climb into the front seat. It wasn't easy as both seats were thick and topped with large head restraints, and he was a big man attempting to squeeze through a small space, but somehow he succeeded. No sooner had he taken his place behind the wheel when, in the rear view mirror, he spotted the killer making his way around the back of the car, heading for one of the doors on the undamaged side.

He started the car. The killer was alongside him now, shouting and banging the roof with his fist, his face locked in an angry stare, but he couldn't hear what he was saying for the roar from the car's over-revving engine and the ringing in his ears. He couldn't seem to move the lever out of 'Park'. He finally got it into 'Drive' and shot past Don, who looked up more in surprise than fright, as he had never seen him driving.

He edged past the damaged Toyota and without looking to see if the road was clear, hit the accelerator and sped off down the rain-streaked street.

THIRTY-FIVE

DI Henderson drove slowly through the centre of Henfield, a large village to the north of Brighton. It would be more appropriate to call it a small town as he passed a couple of garages, several pubs and a smattering of small but smart shops, including a bakery, a mini-supermarket and a wine merchant.

'I used to go out with a guy from Henfield once. Had his own place up there,' DS Walters said as they passed a side road.

'It didn't work out?' Henderson asked. 'But don't give me the long version as we're nearly there.'

'It was difficult for us to get together, so it was over before it started. Between the daft hours we work and his commute to and from London on a train that often arrived late, and added to the mix, an unreliable car, trying to meet him became too much hassle.'

'I can see how it might give you a problem. Perhaps you need to date someone near where you live or one of our fine officers at Sussex House.'

'No chance. It's bad enough having to work beside most of them.'

He stopped the car outside a modest semi-detached house in Northcroft, a bit of a come-down from the former marital home in Woodland Drive. He knocked on the door and when it opened, meeting Emily Grant once again reminded Henderson what a fine looking woman she was.

Deep blue eyes complimented a mop of thick, brown hair, cut to shoulder length, and with the shapely figure of a disciplined dieter or a fitness enthusiast. However, the sight of two young Labradors confirmed the svelte shape was likely a function of long walks in neighbouring fields rather than any pounding done on the streets of Henfield or on a running machine at the nearby Leisure Centre.

With the dogs safely locked away in the kitchen, they moved into the lounge. It was a small, cosy room, filled with a few pieces of furniture which might have looked good in the larger room at her old house, but here they dominated.

'If you remember,' Henderson said, 'when we last spoke I said we were looking into Peter's accident because losing two members of the same band so close to one another looked odd...'

'Yes, and you also said Sarah Corbett asked you to look at it again.'

'That's right.'

'She's been here to see me, you know.'

'Oh, has she?'

'Yes. She called me not long after I saw you and said she would like to come and see me. She's a nice woman, genuine. I think she and Pete were only going out for a short time and she feels bereft at losing him so soon afterwards. Perhaps coming to see me added a little more colour to her memories.'

'Was it a difficult meeting?' Walters asked.

She flicked back her hair in what could be considered a suggestive gesture if they weren't discussing the death of her husband and a conversation with his former lover.

'It was less awkward than you might think, as our

marriage was finished and I was ready to move on, although I don't think I could say the same for Pete.'

'Did Sarah leave a happier person?'

'I think so, she hasn't been in contact since. Did she talk to you again?'

'No, I haven't spoken to her since she first approached me.'

'I hope she finds peace.'

'Emily,' Henderson said, 'can you tell me what was the connection between the band and a guy called Mathew Street?'

'God, there's a name I haven't heard for a long time, Mat Street. His connection with the Crows? Let me think, it's been a while.' She stared at the coffee table for a few seconds. 'I don't know if I told you before, but Pete was the only married man in the band, and to make sure he didn't get into any trouble, as if he would, I often joined him on tour.'

'Yes, you did.'

'We travelled all over, to the north of England and parts of Europe, and even went up to your neck of the woods a couple of times. Mat Street was a roadie and general handyman who only joined us for the big tours, but on the side he could get us anything we wanted like cheap booze, fags and illegal magazines, and for me and the other girls, perfume, clothes, dresses and jeans. I don't know where he got it all from, abandoned warehouses he said, but as we didn't have much money at the time, we didn't care.'

'Drugs?'

'Street could supply drugs, but being a rock band, drug dealers were ten-a-penny. Pete, if you can believe it, didn't do drugs. Even then, he was into keeping fit, he had to be, as he was the drummer. He liked a drink and Street could always lay his hands on some pretty strong Russian vodka, Pete's poison at the time.'

'I get the impression Mat did more for the band than booze and drugs.'

'I'm not sure what you mean.'

'I think something was going on between him and the band, something big was being planned, before they split up.'

Henderson was fishing, trying to fill in the gaps Mathew Street had left unsaid.

She shook her head. 'No, I wasn't aware of anything else.'

She looked calm and unruffled by the question, good. It wouldn't do his reputation any good to be thrown out of two houses in the same week.

'You see,' he continued, 'both Mathew Street and Derek Crow—'

'Have you seen Derek? How is he taking this? It must be awful for him to be the last man standing.'

'We interviewed Derek just before we met you at the house in Woodland Drive. He's pretty concerned as you might expect. Who wouldn't be in such circumstances?'

Her face creased with worry. 'I've called him a couple of times but I must go and see him. I can't begin to understand what he must be going through.'

'You sound like you are quite fond of him,' Walters said.

'Do I? I suppose I still am.' She looked over in the direction of a photograph of her and a bloke Henderson assumed to be her new man, standing behind two grown-up kids. 'I think I can say now as Pete's no longer with us, but Derek and I were lovers back then. I would have left Pete if he'd asked me, but he didn't ask and here I am.'

'When we spoke to Mathew Street and Derek, they both became evasive when asked where the guys got the money to start their various businesses. I don't think they got it from being in the band.'

'Why not? They sold plenty of albums and did loads of tours. I should know, I was with them a good part of the time.'

'Frannie Copeland said–'

'Frannie Copeland? I wouldn't believe a thing that thieving shyster said.'

'No?'

'Derek always said he was conning them, keeping back money promoters had paid them, and all the while making them survive on a shoestring. We once did a gig in Preston and I saw the promoter give Frannie a wad of cash. We never saw any of it.'

'Why didn't they sack him?' Walters asked.

'He had them tied up in a water-tight contract, they couldn't get out of it, even if they wanted to.'

'If we stay with the assumption,' Henderson said, 'that they didn't make much money from the music, and why would they when they walked away from their best-selling album, where did they get it from?'

'Now I think about it, you could be right, life with the Crazy Crows was one long party. When you're in your twenties, you don't think who's paying the bills, the hotels, the road crew, the rent of the hall and everything else. I know now the band paid for it, out of their twenty per cent or whatever that mean swine Frannie Copeland was giving them.'

'Peter needed money to set up Grant's.'

'The business will pass on to my daughter Danielle in a few weeks' time, and with luck she'll use some of the profits to keep her mother in the style to which she has become accustomed,' she said smiling, as her eyes roamed her modest surroundings.

Henderson was beginning to lose patience with all this reminiscing and diversion, she was being as evasive as Derek Crow and Mathew Street. It had begun as an innocent question, almost a throwaway to Crow and Street in an attempt to make them open up and reveal a little more of what went on, but the more he probed, the more he realised it was something no one wanted to talk about.

He tried again. 'This is important, Emily. I need to get to the bottom of this, as it might be the reason someone is killing members of the band and we need to stop the same thing happening to Derek. I think the start-up money question might be the key to the whole thing.'

The room went quiet and he could hear one of the dogs moving in its basket and a pigeon cooing in the trees outside. Walters had been with him long enough to know that silences between words were important in giving witnesses time to consider the options, and she wasn't tempted to open her sizeable mouth, even if the oppressive silence was willing her to do so.

Emily sighed as if deciding something. 'It wasn't like Pete turned up one day with a pile of money.'

'No? What was it like, then?'

She looked at him, chewing her lip. 'I suppose now with Pete and Eric dead...I don't know. It might not reflect well on Derek.'

'I don't think he would care, if the choice was life or death.'

'Derek wasn't involved, you have to take my word for it, but you know what newspapers are like nowadays, he would be tarred by association.'

'I don't want to get heavy handed, Emily but I do need to remind you this is a murder investigation. We believe someone murdered your ex-husband and is planning to kill Derek Crow. Isn't this enough incentive for you to try and stop it?'

She took a deep breath. 'Eric, as you no doubt gathered from your other interviews, liked his dope, but in his more lucid moments he could be a bit of a daredevil. The first time the band were in Germany, he met this Dutch guy who could get drugs, not the little packets people like Mathew Street supplied, but big bricks of top quality Lebanese and Afghani hash, LSD by the thousands, and bags of cocaine. With help from Fast Eddie, one of the band's roadies, who's dead now, they packed out a couple of speaker cabinets and became big-time drug importers.'

It was Henderson's turn to take a deep breath.

'Incredible. How many runs did they make?'

'Five, I think. When it started off, they were doing it for personal consumption and selling a little on the side, but soon it developed into a big business. They were making serious money and pretty soon all of them, except Derek were involved.'

'If they were doing so well importing drugs, why did they pack in the band?' Walters asked. 'I imagine if they didn't tour any more, their little business venture would stop too.'

'It would, but they believed Customs were on to them.

At the time, we just thought it was Eric's paranoia, but when another band got stopped at Dover and busted, he got scared and decided to pack it in.'

'I would imagine by then,' Henderson said, 'they'd made enough money for each of them to start something legitimate.'

'That was the plan. Then, with Danny dying and Eric out of his head most of time as he blamed himself for the accident, finishing the band and starting something new became an easy decision.'

'I see.'

'The main reason they got away with it for so long was because Derek didn't know a thing about it. They never involved him as he would have put a stop to it right away if he did. You see, they always made sure he was driving one of the vans when they went through Dover. He did it, bless him, without a care in the world, convinced it was full of nothing but amplifiers, speakers, instruments and a bunch of knackered musicians.'

THIRTY-SIX

With an almost imperceptible nod, Detective Sergeant Willard Jenkinson indicated to DC Huntington to follow him as they made their way down to the interview suite at Snow Hill police station. At this stage, he would often say something encouraging to the young detective he was mentoring about how he hoped the interview would go well and that with some luck another criminal would be taken off the streets, but not today. He couldn't give a toss if it went well or not.

'What do we know about the suspect, sir?' Huntington asked.

'It's in the arrest papers son, read 'em,' he said. He neither wanted conversation nor the observation of social niceties. He banged the interview room door open, making the suspect sitting inside jump, and took a seat. Huntington would do the technology, as sure as hell, he wasn't doing it.

The papers were lying in front of him, but instead he stared at the suspect. In many respects, a sight to cheer the saddest heart, as she was a lovely looking woman with deep brown eyes, the subtlest of makeup, a small button nose and ruby-lips that looked almost kissable. To add to the pleasant vista, she was wearing a bright flowery dress displaying a generous amount of boob, but as this was a serious conversation, he was more pleased to see her face sporting a worried look. Well, no bloody wonder.

'Good afternoon, Mrs Hannah.'

'Good afternoon, detective.' The voice sounded forced-cheery, a result of never having been in police custody, and in his job a suspect without a criminal record was as rare as a carnivorous hen.

'I am Detective Sergeant Willard Jenkinson and this is Detective Constable Bradley Huntington.'

'Pleased to meet you, I'm sure.'

He talked her through the usual admin stuff about the use of recording devices, her right to a lawyer and how she wasn't under arrest, at least not yet. Based on what she said in the next ten minutes, she would either walk free and go home to her house in Farnham, or be locked in a cell awaiting the arrival of Serious Robbery detectives who would cart her off to Paddington Green or some other dungeon.

'If I can make a start, Mrs Hannah. Early this afternoon you entered the premises of bullion dealers, Stevens, Makepeace and Riedel in Hatton Gardens, and informed them you wanted to sell a gold bar. Is this correct?'

'Yes, it is. But I don't see there's anything wrong with doing it, so why was I taken in here and left to freeze for hours in a draughty corridor?'

'I'm getting around to it, have no fear.'

He took a photograph out of a folder and spun it around for her to see. 'Does this look like your gold bar?'

She looked at the picture. 'I suppose so, but it looks like any gold bar. No hang on, it is mine. I recognise the little flag symbol.'

'Can you tell me what you said to the man you spoke to, Mr Jocelyn Stevens, about where you obtained it?'

'I told him and I'm telling you now, it used to belong to my grandmother, a dear woman who died a few months ago. She told me she brought it over from Poland during the war. She said it might be Nazi gold but I'm not sure if that bit's true.'

'You don't sound very Polish to me.'

'I'm second generation British, but our family still observes Polish tradition.'

'Do these traditions involve robbing airlines?'

Her mouth fell open, goldfish-like. Not a good look for such a pretty face. Shortly afterwards, a single word, 'What?' came out.

'Mr Stevens is a cautious man and he knows there is a lot of dodgy gold around. When he spotted the little logo there,' he said pointing at the photograph, 'he decided to look it up. Sorry, if it's not too clear, someone has tried to file it off. Do you know what he found?'

'No, but I'm sure you are about to tell me.'

He liked this part of police work, the reveal, as comedians called it. He waited a second or two before handing her another photograph, not another shiny gold bar, but a close-up of the logo from the first gold bar, blurred and indistinct.

'What's this?'

'The little symbol or flag as you call it, from your gold bar.'

'Oh.'

'If you look closely, it says, 'Suisse' with a little symbol underneath which I'm told is the Swiss flag. Not a polish flag but a Swiss flag. Can you see it?'

'Just about,' she said in a croaky and dry voice. This interview didn't stretch to refreshments.

'Do you want to know something interesting about your gold bar?'

'No.'

He leaned forward. 'This one and a pile of its mates with a value of £20 million at 1989 prices, along with a couple of mill in cash and securities, were all nicked from the Windlass Security depot at Gatwick Airport in August 1989. The gold and boxes containing the securities and cash were about to be loaded onto an AeroSwiss jet for onward transportation to Switzerland when seven robbers attacked them.'

'I don't know anything about the theft of any gold bars. I got this one from my grandmother.'

'So you say but I think you do. Do you know what a kilogram of gold is worth?'

'About thirty-five thousand pounds, the last time I looked.'

'Very good Suzy, I can see you've done your homework. Now do you know the sentence you would receive for stealing or re-setting gold nicked from the AeroSwiss raid? I might add, five Windlass security personnel were hospitalised. One was shot and the others beaten up and sprayed in the face with CS gas.'

'I didn't steal it,' she said, her face red and flustered, 'I tell you, I found it.'

'Ah, I see we've moved on from the benevolence of your dear, departed Polish grandmother to a remarkable lucky find. In which field or woods did you find it, as I think I might be tempted to go out and buy a metal detector?'

'I didn't find it in a field,' she said.

'No? What a disappointment. Where then?'

She sighed the sigh of the defeated; the lady had been rumbled. 'My husband died two weeks ago. I went through his things and found the gold bar in a bag. In fact, I found two. I swear to God it's the truth.'

'This sounds more like it. Tell me about your husband. I've known people who would kill for a lot less than thirty-five grand.'

She scowled, perhaps he needed to tone down the sarcasm a notch or two.

'He died in a car accident almost two weeks ago when his car went out of control and crashed into a lorry. You might have read about it as it was in all the papers. In his younger days, in the eighties, he was the guitarist in a rock group called the Crazy Crows.'

'What was his name?'

'Eric Hannah.'

He turned and looked at Huntington, his researcher of all things arcane and a skilled user of technology, often of the kind he could barely switch on.

'I believe it happened on the A31 near Farnham, sir.'

'Very good, Huntington. Yes, I remember it now, a big blaze that closed the roundabout for hours.' He looked back at the suspect. 'I'm sorry for your loss, Mrs Hannah.'

'Heartfelt I'm sure, but thanks for saying it anyhow.'

In his mind, she was moving away from his initial assumption that she was a fence, to more like the innocent party trying to pick up the pieces after her husband died. His chances of locating a horde of gold would have to wait for another day.

'So,' he said, trying to sound more conciliatory than previous. 'Where do you think your husband obtained these two gold bars?'

'I don't know because he never told me anything about it. You see, I'm his third wife and as I'm a lot younger than him, I wasn't around in his musical days.'

'I guessed as much.'

'I assume he bought it on his travels when he was still playing with the band, or from one of the dodgy characters who used to hang around with them.'

'Maybe he bought it a few months back without your knowledge.'

She shook her head. 'I don't think so. I think he's had it for a long time. See, the only period in his life when he had any money was when he was in the band and just after, and even then, he seemed to spend it just as fast as he was making it.'

'The bullion raid at Gatwick airport was carried out by seven armed men who fired shots into the ceiling as they helped themselves to the goodies being loaded on to a conveyer belt. All seven were captured and since then, served lengthy prison sentences, but the gold has never been recovered. We assumed it was melted down and sold to dodgy bullion dealers. Most of the gang were released in the last couple of years, so you can see why the sudden appearance of one of the bars from the raid interests me.'

'If the men are now out of prison, you would expect to see a few more of them popping up, I would think.'

'You could be right, and maybe I can look forward to more chats like this one in the future, although something tells me they will not be as pretty as you.'

He gathered his papers together and stood. 'Thank you for coming in Mrs Hannah. I do hope we haven't spoiled your day.'

'What? You're not going to charge me?'

'As you said at the start of this interview, you haven't done anything wrong.'

'I can go?'

'Yes, you can, but we might need to talk with you again.'

'Can I keep the gold bar?'

He shook his head; cheeky mare. 'Unfortunately, no. We'll keep this one and send someone over to collect the other one you have in your possession, so do not try to sell it. They don't belong to you or your late husband, but the insurance company covering the security raid loss.'

'I see.'

'It was a pleasure to meet you, Mrs Hannah. DC Huntington will see you out.'

Jenkinson strode back to his desk, whistling a merry tune, but stopped when he realised it was Rihanna, a song playing every hour on Capital Radio. He was forty-five, for God's sake, and any interest in her was only from the waist down and nothing to do with her singing.

He was happy nonetheless, as there was nothing coppers hated more than unfinished business, and who knows, maybe the finder of the missing AeroSwiss gold would get his name in the papers. If that couldn't please him, nothing would.

THIRTY-SEVEN

DI Henderson was seated at the small table in his office with DS Carol Walters facing him. He felt full of enthusiasm to go out and do something, kick in some doors or haul in some witnesses for questioning, but there didn't seem to be anything he could expend his energies on.

They were discussing the interviews with Derek Crow and other associates of the band, the post-mortem results of the three victims and the research done on police computers and the web. Now, forty minutes later, he believed it was time to draw some conclusions.

'I think we have three motives for the murder of the guys in the Crazy Crows,' he said.

'I think so too.'

'Motive One. Somebody, and it might be Mat Street as he might be his uncle or something, is exacting revenge because he blames the Crows for the death of Danny Winter.'

'He might have some justification,' she said, 'because we know Danny and Eric Hannah didn't get on, and the whole purpose of the boat trip in Dorset could have been a ploy for Eric to get rid of Danny.'

'Could be, because at the inquest Barry said he was flat out on the bottom of the boat and so drunk he didn't see or hear what went on. The police and the coroner could

261

only take Eric's word for what happened.'

'Eric said they started larking about and Danny fell in, and Eric wasn't a good enough swimmer to pull him out, even if he could see him, but he couldn't as it was pitch black.'

'Now,' Henderson said, 'if a relative of Danny is doing the killings, why would he hold a grudge for so long? Why do something now and not ten or twenty years ago?'

'I don't know. You would think if this person was hell bent on revenge, he would start killing them after the inquest returned a verdict of accidental death, or after the CPS decided not to look at the case again following a request by Danny's mother.'

'Something must have prevented him taking action sooner. Maybe he was posted abroad with the Army, was under long-term medical care, or he was in jail.'

'Or after some new information came to light.'

'Good point, but we'll explore the jail angle first. Let's take a look at Street's record again.'

She rummaged through a large spread of papers and reports scattered over the table and the floor, but soon found what she was looking for.

'So,' Henderson said, 'he went to jail for a post office robbery in 1989, not long after the Crows split up.'

'It keeps him away from the band after the inquest as he was on remand awaiting trial.'

'Right. He received a twelve-year sentence for the robbery and while in jail, he received another fifteen for the AeroSwiss robbery at Gatwick Airport and only saw the light of day six months ago.'

'So if it is him,' Walters said, 'the only window of opportunity open to him was in the last six months.'

'Moving on, Motive Two. We know the band imported drugs hidden inside speaker cases, as Emily Grant told us, and this piece of private enterprise we think provided them with the capital to start their various businesses. Now, in the course of drug smuggling, is it possible they fell out with one of the sellers in Holland or Germany, or maybe one of the buyers here in the UK?'

'If so,' she said, 'we're back to the old chestnut. Why wait so long to kill them?'

'Maybe they were locked up or hiding out abroad to avoid arrest, plenty do. Although I do agree with you, it's a long time to wait.'

'You're telling me.'

'Motive Three,' Henderson said, 'something happened to give Mat Street the additional 15-year stretch. What caused it and what if he blames the Crows?'

She rummaged through her fire-hazard of a paper mess once again. A moment or two later she said, 'The police report at the time, said...ah yes, here we are. Superintendent Davis of the Met Police said and I quote, 'as a result of a tip-off from a member of the public, we raided a number of addresses and arrested seven individuals in connection with the AeroSwiss robbery at Gatwick Airport in 1989. None of the gold, cash or securities has yet been recovered."

'You're right. Somebody tipped them off.'

'Now if it was one of the Crows, what did Street do to them to make them so vindictive?'

Henderson scratched his chin, thinking, 'We don't know and Street isn't likely to tell us, but no matter how we cut it, he's still our best and only candidate. Talking of Mat Street, how's the surveillance going?'

She picked up her phone from the desk. 'Shall I call and get an update?'

'Might as well.'

Henderson had requested three two-man teams, the minimum size for any surveillance operation, to watch Street, but then they were dealing with a pensioner suffering from a heart complaint, and not a keep-fit fanatic who would drag them all over town. To his surprise, DCI Edwards signed off his request for manpower without a demand for further justification, perhaps feeling guilty for previously booting him off the case. Just as well, as putting tabs on their only suspect, one who made an unlikely candidate for carrying out three cleverly executed murders, wouldn't stand up to much scrutiny.

He made the call as he believed whoever was behind the killings, either as paymaster or perpetrator, needed to make their move on Derek Crow soon. Derek was edgy and considering moving from an accessible town house in St. John's Wood to a gated community in Surrey or Essex, according to some newspaper reports. In addition, the Prime Minister was facing some awkward questions in the House about what was being done to protect his favourite businessman, and it wouldn't be long before he instructed the Secret Service to watch over him.

Walters placed her phone down on the table. 'Nothing much to report. Today's sum total is one trip outside to put on a bet, drink a pint and buy a newspaper. Oh, life is so boring when you're old.'

'It'll happen to you one day.'

'Yeah, but I'll be kicking up fine Caribbean sand as I walk along the beach to a bar for my morning piña colada, not freezing my chilblains off in windy Eastbourne.'

'On a police pension? Dream on, sister. In essence, we've got three motives and only one suspect,' Henderson said. 'Where do we go from there if Street turns out to be a dead end?'

'Well, for sure we can't wait for whoever it is to kill Derek Crow, if we don't want to lose our jobs and be vilified in all the papers.'

'I think we got everything out of Emily Grant we could,' he said, 'and Sam Schweinsteiger and Frannie Copeland were too much on the periphery to know in detail what was going on. This leaves us Derek Crow and Mat Street.'

'What about the road crew?' Walters asked. 'Emily said a couple of them were involved in the drug shipments.'

'We'll target them if Street draws a blank, but I think they'll know a lot about drug shipments but not much about anything else.'

'It might be enough if our perp is amongst them.'

'Could be, in that case, we'll need to talk to Emily and Derek again and expand our list of suspects and witnesses.' He looked at his watch. It was after six. 'That can be tomorrow's job. You wanted to get off early didn't you? Something about a hot date or was it a hot bath?'

'I do go out on dates now and again, you know,' she said, gathering her papers together, not an easy job. 'It's keeping them that's my problem.'

'I'm sure George could find you a spare holding cell if you really want to make sure they don't run away.'

'I might take him up on it.' She stood, a thick wad of papers clutched to her chest. 'See you tomorrow, boss.'

'It's Saturday, so don't expect to see me in here until ten. Goodnight, Carol.'

Henderson walked back to his desk and for the next half hour worked his way through thirty-odd emails, leaving another forty unread. His penalty for spending so much time out of the office this week.

In addition, he was not sure what to do about Rachel. She was making noises about the cost of running two houses and how she didn't see him for days on end when he worked on a big case. If that wasn't a prelude to, 'let's move in together' he didn't know anything about women.

What she didn't realise, was his flat was his oasis of calm during intensive work periods and the last thing he needed at ten-thirty at night, when he was tired and in dire need of a shower, was her standing at the door asking where the hell he'd been.

His phone rang.

'Henderson.'

'Evening sir, Phil Bentley here.'

'How's our Mr Street getting on? I suppose the lack of activity is allowing you to catch up on gossip and create some of your own.'

'We are sir, but I thought I should let you know, our target's on the move.'

Henderson sat up, pen poised over a note pad.

'What happened?'

'A large blacked-out Mercedes van turned up, one with a big yellow lightning slash down one side. A guy got out and went into Street's house and few minutes later they both came out.'

'Are you following them?'

'Yes sir, Sally Graham's at the wheel.'

'You won't lose them, then.'

'No, sir.'

'It was a statement, Phil, not a question. I know how fast Sally drives.'

'I realise that now from personal experience, but when the van accelerated away from the lights in Eastbourne, the engine roared as if there was something big under the bonnet, so if he did put his foot down, even Sally couldn't catch him. This time, we're in luck, as he's on the A27 heading west towards Brighton and there's a lot of evening traffic, so he couldn't get away from us even if he wanted to.'

Henderson knew the road well, he drove it only last week when he and Walters were in Eastbourne talking to Mathew Street. For the most part, it was single carriageway, but when it moved closer to Brighton, it turned dual. Even then it was still easy to follow a car without losing them as the road was often so busy with traffic there was no room to overtake.

'Phil, call me when he gets closer to Brighton for an update, or if he turns off the A27. Am I clear?'

'No problem, sir.'

Henderson shut down his computer, grabbed his jacket and ran down the corridor, but before heading downstairs to the car park, he returned to his desk. Street was travelling towards Brighton, although equally, he could also be heading for Worthing, Southampton or Penzance, but Brighton stuck in his mind as he remembered Street telling him of a son who lived there. In truth, he'd only told him he had a son, a researcher in Sussex House had found out his name and address. Now where did he put that piece of paper?

A couple of minutes later, he strode towards his car, the address of Neil Street's house implanted in his brain.

He started the car, retuned the radio to Southern FM as Walters had been fiddling with it again, and edged out of the Sussex House car park.

The phone rang: Phil Bentley.

'We're coming into Brighton now, sir. We're just passing Falmer Railway Station and the Amex Stadium.'

'Ok. Do the same again Phil, call me in five minutes or earlier if he turns off.'

'Sir.'

Clear of the car park, Henderson headed for Centurion Road. He didn't need the sat-nav as it was in the same part of the city as his apartment in Seven Dials. Even though Neil Street's property was half a dozen streets away and probably worth as much as his flat, it was in the posher-sounding Clifton Hill district.

He didn't often elbow his way into a surveillance operation, unless what they were doing put the team in mortal danger or they needed additional bodies to help arrest a dangerous criminal, but this change in Mathew Street's behaviour intrigued him. It seemed uncharacteristic for an elderly man who didn't go out much to associate with the owner of a souped-up van and travel with him to Brighton, or wherever he was going, and he wanted to see where they ended up for himself.

He couldn't park on Centurion Road as there wasn't a space, and ended up in the street parallel to it. The last phone call from Phil Bentley told him the van had turned up Trafalgar Street, and as he suspected, it was coming towards him. A few minutes later he spotted it. The van drove past his car and far from searching for a parking space as he had done, it reversed into what he realised was the back garden of Neil Street's house in Centurion Road.

He watched as Street and his slightly taller but stockier companion made their way to the house, unlocked the door and walked in. A few minutes later Phil and Sally's unmarked car drew alongside his. He wound down the window.

'Evening sir. I take my hat off to you, you were right. They were heading to his son's house.'

'Well done to you two for keeping tabs on them and not losing them; it was only a hunch. The two men have gone inside the house.'

'Parking around this area is a total nightmare. I think we'll try further up the hill towards the Dials and keep our eye on the house on foot.'

'Don't bother, Phil. You and Sally are off shift at ten, are you not?'

'Yes sir, we are.'

'It's almost eight now. I'll do the next couple of hours until Terry and Dave come on.'

'Are you sure?'

'Go, Phil, before I change my mind.'

'Thank you, sir, but I do hope you've brought a good book with you, you'll need it with this guy.'

THIRTY-EIGHT

Derek Crow yawned and stretched. At least he could stretch out here in the front seat, because in the rear, the car didn't offer any leg room at all. In the wake of the Jaguar crash and his rapid escape, his insurance company had given him this poxy Vauxhall until his own car was fixed, but at least it wouldn't be his transport for much longer.

'Did you speak to the police?' Don Levinson, his driver and all-round protector, asked.

'What about? Leaving the scene of an accident and being in charge of a car while being useless at driving?'

'No, because I know you sorted that out with the police and they've decided not to take it further. About this meeting Paterson set up with your old mate, Mat Street, a known criminal.'

'No, Street was precise. No police or the meeting's off, and I need this meeting.'

'Yeah, but if this guy's cosha, he knows the identity of someone out there who's gone and killed three of your buddies. You're gonna need to involve the police.'

'Don, you don't know him. He's a wily old fox and will only tell me something if it's on his terms. If not, he'll shut up and tell me nothing, even if he was being tortured.'

'He would if I was in charge of doing it.'

'I'll wait and hear what he's got to say. If he's only got a name, it's not enough. I'm going to need a lot more evidence before I take it to the police. Don't forget, the cops were the ones who said the guys died in accidents, and they're going to be embarrassed, not to mention mighty pissed-off, if I tell them something different. So I need to be sure of my ground.'

'I guess you do,' Levinson said. 'In some ways, I can understand why Street is so wary of cops. He's been in and out of nick so much he must be shit-scared of doing something wrong that might send him back.'

'It isn't his only worry.'

'No? What else?'

'Did you see the article in the paper the other day about one of the gold bars from a robbery at Gatwick twenty-odd years ago turning up?'

'What, this Gatwick?' Levinson said, laughing as they drove past the junction for the airport and continued heading south.

'Yep, at the same Gatwick, a gang of seven villains including our Mr Street, robbed a security company who were in the process of shipping gold and money to a bank in Switzerland. The boys have all done time but none of the gold has been recovered.'

'Until now.'

'Until now, but this is the first bar to turn up.'

'So, you think he's worried in case there's a shake-down of everybody in the gang as they try and find out where the rest of it is hidden? I would if I was a cop.'

'Right.'

'So, the cops are probably out there looking for him.'

'Yeah,' Crow said, 'and maybe it's the reason he's moved out of Eastbourne, to get away for a while until the heat cools down.'

'Sure, but once he's got his thieving mitts on all the money you've got in that bag, he can go where the hell he bloody well likes.'

'He can't go far enough away for my liking.'

Crow slumped down in the uncomfortable seat and stared out of the window. He didn't know if he was doing the right thing but in his experience it was better doing something than sitting at home, twiddling your thumbs and waiting for events to happen all around you.

Street was a street hustler and would do anything for money, including selling out his mates. Derek felt confident if Street knew the identity of the person or persons behind the killings, the lure of fifty grand would be enough to put all thoughts of loyalty, trust and camaraderie behind him.

Fifteen minutes later they reached the outskirts of Brighton, and if his driver had managed to program the sat-nav properly, it would now point them towards Seven Dials. He knew Brighton well and the Dials was a place where he once stayed when he was younger, but he didn't have a clue how to get there now.

'What's the plan when we arrive?' Levinson asked.

'Plan? What plan? Why do we need one? I'm meeting an old mate. We talk, we parley; I get the information, he gets the money, and I get the hell out.'

'I'd like to make sure you get out of there in the same shape you went in.'

He laughed. 'He's a sixty-seven-year-old man for God's sake, what sort of trouble is he likely to cause? Beat me to death with his pension book?'

'All the same, I'm responsible for your safety, Derek. He might have a piece. He's a convicted armed robber for

Christ's-sake.'

'I'm touched by your concern for my welfare, Don, but I think I'll be fine.'

'Think on. He might not be the one carrying out the killings, but he might be sitting in his gaff with the three or four heavies who are.'

'I've thought about that too, but Paterson assures me Street keeps himself to himself. He couldn't rustle up anything heavier than a couple of eight-stone shandy drinkers and frankly, I defer to his better judgement when it comes to the assessment of old cons.'

'What say I give you fifteen minutes and if you don't come out, I kick the door in?'

He shook his head. 'No, don't do that. We might be nattering like a couple of old maids and quaffing some decent malt, and then you come in with your size-fifteens and smash his door into a thousand pieces. He'd probably get mad and stick a kitchen knife into your chest and I would never be welcome to darken his threshold again, would I?'

'Suppose not, but would it bother you?'

'Let's say, if I'm not out in twenty minutes, you phone me and if I don't pick up, you come in, but bloody well knock first.'

'Ok.'

It was good to see Brighton again and it brought back many great memories. Preston Park where he used to kick a ball with a few mates, the seafront where he'd been in a few fights when he was a member of a teenage gang supporting the Albion, and the station, his escape route to London when Brighton became boring, or if somebody was out to get him.

There were more shops around Seven Dials than he remembered, and many with an ethnic flavour. It was not unlike the streets near his house in London where he was never far from Halal food shops, Lebanese restaurants and Polish newsagents offering copies of *Gazeta Wyborcza*.

They couldn't find a parking space near Street's house which gave his driver an excuse to drive past and take a good look, 'reconnoitre' in squaddie parlance.

'I can't see any souped-up BMW's or blacked-out SUVs,' Levinson said, his expression tense.

'Is it a good sign?'

'Yep, a lot of gangsters and drug dealers use them. They're a dead giveaway.'

'Oh. Now I know.'

'Parking's bloody awful around here.'

'It's what the locals get for electing a Green Council, and the PM hates them more than the Trots in his party. They hate cars. They'll be making everybody grow vegetables next.'

'I'll reverse along the road and drop you off outside his gaff and then I'll go find a space. If it's ok with you?'

'Fine.'

'Remember Derek,' he said when he'd stopped outside Street's door, 'twenty minutes max and you better answer the phone or I'm coming in.'

'Got it, captain,' he said, offering a mock salute, making Levinson frown. He stepped out of the car and slammed the door shut.

His knock was answered by Mat Street and after Crow got over the momentary shock of seeing how much the man had aged, moving from a face that looked like a mottled grape to closely resembling a walnut, they shook hands. 'Hello Mathew, good to see you.'

'Good to see you too, Derek, come on in.'

He sat on the settee while Street took the armchair. Street had to be a bit deaf as it took him a few seconds to realise the television was blaring behind him, some bloke with perfect white teeth cheering on two contestants pushing large balls up a slope. He and his wife usually sat down for dinner at this time on a Friday night, so he didn't have a clue what the programme was called or where its entertainment value lay. Street lifted the remote and turned the set off.

'So how are you, Derek? Long time no see.'

'Indeed it is. I'm fine, how's yourself?'

'I got me a dickey heart but as long as I keep taking the tablets, I'm ok. Other than that, they say I'll live to a hundred. Right,' he said, slapping his hands down on the arms of the chair, 'what can I get you to drink?'

'What have you got?'

'Scotch, vodka and beer, I think.'

'Scotch is good.'

'How do you take it?'

'With just a little water.'

He rose from the chair, a tad sprightly for a man with a bad heart, but as an expert on petrol, diesel and 28-second kerosene, Derek didn't know much about cardiac pulmonary disease, atherosclerosis or angina. In fact he was still recovering from the shock of seeing him. His memory harked back twenty-odd years when he'd sported a tousled mop where a sparrow could happily nest and not the sparse back-comb of today, he'd been fuller in the figure and not a nine-stone featherweight, and his face had been chubby and smiling and not sullen, weather-beaten and as craggy as a Shar Pei dog.

Ah well, age came to us all, especially if so much time was spent in the unhealthy environment of HM Prisons and eating such awful food. He made a mental note to have his health checked, not because he was worried about getting old, but if there was a choice, he wanted to do so gracefully.

For a short-term hideaway, his little Brighton house was well-appointed with magazines on the table, pictures on a bookcase and ornaments dotted around the room, as if the occupants were off on holiday, and not a house used for short-term lets. There wasn't much of a view out front, parked cars and houses across the road, and out back it was dark and he couldn't see anything at all.

'Here you are Derek,' Street said handing him a glass, 'your health.'

'Your health Mathew,' he said downing a gulp. It caught the back of his throat, which he put down to it being a cheap blend, as over the years his palate had become accustomed to twelve-year-old malts like Ardmore, but this stuff didn't half light a fire under his shirt.

'Whose place is this?' he said after recovering the power of speech.

'It belongs to my son. He's away with his wife, trying to sort out a rocky marriage.'

'Where did they go?'

'Why, are you heading the same way yourself?'

'Ha, it's too early to be thinking about anything like that. We've only been married five years.'

'Is this the second or third missus you're on?'

'Give me a break, Mathew. It's only my second. The

way things are going, there won't be another.'

'They all say the same at some time or other.' He lifted his glass. 'Let's not be cynical, not tonight. Here's to a long and happy marriage.'

'I'll drink to that. A long and happy marriage.'

Street began to describe the place in the New Forest where his son had gone, and Derek was sure he knew it but somehow his brain didn't seem to be joining the dots together with its usual alacrity. Street's face shifted in and out of focus, making him think the electricity was on the blink or the whisky was stronger than the stuff he was used to; he felt hot.

He rested his head on the sofa and closed his eyes. He could hear voices, as if there was more than one person in the room, but it was too much effort to open his eyes and check. If it was Don, he didn't hear the door being kicked in, or his regimental bark, ordering everyone to lie down with their hands on their heads.

Five minutes or maybe half an hour had elapsed, he couldn't be sure, when strong hands gripped his shoulders and lifted him to his feet and he began to move. It had to be a pair of paramedics, here to take him to hospital and treat him for this strange affliction, making him feel he'd contracted a mysterious tropical disease or his brain was experiencing a stroke.

The paramedics seemed to be taking him on a longer walk than the short hop to the front door, where he assumed the ambulance would be parked. The way he felt now, what did he know and what the hell did he care?

THIRTY-NINE

DC Phil Bentley had told DI Henderson he would need a book to while away the time while watching Mathew Street, but that was before it turned dark. Now, he couldn't read a book or a newspaper even if he had one, but there was enough light for him to see Mat Street and his companion coming out of the door at the back of the house in Centurion Road. To Henderson's surprise, they were carrying a man between them as if he was drunk.

Street's mate opened the rear doors of the van and the two men eased the drunk inside, not an easy thing to do, as he was a big man and Street was smaller and not as strong as his companion. The doors slammed shut and after giving one another a high five for a job well done, the two men climbed into the front seats and seconds later, the engine of the van fired up.

If they intended going back to Eastbourne, he would follow, and let the next two-man surveillance team already down there take on the night shift. If the plan was to go somewhere else, he would follow as the strange threesome rattled his 'curiosity' antenna and convinced him something was going on.

It didn't take long to discover they weren't heading back to Eastbourne, as after cutting through Seven Dials they drove west along the Old Shoreham Road. Bentley had told him the van was powerful, and he could hear and see it was, but the driver did him a favour and stuck to the speed limits. He suspected it was not out of consideration for their hapless passenger in the back, who wasn't, as far as he knew, strapped in, but they were travelling though suburban Brighton and Hove and local cops were good at nabbing the inattentive and the reckless who strayed above the thirty-mile-an-hour speed limit.

He needed to be careful too, as traffic had thinned out from earlier with no slow-moving streams of cars to hide behind, but with the added advantage of darkness. There were side roads every thirty or forty yards on the right, leading to housing estates creeping towards the foothills of the South Downs, and to the left, down to the sea. The next big towns up ahead were Shoreham and Worthing, and more by luck than judgement, he'd recently filled the car with petrol. If they decided to travel to Portsmouth or the New Forest, he was ready to follow; but he wasn't sure if he fancied a trip to Dorset or Cornwall and watching them enjoying their holidays.

He slowed as they approached the crossroads and traffic lights at Boundary Road, and just then, the left-side indicator of the van started to flash, forcing Henderson to jump a red light to keep up. They drove down Station Road, and after rumbling over the railway tracks at Portslade Station, came to a halt at the traffic lights opposite Shoreham Harbour.

He wound down the window to clear his head and caught the familiar smells: a salty tang of fried food and seaweed, with overtones of diesel oil, smoke and sawn timber, reflecting the industrial nature of this part of town.

He was surprised to be here as he expected the van to turn off into any one of the many small streets around the area, as they led to numerous cheap hotels, seedy commercial premises and oil-stained garages, the ideal stomping ground for an old con, his partner and a drunk friend. When the lights changed, they turned left and headed back into Brighton.

Henderson banged his fist on the steering wheel in frustration. They must have seen him and were toying with him, leading him a merry dance and hoping he would get bored and go home but in a few moments, he realised his mistake. The van stopped at the traffic lights leading into Shoreham Harbour.

Henderson needed to be extra careful here, as it was Friday night and no one in their right mind, employed by one of the myriad of grain merchants, metal-crushing businesses, haulage companies and timber warehouses would be within a mile of the place. They would be either curled up on the settee with a six-pack of lager after a stomach-bloating curry, or well on their way to getting plastered in any one of the hundreds of pubs between here and Brighton, mistaking the ugly girl at the bar for the woman of their dreams.

His knowledge of Shoreham Harbour was as good as any of the residents in the area; it was large and split into two parts, called the West Harbour and the East Harbour. The other large docks in the South, Southampton and Dover handled freight and passenger ships, but Shoreham was an industrial harbour and only dealt with smaller and lighter ships, transporting grain, timber and other loose materials between the UK and Europe.

The traffic lights changed and the van, with Henderson following some way behind, drove into the harbour. He passed a sign for Hove Lagoon where he'd once completed a windsurfing course, meaning they were heading into the East Harbour, the lights of the shore slowly diminishing in his rear view mirror. To the left was the sea, glistening cold in the moonlight, and to the right and behind yet more heavy industrial sites, the dark waters of the canal, a calm inlet where ships could dock to unload precious cargos, protected from the swell of the tide and the rocking of the wind.

Close to a skip-collection business, the public road ended and a private road began, replete with a forbidding sign designed to halt ordinary folk who didn't possess a port identity card, police warrant card or were not sitting behind the wheel of an ambulance or fire engine. At the top of a rise, the silos of Southern Grain Merchants reflected eerily over the waters of the canal. He passed the site at a slow speed and at the back of the car park and partly-hidden by shadows, he spotted the black van.

He stopped, killed the lights and reversed into the site, not taking his eyes off the van. He saw no movement but kept well away and drove into a gap between two buildings, making sure the car was parked out of sight and facing the right way to make a speedy getaway. He got out of the car and set off on foot.

He approached the van and could see the front seats were empty. He moved to the back door and listened for a few moments but couldn't hear any signs of life inside. He tapped quietly on the door with his knuckles, but still heard nothing. He tried the handle and opened the door but the van was bare; no passengers and no paralytic drunk.

Sticking close to buildings, he only shifted between them when satisfied no one was lurking around the corner. Set back from the water's edge, the grain silos reared up like mythical giants, small and insignificant from the shore, but huge and foreboding close-up.

Knowing Brighton as he did, he wouldn't be surprised if stoned druids came down here once a year to celebrate the summer solstice, mistaking the strange construction for Sussex's answer to Stonehenge. The buildings closer to the canal were squat and dark, offices rather than warehouses, and as he passed them, he peered inside, trying to spot the slightest flicker of light or the merest hint of movement.

Approaching the canal's edge, he edged around the corner of the last building, and up ahead saw the dark, looming presence of a ship. Moving closer, he could read the name, *Baltic Star*, although the bright blue star emblem looked faded with rust, which continued in a ragged line like a drip down to the waterline.

It was docked beside the grain silos and it didn't take the detective skills of Poirot to determine it was likely a grain carrier and bringing wheat, oats or barley to or from the UK and the Baltic states. This area of the dock was lit, not much but enough for security personnel to ensure nothing was being stolen. It begged the question, where were the security staff? But if something bad was about to go down here, Henderson didn't want some spotty, overweight oik sticking his oar in or ending up at the bottom of the canal.

He searched the buildings lining the docks, an easy job as darkness would highlight the faintest sliver of light inside, but he found no trace of Street or his companions. This left only one logical conclusion, which he knew as soon as he saw it: they were on the ship. He groaned.

Boats like this were narrow, cramped and full of equipment and tools designed to injure or be dropped by the careless. It would be a hard place to move around without being spotted and a difficult place to escape from if he was.

The gangplank creaked and moaned despite his best efforts, making sure everyone aboard would now be alerted to his presence, making him feel even more exposed. Close-up, the ship wasn't as big as it looked from the dock and would be dwarfed by any half-decent-sized cruise ship or cross-channel ferry, but unlike a passenger vessel, most of the capacity of this one, would be given over to the hold.

Walking towards the crew quarters, the ship felt deserted, which was just as well as he didn't know who would be more surprised if he bumped into a large Latvian with his pecker out, doing his best to lift the level of the canal. Perhaps Street had slipped some largesse into the captain's palm to give him and his boys a free night on the town, or they were all down in the galley having a party. The second option made him wince but a little voice was telling him this was foolish as he couldn't see sights or sounds of the crew, and it was being shouted down by another voice called curiosity.

By accident, as ships like this did not have a little map pinned to the wall as they did on cross-Channel ferries, he found the galley. To him, the word conjured up a vision of the one aboard his own boat, *Mingary*, a two-burner hob, a tiny fridge and an oven suitable for cooking nothing bigger than a Guinea Fowl, but this place was on a different scale and would not shame a works canteen or a small school. He could see a full range of modern kitchen appliances, cupboards brimming with pots and crockery and plenty of places for diners to sit. Next door in the sleeping area, were books and magazines, all in a language he couldn't understand but his best guess would be Russian.

In the background, the ship creaked, squeaked and groaned as it pulled on its mooring, the hull stretching and contracting with the changing temperature, and the current in the canal swishing water against the dock and slapping the sides of the ship. With this level of ambient noise, it was little wonder no one came out to enquire why he was climbing the ship's gangplank, either that or no one else was on board.

Listening hard, he could hear another sound lurking there, a low humming. It might be the electricity generator used for lighting the ship or running the air-conditioning, but even though the fridges and freezers were all working and the corridors lit, the air felt hot and stale. In which case, the noise wasn't an air-con system for the crew, but one for the cargo to stop it rotting. It didn't matter if the crew sweated and sweltered through a Baltic summer, God help them if they didn't deliver the cargo in tip-top condition.

He moved further down the corridor where he noticed an improvement in the decor with better lighting, the doors and fittings had fewer scuff marks and scratches, and the floor was covered in a smarter looking material, making him think it was the captain's quarters. He came across what looked like a small dining room, and slipped inside for a breather. Furnished with a table and a couple of cabinets, it looked more spacious than the crowded communal table and benches he'd left behind in the galley area, and not a bad place to be during a long sea voyage.

At the far side of the room and on top of a cabinet, a silver tray with half a dozen small glasses and a bottle of vodka. Curious to discover if Eastern Europeans really did drink high-proof alcohol, or it was a rumour put about by Russians to justify boorish behaviour, he walked over to have a look and maybe try a little taste. He reached out for the bottle and stopped. He heard voices and instinctively ducked down beside the cabinet.

It took him a few seconds to realise the voices were coming not from out in the corridor, as he first assumed, but from the room next door. He stood and reached for the handle of the dining room door, intending to move outside and see if he could get any closer, when he realised he was in an adjoining room. Standing on tip-toes, he could see inside the other room by peering through a small gap at the top of the separating door.

There were times when being a lanky six-foot-two could be a royal pain in the arse, like trying to sleep in a standard-sized bed in a budget hotel, or flying in an aeroplane with seats designed for a slim, five-foot teenager, but at times like this, it was a Godsend.

He had a good view inside the other room and to his utter shock, there was Derek Crow, bound to a chair, his face covered in blood.

FORTY

Don Levinson was well agitated and when this happened, somebody usually got hurt. He waited twenty minutes outside Mat Street's house in Brighton and as agreed, he called Derek, but the call defaulted to voicemail. He was not an impetuous man, a comment Derek would dispute, and so rather than rushing over to the door and sticking his boot into it, as he'd first suggested, he rang the doorbell. When the door didn't open, he dialled Derek's number but with the same negative result.

He lifted the letter box and listened but couldn't hear the sound of people talking and moving, or the bloody annoying Ride of the Valkyries ringtone on Derek's mobile phone. Feeling like a Peeping Tom, he peered through the front window but his heart sank when he realised neither Derek nor anyone else was sitting inside.

His Special Forces training bawled in his ear, 'Kick the Fucking Door In!' He turned around. It looked a compact little street and any one of half a dozen neighbours would be only too happy to lift the phone and call the bizzies, and he was sure a few of them had clocked his odd behaviour by now and were watching him or jotting down the 'incident' in their notebooks. Walking quickly, as if he knew which way to go, he turned into the path leading to the back garden. He saw only one doorbell on Street's house, a sign to him that his son owned the whole house and it hadn't been converted to flats, as he didn't fancy wandering into the garden and meeting a dozen half-dressed students enjoying a foam party.

The back door stood at the top of a couple of steps, exposing him to all and sundry who might be looking out their back windows or walking past, but at least it was dark and he didn't have a security light above his head. Using the width of the step, he charged forward and rammed the door with his shoulder. To his complete surprise, it gave way without trouble and he almost sprawled head-first over the kitchen floor. A quick inspection of the door confirmed wet rot in the door frame, the bloody cheapskates.

He didn't need to be quiet as his ungainly entry had made his presence known to anyone inside, and the noise he made was an Army tactic used to scare the occupants and to make them think there were two or three other people with him. The downstairs area was empty, and without hesitation, and with the voice of his former RSM ringing in his head, 'The bastard who hesitates is fucking dead,' he charged upstairs. One by one he shoved open bedroom and bathroom doors but found nothing.

He headed downstairs and spotted a door under the stairs and was surprised to find it led to a basement, as the house looked too small to have one. The footprint of the house wasn't large and neither was the basement, and so it was filled with only a couple of bikes, a spare bed and a few boxes.

Now if he was a titty sucker, and there were plenty of them around, even in the Army, this was the time when he would break down and blubber, as he could see his job, his credibility, and his future prospects as a personal protection specialist all go up in a puff of artillery smoke.

He straightened his shoulders. This was not going to happen as Don Levinson was made of tougher stuff, one of the reasons they made him Captain. Instead of whimpering like a reality show contestant who'd just received severe criticism from a judge, he grabbed a seat in the living room and sat down to think.

Given the complete absence of expected personnel, it was safe to assume Derek had been kidnapped by the criminal Mathew Street and one or more of his accomplices, and taken to a place of their choosing, to be tortured, killed or held for ransom. He was convinced this was the case because if they'd instead popped out for a pint or were walking down the road munching a take-away Shish Kebab, Derek would have answered his phone or called him. Derek knew if Don said he would come to the door in twenty minutes, he would do so.

Ipso facto, this little episode was not some spur-of-the-moment jape, dreamed up for a laugh after one-too-many tinctures or a puff at the happy-baccy, but a well-planned and a bloody well-executed snatch. If all his assumptions were correct, the only thing left to determine was, where had they taken him?

Think Don, think. He knew this house was being used only as a bolt-hole for Street, as he owned a house in Eastbourne. If anything was written down or he'd received a glossy brochure of the castle-cum-dungeon or caravan-cum-prison where Derek was being held, Street wouldn't know the good places in this house to hide it, providing of course, he didn't take the bloody thing with him. He started to formulate a plan. He would take this place apart room by room and find an address, letter or photograph, anything to give him a clue, any clue, as he sure didn't have one now. He hoped to God it didn't sit on a computer, as kicking in doors and interrogating subjects was meat and drink to a man like him, but the one thing he hated more than the Taliban was computers.

He would first concentrate his search in this room, Street's bedroom, and finish with the kitchen. He felt sure Street would keep anything important close to hand, especially if he was nervous about a visit from the bizzies. With the methodical approach of a man with dozens of house searches in numerous towns and villages in Afghanistan under his belt, he began to search.

After five minutes he realised most of the stuff he found didn't belong to a sixty-seven-year-old man whose main interests were likely to be beer, right-wing politics and the weather, but a young couple with a couple of kids. He didn't know any old geezer who shopped at Next, did a bit of hair styling on the side and owned a brilliant collection of *Top Gear* magazines. This place reminded him of one of the apartments he and his ex-girlfriend, Elaine, used to rent in the Lake District when they went hill walking. He remembered how strange it felt to be surrounded by someone else's taste in CDs, DVDs and books.

He finished the search, moved to the door and took a last look, his eyes scanning across the room as if wearing a head camera, looking for anything odd or out of place. He spotted something in such an obvious place he felt stupid for missing it the first time and almost punched himself for the error. Tucked behind the clock on the mock-fireplace, he could see a small pile of mail.

He picked them up and one by one flicked through. He found utility bills, adverts for a pizza delivery service and unopened letters addressed to Neil and Angela Street, he guessed Mat's son and daughter in-law. At the back he lifted out a folded sheet of A4 paper. It was a print-out of an email message sent to Mathew Street from someone called Malcolm Richards at Sussex Grain Ltd.

He read it, taking care over each word, feeling like a hard-pressed detective holding a clue, crucial to cracking the case, but he still didn't like looking through other people's stuff.

> *Mat,*
>
> *The Baltic Star is due into harbour this Friday at four. It'll be loaded with wheat and at five when we're finished, we'll take the ship's crew down the pub. If everyone turns up for work on Monday morning and we don't need to go out looking for them, they'll depart for Tallinn mid-morning.*
>
> *I persuaded Lenny the security guard to come down to the Propeller with us and I'll make sure he stays even if it means spiking his drink, ha, ha - the old git doesn't need an excuse to drink. Hope you sort out your problem mate, but don't leave a bloody mess.*
>
> *See ya,*
> *Malc*

He read it again and stood for a moment, thinking. He always did this, even in the heat of battle, as he needed to be confident the information he was about to use would move the fight forward and was not the fruits of wishful thinking or clutching the only straw left in the basket. Confident it was the real deal and not a ruse or diversionary tactic, designed to fool a harassed personal protection specialist, he pulled out his phone and used it to look up Sussex Grain.

The company was based at Shoreham Harbour, and just to confirm, he searched for the *Baltic Star*. This took a little longer but finally he found a web site tracking merchant shipping movements to and from the UK, and it confirmed the *Baltic Star* had indeed docked at Shoreham Harbour this morning. Yet again, the amount of information he could glean from the web amazed him, as he was a 'touch-it, feel-it, kick-it' sort of a guy and suspicious of computer geeks and their knowledge and nerdy ways; come to think of it, he didn't like any kind of geek.

One day, he thought, as he strode back to the car, technology would be so advanced wars would be fought by computers and younger guys than him hoping for a career in the Armed Services would be sorely disappointed. Even now, the RAF flew drones over Syria and Iraq, flown by pilots who might never fly a real aircraft. In his mind, it was only a matter of time before armies of robots were deposited on battlefields and programmed to fight other robot armies or attack a town.

For the moment though, he would be delighted to have his finger on the trigger of a Predator drone equipped with Hellfire missiles. Its first target would be to find Mathew Street, then he would ram one of its lethal projectiles right up his arse.

FORTY-ONE

From his vantage position in the neighbouring cabin, DI Henderson watched as Mathew Street paced up and down the cabin in the *Baltic Star*. He didn't look like a sixty-seven-year-old pensioner with a heart condition anymore. He bent down and pushed his face into Derek Crow's.

'I'm asking you again Crow, where's my fucking gold?'

'And I'll tell you again, I don't know what you're talking about.'

'Look pal, I know you nicked it, so where the fuck did you hide it? Tell me and all this will be over.'

'Pigs might fly. What are we discussing here?'

Street grabbed a handful of Derek Crow's hair and lifted his head. 'The gold me and Blakey's crew nicked from Gatwick airport in '89; £20 mil worth.'

'Ah right, that gold, but why do you think I would know anything about it?'

Street slapped his face. 'Because you and your mates are the only other people who knew where it was hid.'

'You've lost me there.'

'You're a fucking liar Crow,' Street said, pointing a finger a couple of inches away from his face as if trying to decide if he should poke him in the eye. The prisoner coughed and spat blood on the floor, attempting to clear his throat and mouth. He couldn't move much as his legs were bound together and his hands were tied behind him to the back of the chair.

The three men were in what Henderson assumed to be the captain's cabin with a bed along one wall, a writing desk, a couple of chairs and little else. At least if the captain had a boozy night drinking too much high-proof vodka in the dining room, the place where he was standing, he didn't have far to travel to fall into bed.

'I'm telling you, I didn't have anything to do with stealing your gold, and as far as I know, neither did my brother, Pete, or Eric Hannah.'

Street whacked him in the guts and raised his fist to give him another when his companion intervened. 'Pack it in Mat,' he said, 'we need to hear what he's got to say.'

'Humph.'

In this setting, Street looked no longer the model pensioner who liked a little flutter and an occasional pint of ale, but a silver-streaked wolf circling its injured prey. His face was alive with emotion and expression and he was bursting with energy, moving around the debilitated figure in the chair like a man ten or fifteen years his junior.

Close-up, Street's mate Ace was bigger than Henderson first thought. He was tall, although smaller than the DI, and towered over Street by a foot or more, well-built with thick, tattooed arms and large muscles. He would have been a menacing figure to look at from Derek Crow's position in the chair, but the lack of emotion and the coldness in his eyes was worrying Henderson.

After allowing Derek a few minutes to recover, they resumed their questioning.

'We'll take it from the top. I went on the raid with Blakey and the boys at Gatwick, and we got away with £20 mill in gold, about 5 in cash and 10 in bonds. I was the one looking after the gold, Blakey the cash, and Ernie the securities. Are you cushtie so far?'

Crow nodded.

'Right. Before I know it, we get fingered by some bastard and we all get sent down. I come out half a bloody lifetime later and when I get to my lock-up in Plaistow, the gold's gone.' He bent down to face Crow. 'The guys in the team blame me and want my balls in a sling for nicking it, but I told them as I'm telling you now, it was nicked by you and your mates. You were the only ones who knew about the lock-up.'

'I hear what you're saying, but you've got the wrong guy. I didn't nick any gold.'

The big guy made to hit him but a sharp look from Street stopped him. The little man seemed to have some control over his big mate.

'If you didn't nick it, how come you and the other guys in the band all had money to set yourselves up in businesses, where the fuck did you get it?'

'Bloody hell. If I had a pound for every time I get asked this.'

The big man punched him on the side of the face but he must have been taking it easy as Derek's jaw didn't seem to be broken.

'Stop flannelling Crow and get on with it, or you'll get more of the same,' Street said.

Derek winced, exercising his facial muscles, trying to dissipate the pain. 'I found out later the guys were bringing in dope from Germany and Holland and they were making a packet, this was in the days before the big, organised drug dealers moved in on the scene. That's where they got the money from, not from any gold theft at

Gatwick.'

'What a fucking fairy story. You expect me to believe they did it all behind your back? If I remember right, you couldn't keep your snout out of the trough back then and you're the same now.' He tapped the side of his head. 'See mate, I might be sixty-seven but there's fuck-all wrong with my memory.'

'I always drove one of the vans, sure I did, but I didn't know about the drug dealing and wouldn't want to have been part of it if I had. When I left the band one of our albums started selling well in Japan and Korea, and since I wrote much of it, I made a fair bit from royalties. I would have given the guys some of the money but they didn't need it.'

'What the fuck's this, Mat? This isn't what you told me when we was in Wakefield,' the big man said.

'Shurrup Ace. He's lying. I'll handle this.'

'If you lot didn't steal my gold,' Street continued with a sly smile, raising his voice, 'how come we found gold bars from the raid in each of your mates' fucking houses?' His face betrayed a look of triumph as if playing a winning hand at the end of a twelve-hour poker marathon.

'So, it was you, you bastard! You killed Eric, Pete and Barry!'

Street turned to Ace. 'Give this guy a Mastermind rose bowl, he's cracked it!' Street said, guffawing at his own humour.

'You bastard Street, you'll spend the rest of your life rotting inside a jail cell if I've got anything to do with it.'

'Fat chance of that happening is there, with you all tied up? So c'mon, tell me. How come your lot had gold?'

Derek shifted in his seat, the trace of a smile on his

face. 'I can see it now, you believe the crap some old con told you, don't you? Somehow you think I nicked the gold from the raid and used it to set everyone up in business. Is this the reason you killed them?'

'It was my fucking gold,' he said tapping his chest, his face twisted in hate. 'The heist was my idea and went off as sweet as a nut. If I hadn't got sent down three weeks later, I would still have it.' He paused for a second, reminiscing. 'So if your mates didn't get the gold from you, where did they get it from?'

Henderson could feel the last piece of the jigsaw falling into place, and for a moment he wished his voice recorder was switched on to capture some of this stuff, but he was sure if he pulled it out now, even the noise of it powering up would be enough to blow his cover.

Ace and Street began to argue but he couldn't hear what they were saying as both men were shouting at the same time. The gist of it seemed to be that Ace felt he had been employed under false pretences, although Henderson didn't expect to see him at an Employment Tribunal any time soon. Street told him everything was fine, as they had recovered loads of money and part of the gold, but it didn't seem to mollify the big man who kept whining like a spoiled child.

'Enough Ace!' Street said.

'But Mat!'

'I said enough!' Street looked livid, angry enough to deck the big man. 'This is getting us nowhere.'

Ace stood for a half-minute, not moving, staring at him. Such odd behaviour would unnerve most people but Henderson was learning from this little show that Mathew Street was not like most people.

'Ok,' Ace said when normal service had been resumed. 'We'll get nothing more out of him, what do we do with him?'

'Beat him up some more. I still think he knows something.'

Ace punched Crow in the chest, kidneys, the face and kicked him in the shins. It was horrible to watch and it took Henderson a strong measure of self-restraint not to go in there and give Derek a hand. After suffering this for a minute or more, Crow said, 'All right, all right, I'll tell you.' At least that's what it sounded like, his mouth was bloody and split and his nose distorted.

Crow tried to clear his throat but winced in pain at the effort and spat loose teeth on the floor.

'I'm waiting.'

'You're not going to like it.'

'Try me.'

'Eric Hannah stole your gold. You and him were mates at the time and he knew about the gold. He told the other guys and hatched a plan to nick it, but first he needed to get you out of the way.' He paused trying to clear something from his throat that was making his voice garbled.

'He told the cops about what you and your thieving pals did—'

'You bastard!' Street made to punch Crow but in a lightning movement, Ace caught his fist.

'Leave it Mat, I wanna hear the rest.'

'I spent 25 years inside thanks to this fucking bastard.'

'They would have caught you eventually,' Crow said, 'it was only a matter of time.'

'No chance. We had—'

'Finish your story,' Ace said.

He shifted in the seat trying to get comfortable, wincing when his bruised kidney rebelled. 'After they arrested you, Eric broke into the lock-up and nicked the gold. He gave some to Barry and Pete but I wouldn't touch it.'

'You expect me to believe this?'

'Why the hell not? Did you find the remains of the stash at Eric's place? He only cashed in a couple of bars each year to fund a holiday in the Caribbean. He must have had loads left.'

Street looked at Ace. 'You searched Hannah's place, didn't you? You're not trying to hold out on me are you, big man?'

'No, Mat don't be daft, I would never do that. I told you, Hannah's woman's been there all the time. I couldn't get in, but I've still got her old man's keys.'

'Fuck!' Street said.

'I need to go back there and look again.'

'Yeah,' Street said. 'Soonest. Tomorrow and if she's still there, don't fuck about, use the knife.'

'What about him?'

'We stick to the plan.'

Ace walked over to Derek. In a slick movement indicating the actions of a seasoned professional, he pulled a small cosh from his pocket and whacked him over the head several times until Derek lost consciousness.

'Right,' Street said, 'let's get him out of the chair and upstairs.'

Ace made to grab Crow but stopped. 'What about the dope?'

'Christ, I forgot about it. Good thinking big man, it's in

the bag.'

Ace reached into a holdall and pulled out a well-wrapped package about the size of half a kilogram of cheese and put it in Derek's pocket. Henderson didn't have a good view of the bag, but he saw it also contained cash, thousands of pounds in his opinion.

A bag of dope in the pocket was an old trick. When the body is discovered, the police assume the murder is the result of a drug deal gone wrong, leading them down the wrong path. The added twist to this one, and the reason he believed they were intending to kill Derek aboard this boat, was his body wouldn't be noticed until the ship reached port and its cargo unloaded. Local police would have no idea if the murder had happened on their patch or in the UK, adding more fuel to a confused situation.

Henderson watched as Ace untied the inert figure, gripped him under the armpits and hauled him towards the door. When he pulled Derek into the corridor and clear of the narrow cabin doorway, Street moved out to join him. With Ace at the shoulders and Street at the legs, they lifted him and slowly made their way along the corridor. In a few minutes, when he could no longer hear any grunting and swearing, and it sounded like they were now negotiating a staircase at the end of the corridor, Henderson poked his head out of the dining room.

He stood there for several seconds until he was sure neither man would come back to retrieve something left behind in the cabin. He left the dining room and retraced his steps back to the galley. When he got there, he stopped and looked around to make sure everything looked the same. Satisfied, he climbed the staircase, and headed up in the direction of the star-laden night sky.

FORTY-TWO

The more Carol Walters downed the fruity Marlborough Sauvignon Blanc, the more relaxed she became, but with it surfaced the regret of her earlier outburst. She was a cop and even though she hadn't been working late these last few weeks and didn't often go into the office on weekends, there were times when she needed to cry-off a date. Therefore, it was childish for her to throw a flaky with her new friend Simon when he put in an appearance forty minutes behind the agreed time because his boss wanted a word about his up-coming pay rise.

Her main problem with relationships was she didn't understand how they worked. Was she supposed to be on the lookout for someone who would be one hundred per cent compatible in character, humour, sexual preferences and their choice of job, or was 'true love' the only criteria and when she found it, everything else would fall into place? In her experience, it never seemed to work either way and she was coming to the conclusion that she was a lousy compromiser.

What Simon didn't know, her hair was at the heart of the problem. For more years than she cared to remember, her hair was cut to shoulder-length and parted in the middle. Based on a whim or on something he might have said on their last date, it was now short, only covering her ears, and, another first, coloured with a parting to one side. When she first came out of Coco's in East Street, feeling self-conscious and ninety-quid poorer, it wasn't an exaggeration to say she felt violated and regretted parking the car so far away in Churchill Square.

Simon's first mistake was to call round after she had bumped into her friend Melissa. Using a deadpan expression Melissa last used when she re-told the story of when she caught her son masturbating, she said her new look was 'interesting' and 'a bit of a change,' with no mention of the years it took off her age or how it suited her pretty, rounded face.

Simon's second mistake occurred when he didn't say anything about her hair. Whilst he apologised for being late and prattled on about his boss and the size of his next pay rise, he failed to notice a woman in need of massive reassurance and a healthy dose of TLC. A quick altercation later, he returned to his car and was on the way home before she could say, 're-modelled', 're-styled' or 'meet the new me.'

She started watching a film on television but she couldn't concentrate and decided to stop boozing as the alcohol was making her feel melancholy. With some difficulty, she rose from the chair and walked into the kitchen. She made a mug of coffee and carried it back into the living room with a bag of crisps, a vain attempt to try and soak up the booze.

Friday night television, as usual, was a load of crap. She flicked through the channels looking for something not involving answering asinine questions against a ticking clock, trying to imagine a bygone age with actors who sounded modern in voice and with hairstyles that wouldn't look out of place now, or an action film with crash-bang pyrotechnics designed to wake the kids upstairs and with hard-to-hear, mumbled American dialogue.

She started watching a stupid comedy about two straight guys living together, but the jokes sounded familiar. The phone rang. Keep calm girl, she said to herself, if it's Simon, he's the one who needs to apologise.

'Carol, it's Angus,' he said in a quiet voice, almost a whisper.

'Where are you? Have you been drinking? You sound like you've been drinking?'

'I could say the same to you, but no, I haven't had a drink all night. I'm on a ship at Shoreham Harbour—'

'Bloody hell! Was it something I said? You're not thinking of emigrating are you?'

'Shut up, Carol and listen. There's a ship docked in Shoreham Harbour, the east side of the harbour, called the *Baltic Star*. Mathew Street and his mate Ace have abducted Derek Crow and brought him here. They've bashed Derek around and I think they're about to kill him.'

'Derek Crow? Are you sure?'

'Of course I'm bloody sure. I know what Derek Crow looks like, I've been watching him being tortured for the last fifteen minutes. They think he stole their gold.'

'What gold?'

'Don't you start. It doesn't matter about the gold, I'll tell you later. What's important is you need to get our people down here, armed and plenty of them.'

'Right ok, I understand. Where's Derek now?'

'He's lying on the deck. He's unconscious.' He paused. 'I think they're going to dump him in the hold.'

'Why would they do that? Are they not just going to

dump him overboard?'

'I think, although I haven't seen inside it yet, the hold is full of grain and his body will end up—'

She heard scuffling, a yelp, and a series of soft thumps, which to a suspicious copper sounded like repeated blows from a fist or a boot. Seconds later, the line went dead as if the phone network had failed or someone had stamped on Henderson's phone.

The Sauvignon Blanc haze disappeared as the copper inside seized her attention. Still holding the phone, she called Lewes Control and resolved to speak with as much poise and clarity as she could muster, not wanting to sound like a hysterical teenager or a drunken bum who called in for a laugh. All calls were recorded and often played back in court where they were picked over by a team of defence lawyers, sober as judges and as thorough as crows picking over carrion.

She identified herself and said in a voice less pissed than she felt, she needed the armed response team down at Shoreham Harbour, and to her surprise, the operator responded. If the call to Lewes Control sounded business-like and went according to plan, there remained a high probability the next one wouldn't. She gathered her thoughts, dialled the number and took a deep breath.

'Edwards here.' In the background Walters could hear the clinking of glasses and raucous, drink-infused laughter.

'Good evening, ma'am, DS Walters here. Sorry to disturb you.'

'DS Walters, you're not still on duty are you? It's after ten on a Friday night.'

'No, ma'am, I'm at home. I've just received a call from

DI Henderson–'

A loud voice faded in, then out, but she couldn't make out the words. 'It's my husband telling me I'm neglecting my supper guests. Will this take long DS Walters?'

'I'm sorry to interrupt your dinner party, so I'll cut straight to the chase. Derek Crow, he of the Crazy Crows rock band and the Prime Minister's businessman friend, has been kidnapped. DI Henderson followed him and now believes Derek Crow is in mortal danger.'

'Have you been drinking, DS Walters?'

'Yes, I have. As you say, ma'am, it is Friday night, but this isn't me telling you all this. DI Henderson told me before the phone went dead and we were cut-off.'

'Why was he calling you? Did he ask you to do something?'

'Yes, he told me to send back-up as he's sure Derek Crow is about to be killed.'

'Did you?'

'Yes, I've instructed Lewes Control to give me as many cars as they can find and an armed response team.'

'I'm on my way. Where am I going?'

'To the east side of Shoreham Harbour. He's on a ship called the *Baltic Star*.'

The phone went quiet for a moment and she heard the muffled sounds of CI Edwards talking to someone. 'Right,' she said when she came back on the line. 'I'll go back in and say goodbye to my guests but I bet they'll be well chuffed to see me leaving as I haven't yet served dessert.'

'I'm sorry about the interruption ma'am, but thank you. There's just one other thing. Could you pick me up on the way?'

FORTY-THREE

Henderson could see the night sky as he reached the top of the ladder, ascending out of the ship's bowels and welcoming the clean, night air, a change from the stale atmosphere below decks.

In the shadow of the funnel, he pulled out his phone and called DS Walters. He was two minutes into the phone call when he fell on the deck in a heap after receiving a whack on the head which turned his knees to jelly. He dropped his phone and heard a crunch as his attacker stood on it.

Kicks came in but he'd been in this position enough times to realise he couldn't just lie there and take a beating otherwise he'd be finished, as it seemed this guy meant business. When the next kick came in, he grabbed the leg and pushed it back with as much force as he could muster. The guy staggered backwards, more in surprise than from the force of the shove, and fell against a rail.

Henderson got to his feet but to his amazement, the other guy leapt up in a flash, like a fairground target felled by an air rifle, and turned to face him. He now adopted a martial arts stance, his hands in karate-chop shapes and walking towards him in cautious steps. Whoa, fists and kicks he could deal with, but oriental stuff was out of his league.

The attacker edged closer, his movements stealthy for such a big man.

'Police!' Henderson said in a voice as strong as he could muster, the last desperate attempt of a man with a groggy head and a ship's funnel at his back.

'What!' he said, his face incredulous. 'Show me your ID.'

Henderson reached into his pocket and pulled out his warrant card.

He leaned over and grabbed it, took a quick look before handing it back.

'Ah fuck, sorry man for whacking you on the nut. I thought you were Mat Street's big mate. It was dark like.'

'I'll live,' Henderson said, rubbing his head where he felt a large lump. 'Who the hell are you?'

'Don Levinson, Derek Crow's personal protection specialist, bodyguard in old money. What are you people doing here?'

'I could ask you the same thing.'

'I followed Derek to this place but—Hey, look out!'

Henderson turned to see Ace's impassive face and the cosh he'd been bashing Derek Crow with swinging towards him. There was little he could do to get out of the way and it caught him straight across the temple. On this occasion, there wasn't time for knees to buckle, his lights suddenly had no power.

He woke up, his cheek resting on a lumpy rivet, adding more pain to the rhythmic bass playing in his head. He eased himself up into a sitting position. The cons had pulled back the cover of the ship's hold and he was lying close to the edge, and even though he considered himself a strong swimmer, he didn't fancy his chances in a pool full of wheat or oats or whatever the stuff down there might be. Up close, the space looked cavernous and gauging by the height of the ship, ran to a depth of about thirty or forty feet.

His head was spinning and he felt nauseous, but a few moments later everything cleared, except for the rhythmic thumping of a mini bass player performing inside his head. He didn't know if he had been out for one minute or five, but he could still see Don. He must have squared up to his attacker, Ace didn't take him by surprise, as the cosh was no longer in Ace's hand, no doubt felled by one of Don's karate kicks. Instead, Ace held a knife. This was no cheap punk, jabbing and slashing as if trying to clear a path in a dense jungle, but taking a calm, measured approach, receiving a kick to the head in return for a better opening. Henderson stood and was about to go over and lend a hand when he remembered Derek.

He turned. At the far end of the ship, close to the bow, Mathew Street was pulling the motionless figure of Derek Crow towards the edge of the hold, a job made more difficult due to the absence of his big mate. Henderson staggered and limped the length of the ship, the noise of his exaggerated movement drowned by Street's puffing and wheezing and the shouting and grunting of the two men fighting behind him, so Street didn't look up. A look of triumph appeared on the old geezer's face as he wound up to make a last, final heave when Henderson's fist smacked him in the jaw and he staggered back.

Henderson bent down to help Derek. He looked a mess, his face covered in blood, drifting in and out of consciousness. He tried sitting him up but he flopped back down like a rag doll. Henderson gripped his shoulders and pulled him away from the edge but he was a dead weight, his body snagging on every rivet and seam.

He heard a noise behind him and turned. The warning was enough to prevent Street burying his knife somewhere between his shoulder blades, but not to avoid him sticking it into his left shoulder. Street pulled the knife out, but before he could make another lunge and finish him off, Henderson let go of Derek and rolled away. The pain in his arm began as a serious sting and then it hit him in waves of torment, making him sweat, nauseous and distorting his sense of balance.

Henderson staggered to his feet and moved away before Street realised where he was and dodged into the shadows. He bent down on his knees and took a succession of deep breaths. 'C'mon Henderson,' he said to himself, 'you're not going to die here.'

Enveloped in darkness, in the shadow of a large piece of winding equipment, he felt safe for the moment, as Street didn't look like he fancied diving in after him. He stood on the deck waving the knife from side to side, urging him to come out. He might be a sixty-seven-year-old man, but by the way he handled the knife it looked like his weapon of choice, wielded by his hand many times in the past.

Henderson reached out around him, feeling for a weapon. His hand touched a thick, coiled rope, and never taking his eyes off the demonic face of his armed assailant, in case he felt emboldened and ventured after him, felt for the end. He found it and pulled a section free. Street, realising he might be up to something, decided to go for broke and stepped into the shadow.

He came closer, slashing at Henderson's chest, the blade parting the material of his shirt and leaving an untidy line of blood in its wake. Before he could strike again, Henderson lifted the rope with two hands and swung a length at Street's face, as if chopping a tree. The rope was heavy, as thick as his wrists and wet from rain or seawater and it made a satisfying 'thurump' noise as it made contact with the side of Street's head. The swipe took a huge effort from his damaged shoulder, the pain surging with a constant throb as he tried to put his arms down, almost forcing him to black out.

Street had stepped backwards into the light, shaking his head, trying to clear it, but before he could come at him again, as Henderson knew he couldn't keep this up, he pulled more rope free and swung it again. It hit Street full-force on the side of the head and he stumbled backwards as if drunk. He lurched towards the hold but he couldn't control his own momentum. His foot snagged on a raised edge and he tumbled headlong into the abyss.

Henderson waited for a sudden bolt of pain to ease and then lurched over to the edge of the hold and looked down. Street flailed around like a drowning man, but the consistency of the 'pool' was more like quicksand than water and his strokes only seemed to make the situation worse. Henderson looked around for help and then he spotted Ace coming towards him. On the other side of the hold, under the harsh scrutiny of a security light, Don's immobile body was lying in a heap, blood pooling around him.

Henderson moved back to the dark place where he'd found the rope, and started searching around for something else; he knew he couldn't lift it again and a wet rope wouldn't stop this guy. His hand touched something heavy and he picked it up. It was a heavyweight chisel or riveter, he couldn't be sure, but too short to use against

Ace. When he moved closer, he threw it towards his face. It was crap shot with a tool as un-aerodynamic as a Dodo and missed the intended target but bounced off his shoulder. It didn't seem to bother him much as after a quick rub, he kept coming.

Henderson moved in the direction of the bow and put all stupid thoughts of jumping overboard or climbing down a mooring rope firmly out of his mind when he found a large box and pulled it open, hoping for a fish-gutting knife or a gun. It took him a few seconds to realise he wasn't looking at a box of fireworks but distress flares. He knew enough about sailing to appreciate the different types of flares and if these were the warning or smoke variety, he would be as sunk as a capsized yacht.

In the past, he had fired one or two in practice drills but could he remember how? On the side of the tube, he saw helpful multi-language instructions, just the ticket for the owner of a sinking boat, seconds away from jumping for his life into the grey water, or a panicking detective trying to stop a psychopath. He picked out a flare, pulled off the cap and pointed it at Ace who was about ten feet away. Nothing happened. If the light was better he would have a chance of seeing what he was doing, as there was also a little picture-diagram on the side, necessary as there were many types of flare. He turned it towards the light, spotted the hanging tape, pointed the flare at Ace and pulled the tape. The flare kicked in his hand and a bolt of white light shot out from the end and rocketed towards the ship's control tower.

He bent down and reached for another but when he turned, Ace was almost upon him. He yanked the cap off, pulled the tab and Ace's face exploded in an intense white light, temporarily blinding Henderson. He felt for another, just in case Ace could see better than he could, but when his sight cleared, Ace was backing away, clutching his face.

Henderson moved towards him, aiming to pick up Street's abandoned knife from the deck, but as he got closer, Ace, his face blackened and marked, straightened and charged towards him. Henderson lifted the flare in his hand and fired it. It hit Ace smack in the face and he roared in agony and staggered backwards clutching his eyes. He started to run, perhaps thinking he could find water in the crew's quarters, but instead of running down the length of the ship, he ran across it. Before Henderson could shout a warning, he hit the side rail and toppled into the dark waters of the canal.

Henderson ran over, expecting to see this seemingly indestructible man stroking for the shore but no, a few minutes later he spotted his body; face down and motionless.

FORTY-FOUR

Henderson pressed the 'send' icon and pushed his chair back from the desk. Doing things with one hand was more tiring than it looked, including dialling a number on a mobile, buttoning a shirt and now added to the list, writing an email. He couldn't touch-type, but he usually did a reasonable job using two or three fingers from each hand, but now with one arm in a sling, even this was beyond him.

He had walked out of the Royal Sussex Hospital on Sunday, two days after being stabbed aboard the *Baltic Star*. Street's knife wound to his shoulder had been deep, but it missed slicing nearby arteries. Equally important, at least the doctors seemed to think so, the knife didn't appear to be stained with any gunk or bacteria, as the wound hadn't become infected.

He returned home to his flat in Seven Dials to convalesce. After a few days, the pain was about manageable and some feeling was returning to his hand, but the inactivity was driving him up the wall. In addition, his mind was buzzing, not from the antibiotics or painkillers, but from all the loose ends which needed tidying up.

It took a couple of calls to CI Edwards, from him and his doctor, before she relented and allowed him to return to the office. He was under strict instructions not to go out on any operations but to stay at his desk and let DS Hobbs or DS Walters take the strain. This suited him fine as he had hundreds of emails to read, reports to write and a murder team to manage.

Another reason for coming back was to escape the negative thoughts crowding his head in the middle of the night. Was he was getting too old for this? Were wounds like this taking longer to heal? Would a desk job or the inside of a motorway patrol car suit him better? Should he consider doing something else altogether?

With his good hand, he picked up a file from his desk and went in search of the murder team. It wasn't the first time he had put together such a group after a series of murders, but it was the first time he'd done so after the perpetrators had been killed. It made sense, not only to keep the records straight, inform the media and notify the families, but also to determine if anyone else was involved.

The team were located in a corner of the Murder Suite, overlooking the car park. The whole group were there, not because they found his status meetings so riveting, but because the bulk of the investigation work could be done from their desks by phone and email.

'Afternoon all,' he said.

'Afternoon sir,' came the sullen reply. It was the sound of a team, leggy and tired at the end of a long investigation, when all they could look forward to was compiling reports and updating files for the CPS. He would excuse them this time.

'First up,' Henderson said, perching himself on the edge of a desk as pulling out a chair and sitting down was too much of a faff, 'what's the status on Don Levinson and Derek Crow?'

'I called the hospital an hour ago,' Sally Graham said.

'Mr Levinson is now out of a coma but still in Intensive Care.'

'Good to hear. Did they say what his chances are of making a full recovery?'

'They were cagey on the subject, I'm afraid. So many things can still go wrong, but they think it's unlikely he will return to his job as a personal protection specialist. In time, he should recover most of his faculties, but he'll need to do something more sedentary in future.'

'At least the news is on the positive side. Thanks Sally. What about Derek Crow?'

'That's me, sir,' Seb Young said. 'As we know, he didn't suffer any stab wounds, but multiple broken bones, including ribs, cheek and skull. He could be in hospital for another few weeks and this will be followed by a long convalescence, possibly two or three months, before he's back to any sense of normality.'

'Is he conscious?'

'He is.'

'Who's handling the interviews? It's you, isn't it, DS Walters?'

'Yes sir, it is.'

'Good. Get somebody down to the hospital over the next few days and take a statement from Derek. It shouldn't be much different from all the stuff I overheard aboard the *Baltic Star*, but you never know.'

'No problem.'

'Phil, you're covering the P-M's, if my memory serves me right. How did they go?'

'Much as we expected.' He lifted some papers from the desk beside him. 'Mathew Street's body was recovered from the hold of the *Baltic Star* on Sunday.'

'How did they get him out? Did they have to drain the hold?'

'No, they didn't. They used a tall crane belonging to a ship repairer on the other side of the canal.'

'What happened to all the wheat?' Walters asked. 'Would they scrap it knowing a dead body had been found in there?'

'Maybe not,' Henderson said. 'They gets rats in ships' holds, dead and alive, and that doesn't deter owners from selling the cargo.'

'No wonder I don't like bread,' Seb Young said.

'I thought you were gluten intolerant,' Sally Graham said.

'Phil, what was the P-M verdict on Street?' Henderson asked.

'Asphyxiation.'

'What about Ace?'

'Ace, or to give him his real name, Stephen Watson, drowning. Apparently he could swim, but when he fell overboard on the *Baltic Star,* he hit his head on something in the water, like a plank of wood, rendering him unconscious.'

'Why was he called Ace? Was he good at cards?' Seb Young asked.

'According to a fellow prisoner,' Walters said, 'his favourite song was *How Long* by the band, Ace.'

'Oh, I get it,' Young said. 'Prison, how long; very clever.'

'Apparently not,' she continued. 'He sang it all the time, driving all the other cons spare as it reminded them of how long they had to go. The guy I spoke to said, if Ace hadn't been such a nutter, they would have done him in ages ago.'

'What do we know about him?' Henderson asked.

'He had been orphaned at the age of ten when his parents died in a house fire,' Seb Young continued. 'He lived with a succession of foster parents when, at the age of seventeen, he murdered the last couple he stayed with. Sentenced to life and released on licence around the same time as Street, the man he befriended in jail and who according to some, became a sort of father figure to Ace.'

'Some role model,' Walters said.

'Does Ace have any living relatives?'

'No.'

'Where did we get with the 'Blakey' reference?'

'His real name is John Blake,' Phil Bentley said, 'and he was identified as the ringleader of the AeroSwiss robbery gang when they appeared at the Old Bailey in 1990. We believe he was putting Street under pressure to locate the missing gold.'

'Did you interview Blake?'

'I did, sir. He's a nasty bit of work, but he's over seventy now and in poor health. I think his sons are running the criminal show now. Enquires are continuing.'

'For those who don't know or didn't read my statement, a few weeks ago, Eric Hannah's wife Suzy tried to sell a bar of gold stolen in the Gatwick Airport robbery. As Phil said, this robbery looks to be the motive behind the murder of the Crazy Crows, as Street was convinced the Crows stole their gold.'

He stopped to take a drink of water as his throat was parched. Coffee was off the menu for the moment as even the smell of it made him feel sick.

'Going by what I heard, it was Eric Hannah who stole the gold, and the bars found at the houses of Barry Crow and Peter Grant by Ace, were given to them by Hannah to help kick-start a new career after the band split.'

'So, by implication,' Walters said, 'Eric Hannah had possession of most of the gold, and providing he didn't spend it in the intervening years, some of it may still be hidden at his house.'

'You're quite right. Before this meeting, I sent an email to the Met's Serious Robbery Squad and told them the story. It's their problem now.'

'Knowing them,' Walters said, 'the next time we hear about it will be on the front pages of several national newspapers, telling everyone what a great job they did and what brilliant detectives they are.'

'They didn't turn you down again, Carol, did they?' Phil Bentley said.

'Bugger off.'

'Phil, did you get a sense from this guy Blakey when you met him as to whether he knows any of this?'

'It's hard to tell, sir, as he denied having anything to do with the gold since the robbery, but I would take anything he said with a pinch of salt as I'm sure he would grab it all tomorrow if he could. However, I didn't detect any urgency around the place and all three sons were there.'

'Maybe he's got it already. Keep your eye on this one, Phil.'

'Yes, sir.'

'I've got nothing more, does anyone have anything else they want to add?'

'Just one more thing,' Seb Young said. 'A local promoter by the name of Ainslie Wicks is aiming to stage a tribute concert at the Brighton Dome in May. He says he'll have two or three bands on the bill and they'll play a selection of Crazy Crows songs. All proceeds will be donated to Barry Crow's breast cancer charity.'

'A fitting memorial,' Henderson said. 'I'll certainly be buying a ticket.' He rose stiffly and stretched. 'Is there anything else?' He looked around at their faces. 'No? Same time tomorrow.'

He turned and walked back to his office. He had just slumped in the seat when his phone rang. It was tricky dialling a number on a mobile, but he'd perfected the technique for answering it, as long as the caller didn't mind waiting while he transferred from one hand to another.

'Henderson.'

'Good afternoon, DI Henderson, DI Long of the Serious Robbery Squad.'

'You got my email?'

'I did and thank you for all the good work you and your team have done. This robbery has been on our books for over twenty years without a dicky bird and now I can see it being wrapped up in the space of a week.'

'I'm pleased to hear it.'

'The thing is, we're conducting a search of the Hannah household in the morning. Since you gave us the lead, I would like to ask you to come along as an observer.'

FORTY-FIVE

Henderson arrived at the Farnham house of Suzy Hannah five minutes before DI Long of the Serious Robbery Squad pulled up in a grubby Vectra, and following behind, a van with a six-man search team. While Henderson and DI Long went to the door to present the search warrant, the forensic team decamped from the van and donned over-suits, gloves and unpacked detectors.

It must have been a scary prospect for the diminutive Suzy Hannah to be confronted by the over-size figure of DI Ken Long and half-a-dozen eager blokes intent on rustling through her smalls, but she took it in good grace and after inspecting the paperwork, allowed them to get on with it.

Henderson was nothing but a spectator, there to admire the professional approach of the Serious Robbery guys, a reward for re-awakening the AeroSwiss case when without it, they would still be in the Dark Ages. With much stomping and rummaging going on upstairs, he approached Mrs Hannah and asked to see the place where she had found the two gold bars.

'We need to get the steps.'

They walked out the back door and when he got over the untidy state of the garden, he could see two sheds. A large, well-maintained shed at the back, looking like a smart summer house, and a smaller tatty shed behind it.

'What do you use the big place for?'

'Did you know my husband was a musician?'

'Yes, I did.'

'Well, this was his rehearsal space.'

'I'll take a look in there later. Let's get the steps.'

He carried the aluminium stepladder back to the bedroom and Mrs Hannah placed them close to a large, dark-varnished wardrobe and climbed up. It was rude to stare, but he couldn't keep his eyes off her beautiful legs, the dress creeping up to mid-thigh as she reached for something at the top of the wardrobe.

She stepped down holding a small case and handed it to him. It looked old and tatty.

He placed it on the bed and undid the zip.

'This is where you found two gold bars?'

'Yes.'

'You didn't find any more?'

'No,' she said with a steely stare. He was a student of Neuro-Linguistic Programming, NLP for short, a methodology to help him understand not only what people said but how they said it based on facial expressions and body language. Her face didn't exhibit one trace of a lie and in fact, her expression was saying to him, 'Are you doubting me?'

'Aside from the two gold bars, you found nothing else?'

'No,' she said, as emphatic as before.

Henderson climbed the ladder to made sure there weren't any more bags with gold up there, but he didn't see any.

Everyone was still busy upstairs and Henderson, looking for something to do, picked up the shed keys and walked out the back door, this time without the delectable Mrs Suzy Hannah in tow. He opened the door of the big shed but his glance through the window didn't prepare him for the sight which confronted him; a grown man's paradise and no mistake. Guitars tastefully strung along the wall, a fridge stocked with beers, a television hung from another wall, and a sofa, a comfortable place to sit down and enjoy it all.

Against one wall stood a tall cupboard which he opened, half-expecting it to be full of gold, disappointed to see it was crammed with music paraphernalia; pick-ups, cables, bits of old amps, music books, but alas nothing that glittered. A beautiful Oriental rug caught his eye. It covered a large section of the wooden floorboards, a red dragon surrounded by a variety of Chinese symbols, but the mystical image was sullied with numerous cigarette burns and what looked like beer stains.

He pushed the settee back and rolled up the carpet. To his disappointment, there was no hatch leading to a gold vault, and going by the booze fridge and his luck, if there was one, it would likely be a spiral wine cellar. He sat on the settee and slumped back, resigned to his position as the spare part in the search party for the rest of the morning.

The sun poked through a cloud and rays of bright light, filtered by tall trees, forked through the window. A ray touched his face, warming it. He closed his eyes and enjoyed its pleasant glow, the only source available inside the unheated rehearsal studio of a dead musician on a cold day.

He sat there for three or four minutes thinking about Eric Hannah playing in here, before easing himself up from a slouch and rubbing his eyes. He then noticed some of the floorboards weren't the same shade as the surrounding floor. Keeping his eye on the spot in case he lost it, he bent down. He pulled out his key ring and eased the small screwdriver attachment between the boards. The board moved as if they weren't stuck down and he found the same thing happened on three sides of the discoloured area.

Utilising a bit of logic, he reasoned that if Eric Hannah built it, he must have had an easy method of opening it. He rummaged through the cupboard again and found two flat pieces of metal that appeared to be likely candidates. At first glance, they looked the same as all the other guitar accessories, a sort of powder black, but even with his limited musical knowledge, he couldn't think they would be of any use on a guitar or sound system.

He eased both pieces under the floorboards and pressing one with his good hand and the other with his knee, lifted a hatch. When there was enough space to fit in his hand, he let go of the metal plates and lifted the hatch. It was hinged on one side and he pushed it until it stood perpendicular with the floor.

It revealed a space three-foot-by-three-foot square and a couple of foot deep, lined in wood. His breath was coming in short gasps and his heart thumping a crazy beat, a better stimulant than standing close to the delectable Suzy Hannah. At the bottom of the space, a grey, musty blanket was spread out as if covering something. He reached down with a trembling hand and lifted the blanket.

Nothing. Zilch. Nada. Nought. His heart fell; he was convinced it would be here. He heard a noise behind him but it wasn't DI Ken Long coming to gloat as he'd found the gold in the loft, but Mrs Hannah.

'Where are they?' he said. 'The gold; the gold bars.'

'I showed you where I got them. At the top of the wardrobe.'

'I don't mean two gold bars, your husband's stash.'

'The only stash he ever kept in here was his dope. He thought I didn't know about it, but I did.'

He stood to face her. 'Where have put them?'

She looked at him, steady as an oil tanker. 'I don't know what you're talking about.'

He tried to look through her deception but his NLP training wasn't helping; she was good.

'I know there was gold in there,' Henderson said. 'Forensics will prove it.'

'Well it's not there now, is it?'

'I can see that. So where is it?'

'If there used to be gold in there as you say, my recently deceased husband must have spent it.'

'I don't believe that for an instant. I think you took it.'

She gave him a long, slow look and reached over to his injured arm and rubbed his discoloured hand gently. 'You're not sure, are you, Mr Detective?' She said, looking up into his eyes. 'If you want to find out, you're just going to have to prove it, aren't you?'

FORTY-SIX

2 Months Later

At the corner of Lower John Street and Golden Square in London, a man stopped walking and stood to the side to rest on his stick. Derek Crow didn't injure his ankle aboard the *Baltic Star,* but fell out of bed when he took a dizzy turn and damaged ligaments in his leg.

He was tempted to stay where he was, leaning against the wall and have a well deserved cigarette, after negotiating the Underground from St John's Wood all by himself, but a voice in his head told him not to. Doctor Said, a Pakistani heart specialist came to see him as he lay helpless between the crisp clean sheets at the hospital. In his hand, he held x-rays allegedly of his insides, but Derek reckoned they belonged to some poor unfortunate and were used by the good doctor to scare the rest of us.

Doctor Said sat at his bedside and banged on about visceral fat and the hidden dangers of eating rich food and the only way he could get rid of him and return to watching *Wanted Down Under*, was to take the proffered leaflet and agree to adopt his diet plan. Like a bad penny, he kept returning and Derek realised his lack of mobility made him a target for numerous evangelistic medical staff who roamed the corridors and wards of the Sussex hospital like bees looking for nectar.

He hobbled on, the cigarettes staying put inside his

jacket pocket. In fact, he didn't need a jacket as away from the shadows of the buildings in Lower John Street, he was bathed in the warm sunlight of a beautiful May morning. If he could find a way of carrying his jacket while walking with a stick he would, but it would leave him without a hand free to stop him falling if another dizzy spell came along, or to prevent him colliding into some hurrying pedestrian, too engrossed in a text to notice him in their path.

He had taken the Underground this morning as he no longer employed Don Levinson as his driver and personal protection specialist. After leaving hospital two weeks ago, Don went home to convalesce and currently moved around with the aid of a pair of crutches. One of Derek's first acts on regaining his marbles was to instruct his HR Director to find Don a management job within the company. He was now being paid an enhanced salary and one day, in perhaps three or four months time, he would take his place behind a shiny new desk.

He pushed open the door to a building and climbed the stairs. Ten minutes later, he took a seat in a comfortable chair with mug of hot coffee at his side while watching the late morning DJ on Planet Rock, Paul Faraday, do his stuff. He'd been in dozens of radio studios before, mainly in Holland and Germany, but none in the last twenty years, except two interviews he did for the Radio 4 *Today* programme inside their radio van, parked outside his house.

In the days of the band, studio gear was large, the desks were cluttered with kit and the studio was alive with harassed assistants as they cued CDs and searched boxes of tapes for jingles. In contrast, Paul was seated on the opposite side of a tidy table, his face partially obscured by three computer screens and above his head, a fat microphone positioned to pick up his every word.

A few minutes later Paul leaned towards the mike and said. 'You've been listening to *Ain't No Love in The Heart of The City* by Whitesnake. This is Planet Rock and today, I have a very special guest with me; Derek Crow of the Crazy Crows. Welcome to Planet Rock, Derek.'

'Thanks for inviting me here, Paul.'

The third guy in the room, Hal, the sound Engineer gave Derek the thumbs-up to indicate that he sounded fine, necessary as Derek had put on large headphones and couldn't hear himself speak.

'As I'm sure everyone is aware now, as the case was all over the media for weeks, Derek was stalked by a pair of vicious criminals who killed three members of the Crazy Crows band; Barry Crow, Peter Grant and Eric Hannah. So, how are you now Derek? Have you recovered from your ordeal?'

'Just about. I looked a sorry sight a month or so back with a swollen face and strapped ribs, but I'm back to normal. The face you see today is as good as it gets.'

'Ha. Derek, you probably know, I go to a lot of gigs and when news of Barry and then Eric's death filtered out, many bands were asking themselves if they might be next. I came across plenty of nervy musicians, I can tell you.'

'I was asking myself the same question. Although it did strike me odd at the time, why it was only the Crazy Crows being targeted. If it was an attack against rock bands from the same era, or only those singing about black magic or devil worship, it's possible some of them might have become involved as well, but thankfully it wasn't.'

'Perish the thought. Let's talk about the music. The Crazy Crows made four albums over the seven years you guys played together, *Breakaway*, *The Long Road*, *Tropical Storm* and *Black Saturday*. I don't know if you're aware, but judging by the amount of texts and emails I receive every week, you've still got a lot of fans out there.'

'I'm pleased to hear it.'

'A couple of weeks back, we ran a poll to find out our listeners' favourite Crazy Crows track. Before I tell you what they've selected, I'd like to put you on the spot. What's yours?'

He paused for a moment. 'I think I would pick *Bad Luck* from *Black Saturday*. It just feels like a complete song to me. Sometimes when I've finished a song and we record it, I often feel like I should have added a phrase or taken out a word, but not with *Bad Luck*. It feels, you know, finished.'

'It's a great song but it wasn't the top choice of our listeners. The favourite Crazy Crows track of Planet Rock listeners is...' Paul paused and played a ticking jingle, ' *Forked Lightning,* from *Tropical Storm.*'

'I can't disagree, it's a great choice.'

'Tell us something about the song, Derek.'

'It came to me one night when me and the rest of the band were in Brighton. After a gig at the Dome, we joined about thirty others for a barbeque on the beach. It was a beautiful summer's night, and about midnight and with little warning, a storm erupted out at sea, sending huge forks of lightning into the sky. It was so powerful, it lit up ships in the Channel, we could see clearly Brighton's two piers and hundreds of people were watching it from the promenade. I sat down on the pebbles and wrote the song in about half an hour.'

'Let's hear it.'

He cued the record and seconds later, Eric Hannah's familiar guitar riff came ripping through a couple of small speakers hanging from the ceiling.

'You're doing great, Derek,' Paul said. 'Do you feel ok?'

'Yeah, I'm fine, I'm enjoying myself.'

'That's good to hear. When the track's finished, I'd like to talk a bit more about the case, if you're ok with it.'

'Yeah, no problem, ask away.'

'Cool. Enjoy listening to your singing.'

In truth, it sounded like someone else was singing. He had done so much since leaving the band, setting up the tanker business, working with the Prime Minister and now this vendetta with Mathew Street, the band was becoming a distant, albeit pleasant, memory. A few minutes later, as cracks of real forked lighting faded out, recorded by Eric in Antigua when the weather in Brighton refused to play ball, Paul resumed talking.

'You're listening to Planet Rock and in the studio today is Derek Crow of the Crazy Crows. Derek, one aspect of the terrible incident that happened to you and the other members of the Crazy Crows, and still has a lot of people talking, is what happened to the gold? If you can believe it, people with metal detectors are out every weekend scouring fields near Eric Hannah's former house.'

'Ha, they're wasting their time. It's true, Eric did have a lot of gold at one time, but the police conducted a thorough search of his house and garden and found nothing.'

'So what do think happened to it?'

'Eric must have been more generous than I or anyone

else thought and either gave it away to friends or spent it.'

'There you have it, all you fans of metal detectors and lovers of conspiracy theories. Derek Crow says there isn't any gold there, so stop wasting your weekends and stay at home and listen to Planet Rock. Derek, we know Eric's wife Suzy was hounded by reporters and camera crews and she got so fed up, she left the country. Have you heard from her? How's she doing?'

'She's doing fine. She's moved to the Caribbean, but I won't tell you which island for obvious reasons. She is buying an old dilapidated hotel and plans to turn it into a luxury spa retreat for rich travellers. She's promised that the bar will be called *Hannah's Retreat* in Eric's memory. A fitting gesture, I believe, for a man who spent so much time warming a bar stool.'

'Good luck Suzy. This dovetails nicely into the next track which features some fine guitar playing by Eric. Derek, can you please introduce the title track from the *Black Saturday* album.'

'It's a pleasure.'

About the Author

Iain Cameron was born in Glasgow and moved to Brighton in the early eighties. He has worked as a management accountant, business consultant and a nursery goods retailer. He is now a full-time writer and lives in a village outside Horsham in West Sussex with his wife, two daughters and a lively Collie dog.

Hunting for Crows is the fourth book in the DI Henderson series, the calm Scottish detective with the hidden ruthless streak.

Acknowledgements

In writing a book about a rock band, I needed to go no further than plunder the memories of a misspent youth, attending concerts by Genesis, the Rolling Stones and Thin Lizzy. I have read many books on the subject too, not just band biographies with tour dates, album lists and the 'sexploits' of a wild lead singer, but also those focussing on other people on the tour. Of particular help were: *It's Only Rock 'n' Roll* by Jo Wood for the wives' story, *Roadie: My Life on the Road With Coldplay* by Matt McGinn for the roadies, and *Life* by Keith Richards for the guitarists.

It is often assumed a book is written by one person but that's only partly true. I would like to thank my wife, Vari, for meticulous proof-reading; Zoe Markham, for peerless editing; Bob Carter, for making me delete words, sentences and chapters if I strayed too far from the story; Peter O'Conner, at BespokeBookCovers.com for designing such a great cover; and to family and friends for championing the Iain Cameron cause, their influence goes way beyond simple advertising.

It only remains for me to thank you, dear reader, for taking the time to read this book. I hope you enjoyed reading the book as much as I did writing it.

The Story So Far

The first three books in the DI Angus Henderson series.

One Last Lesson
The body of a popular university student is found on a golf course. DI Angus Henderson hasn't a clue as the killer did a thorough job. That is, until he finds out she used to be a model on an adult web site run by two of her lecturers.

Driving into Darkness
A gang of car thieves are smashing down doors and stealing the keys of expensive cars. Their violence is escalating and all are fearful they will soon kill someone. They do, but DI Henderson suspects it might be cover for something else.

Fear the Silence
A missing woman is not what DI Henderson needs right now. She is none other than Kelly Langton, once the glamour model 'Kelly,' and now an astute businesswoman. The investigation focuses on her husband, but then another woman goes missing.

For information about characters, Q&A and more, see: www.iain-cameron.com

I can also be contacted:
✉ mailto:admin@iain-cameron.com
f www.facebook.com/IainCameronAuthor
t https://twitter.com/IainsBooks

15999613R00197

Printed in Great Britain
by Amazon